TALES OF L

Other books by Knut Hamsun
published by Souvenir Press

MYSTERIES *translated by Gerry Bothmer*
VICTORIA *translated by Oliver Stallybrass*
THE WANDERER *translated by Oliver and Gunnvor Stallybrass*
GROWTH OF THE SOIL *translated by W. Worster*
THE WOMEN AT THE PUMP *translated by Oliver and Gunnvor Stallybrass*
WAYFARERS *translated by James McFarlane*
DREAMERS *translated by Tom Geddes*

TALES OF LOVE AND LOSS

Knut Hamsun

Translated by
Robert Ferguson

A CONDOR BOOK
SOUVENIR PRESS (E&A) Ltd

The stories included in this volume were first published
in Norwegian by Gyldendal Norsk Forlag, Oslo
in the collected volumes *Siesta, Kratskog* and *Stridende liv*

This translation first published 1997 by
Souvenir Press (Educational & Academic) Ltd,
43 Great Russell Street, London WC1B 3PA
and simultaneously in Canada

Published with a translation grant from NORLA

ISBN 0 285 63383 X

Typeset by Rowland Phototypesetting Ltd,
Bury St Edmunds, Suffolk

Printed in Great Britain by
The Guernsey Press Company Ltd,
Guernsey, Channel Islands

CONTENTS

INTRODUCTION

Knut Hamsun (1859–1952) is best known as a novelist, the author of *Hunger*, *Mysteries*, *Pan*, *Victoria* and *Growth of the Soil*, for which he was awarded the Nobel Prize for Literature in 1920. But during the early years of his career he experimented briefly and intensely with a variety of other literary forms. Between 1895 and 1905, as well as writing two novels and a travel book, he wrote four stage-plays and a verse-drama, published a collection of poems, and produced three volumes of short stories.

The stage-plays were all performed and enjoyed a degree of success among contemporary audiences. Stanislavski devotes a chapter of his autobiography to one of them, *The Game of Life*, describing his production of the play in 1905 as 'a turning point in my artistic career'. But posterity has not been kind to them and apart from occasional revivals in Norway the plays have fallen into disuse. Hamsun himself came to feel that they were failures, and after one final attempt to master the form in 1910 he abandoned drama. *The Wild Choir*, published in 1904, contains some remarkable poetry which came to influence a whole generation of young Norwegian poets, notably Herman Wildenvey; but again, Hamsun more or less abandoned the form after this.

Much the most interesting products of this extended experimental *raptus* of the 1890s were the 34 short stories he wrote and collected in *Siesta*, *Brushwood*, and *Striving Life*, of which 20 are presented here.

These are interesting on two counts: firstly, because many of them feature that enigmatic blurring of autobiography and fiction that is such an attractive and compelling aspect of Hamsun's art; secondly, because the stories often provide an interesting commentary on the novels. 'Secret Sorrow', 'Jon Tro' and 'The Call of Life' all feature, as it were, the narrator of *Hunger*, while the central figure in 'The

Queen of Sheba' is obviously a close cousin of *Mysteries*' Nagel. And although its central character Marcelius is a more prosaic creation than *Pan*'s Lieutenant Glahn, 'On Blue Man's Island' reflects in similar fashion to the novel Hamsun's obsession with doomed love. Other stories, like 'Reiersen of the *Southern Star*' and 'Life in a Small Town', look ahead to the novels of Hamsun's middle age. 'Christmas on the Hillside' has affinities with *Growth of the Soil*, and 'Life in a Small Town', published in *Brushwood* in 1903, is in all-important essentials a sketch for *The Women at the Pump*, a novel which did not appear until 17 years later, in 1920.

In this perspective the short stories provide a fascinating glimpse of an author shedding one literary skin to reveal another, very different skin, as the lonely and intense young romantic of *Pan* and *Victoria* gives way to the older, less personal, more distanced and more cynical creator of such densely populated novels as *Children of the Age*, *Segelfoss Town* and the late trilogy about August the wanderer. In a story like 'On Blue Man's Island' the process of change is almost visible on the turning page.

On the other hand there are stories here with no direct stylistic or thematic link to any of Hamsun's novels. Of the three that are set in America 'Zachæus' is untypical in that the narrator plays almost no part in the grotesque development of the feud between the two main characters; yet it derives a powerful authority from the fact that Hamsun himself worked on the kind of prairie farm described here during his years in America in the 1880s. Similarly, the macabre sequence of events related in 'A Woman's Triumph' is rendered curiously believable by our knowledge of the fact that Hamsun himself worked as a tram-car conductor in Chicago. The third story, 'On the Prairie', is a more typically impressionistic and generalised account of life as a member of a migrant work gang on a Midwest prairie farm, strong in well-caught detail and characterisation, but eschewing plot. What unites all three stories is their unforced acceptance of all kinds of people and all kinds—even the most extreme kinds—of human behaviour.

The most memorable character in 'On the Prairie' is the gambler, Evans, with his silk shirts and his stoical indifference to money. 'Father and Son: A Gambling Story', set in an unnamed country, deals in its entirety with the addictive power of gambling. 'Secret Sorrow' refers in passing to roulette. In this too Hamsun's fiction sounds an echo from his personal life. Newly married to a rich wife in 1898, he shortly afterwards began gambling with her money and lost a great deal of it at the casinos in Namur and Ostend. A mercenary element in the appearance of so many books—ten—in the seven years between *Siesta* in 1897 and *Striving Life* in 1905 is perhaps that Hamsun was trying by the only means he knew how to earn enough money to pay back his debt to Bergljot.

The range of styles and themes on display here is remarkable, and in those stories which concern themselves with the art of story-telling itself we are reminded once again of the truth of Isaac Bashevis Singer's observation, that 'the whole modern school of fiction in the twentieth century stems from Hamsun', a fact so often obscured by the political aberrations of Hamsun's problematic last years in which he publicly supported the Nazis. Many of the stories are funny in a way that gives the lie to the cliché, based on a perception of Ibsen's plays and bolstered by Edvard Munch's paintings, that the Norwegians are a dour people with little sense of humour. 'A Real Rascal' is a superbly mischievous account of the relationship between storyteller and reader, and 'Revolution on the Streets', an almost straight piece of historical reporting from Paris, mounts a rare and witty defence of the right to find political passion a bore. Would that he had managed to hang on to his pragmatic indifference to the end!

'A Lecture Tour' is of particular interest. Written as early as 1886, two years before he began work on *Hunger*, and revised later for inclusion in *Brushwood*, it shows Hamsun in the process of learning to laugh at himself and his literary pretensions and ambitions in a way that he was to display more extensively in the novel in 1890. In 'The Queen of Sheba' he gives us the same sort of narrator as Nagel in *Mysteries*, an existential clown playing with life, making stories up out of nothing and reinventing a dull old world out of sheer boredom. *Mysteries* ends badly for Nagel, but the conclusion of 'The Queen of Sheba' is a triumph of sorts for its narrator. 'The Call of Life' and 'The Lady from the Tivoli' similarly introduce us to street-walking, loitering Hamsun, bored by the everyday and hanging around in the hope that something will happen to lift him out of it.

As well as using the short-story form as a laboratory for trying out new themes, Hamsun used it to experiment with different styles of writing in pursuit of an ever more immediate, direct, 'speaking' style. He often switches tenses in mid-sentence, and indulges a marked preference for the comma over the full-stop, that gives the prose at times a rushing effect. I have tried to reproduce these effects faithfully in translation, and if the result is a style that seems at times un-English the consolation must be that the original Norwegian involves a similarly unique, personal and untypical use of language.

Some of these stories are fragmentary, some are impressionistic. All of them, it seems to me, are interesting, and the best of them show a talent Hamsun could have taken to mastery had he wished to. But with the publication of *Striving Life* in 1905 this extraordinary period of formal experimentation came to an end, and apart from that last stage play, *In the Grip of Life*, in 1910, written largely as a gift to his second wife—an actress—he never again wrote anything but novels.

A LECTURE TOUR

I was going to give a lecture on modern literature in Drammen. I was short of money, and this seemed to me a good way to get hold of a little. I didn't think it would be all that difficult either. So one fine day in the late summer of 1886 I boarded a train bound for that splendid town.

I didn't know a soul in Drammen, nor did anyone there know me. Nor had I advertised my lecture in the papers, although earlier that summer, in an expansive moment, I had had 500 cards printed, and I intended to distribute these in the hotels and bars and large shops, to let people know what was in store for them. These cards were not wholly to my liking in that they contained a misprint in the spelling of my name; yet I was so comprehensively unknown in Drammen that a misprint was neither here nor there.

As I sat in the train I took stock of my situation. The prospects did not dishearten me. I had overcome many difficulties in my life with little or no money, and though I was not rich enough to live in a style befitting the dignity of my aesthetic mission in this town I was confident everything would be all right if I took care with my money. No fancy gestures now! As for food, I could always slip down to some basement-café after dark and get something to eat there, and I would lodge at a bed-and-breakfast that catered for travelling salesmen. Apart from that, what other outgoings would I have?

On the train I sat and studied my lecture. I was going to talk about the novelist Alexander Kielland. My fellow-passengers were a group of high-spirited farmers returning from a trip to Kristiania. They were passing a bottle round and offered me a drink, to which I said no thank you. Later, in the manner of all friendly drunks, they made other approaches to me; but I continued to ignore them until finally they realised, from my general demeanour and from all the notes I was making, that I was a learned man with a lot of important things on my mind. After that they left me in peace.

On arriving in Drammen I got off the train and carried my carpet-bag over to a bench in order to compose myself before setting off into town. As it happens I had no use for this carpet-bag at all, I took it with me solely because I had heard that it was easier to book in and out of a bed-and-breakfast if one were carrying such a bag. It was anyway a wretched old worn-out yellow cloth bag, not really suitable for a travelling man of letters. My outfit, including a dark blue jacket, was considerably more respectable.

A hotel porter with writing on his hat came over and wanted to carry my bag.

I declined the offer, explaining that I had not yet made up my mind about a hotel, I had first to meet a couple of newspaper editors in town. It was I who was going to give this lecture on literature.

Well, I would need a hotel whatever, I had to stay somewhere, didn't I? His hotel was beyond all comparison the best in its class, with electric bells, a bath, a reading room. It's just round the corner here, up this street then left.

He picked up my bag by the strap.

I detained him.

Did I want to carry the bag to the hotel *myself*?

Well, I was going the same way as my bag so I might just as well hang it over the crook of my finger and that way we'd both get there.

At this the man looked at me, and realising that I was not a wealthy gentleman he headed off down towards the train again on the lookout for someone else. But there were no other travellers, so he returned and again began touting for my custom, persuading me finally that in fact he had come down to the station for the specific purpose of meeting me.

Well, that changed matters. The man had perhaps been sent by the committee of some society—the Workers' Educational Society, for example—who had got wind of my arrival. Drammen was obviously a town with an active cultural life and a healthy awareness of the need for good lectures. As a matter of fact, in this regard it seemed to me somewhat ahead of the capital itself, Kristiania.

'Of course you may carry my things,' I said to the man. 'Oh, by the way, I presume the hotel serves wine? Wine to drink with one's meal?'

'Wine? The best there is.'

'Right. You can go now. I'll be along later. I must just pop into these newspaper offices.'

The man looked as if he might know a thing or two so I took a chance on him:

'Which editor do you recommend? I can't be bothered to visit them all.'

'Arentsen is the best man. Everyone goes to him.'

*   *   *

Arentsen the editor was naturally not in his office, so I visited him at home. I told him my business, that I had come in the service of literature.

'Not much interest in such things here. We had a Swedish student come last year with a talk about everlasting peace. He lost money on it.'

'I am going to talk about literature,' I repeated.

'Yes,' he said, 'I realise that. I'm just warning you, you'll probably lose money on it.'

Lose money on it? Priceless! Perhaps he thought I was a salesman travelling for a firm. I said merely:

'Is the large Workers' Hall available for hire?'

'No it isn't,' he replied. 'It's booked out for tomorrow evening by an anti-spiritualist. There are apes and wild beasts on the programme too. The only other venue I can suggest is the Park Pavilion.'

'Do you recommend it?'

'It's very large. Spacious. The cost? Well, I don't know. It certainly won't cost you much. You'll have to speak to the committee.'

I decided on the Park Pavilion. It sounded just right. Those Workers' Society halls were often such small, uncomfortable places. Who were the committee?

Carlsen the lawyer, so and so the furrier, and bookseller somebody else.

I set off for Carlsen the lawyer's house. He lived out in the country, and I walked and I walked until eventually the road came to an end. I told him my business, and that I wanted to hire the Park Pavilion.

It sounded the perfect place for a unique event like a lecture on literature.

The lawyer thought for a moment, and then said he doubted that it was.

No? Was it really *so* big? Surely he could see for himself how unfortunate it would be if people had to be turned away at the door simply because there wasn't enough room for them inside.

But in fact the lawyer went on to advise me against the whole enterprise. There really wasn't much interest in such things here. Only last year we had a Swedish student . . .

'Yes yes, but his talk was about everlasting peace,' I interrupted. 'I'm going to talk about literature. Serious literature.'

'In any case,' he went on, 'you've come at a bad time. An anti-spiritualist is doing a show at the Workers' Hall. He has apes and wild beasts with him.'

I gave him a pitying smile. He seemed to believe what he said so I gave him up as hopeless.

'How much for the hire of the Park Pavilion?' I said curtly.

'Eight kroner,' he replied. 'I'll have to put it to the committee, but I can promise you an answer in two days' time. Informally I think I can safely say that the place is yours if you want it.'

I did some quick mental arithmetic: two days' waiting would cost me three kroner, the hire of the pavilion eight, that was 11. A ticket-seller 12. An audience of 25 at 50 øre each would cover my entire outlay. The other couple of hundred who turned up would represent clear profit.

I agreed. The pavilion was hired.

*   *   *

At the hotel a maid asked:

'Do you want a room on the first or second floor?'

I replied quietly and modestly:

'I want a cheap room. The cheapest you have.'

The maid looked me up and down, trying to work out if perhaps I was a gentleman who found his amusement in asking for cheap rooms. Wasn't I the one who had been asking the hotel porter about wine with the meals? Or was I being so modest in order to avoid embarrassing the hotel? Whatever, she opened a door. I caught my breath.

'Yes, it's empty all right,' she said. 'This is your room. Your bag's got put here already look.'

There was no way out of it, so in I went. It was the finest room in the whole hotel.

'Where's the bed?'

'There. It's a sofa-bed. An ordinary bed in a room like this would spoil it. You just pull it out at night.'

The maid left.

I was in a bad mood. My bag looked so scruffy in such surroundings, and after that long walk along the country roads my shoes were a mess. I swore out loud.

At once the maid popped her head round the door:

'Can I help you?'

Well how about that? All I have to do is open my mouth and a crowd of servants comes swarming in!

'No,' I answered curtly. 'I want some sandwiches.'

She looks at me.

'Nothing hot?'

'No.'

Then she understood. The stomach. It was spring. My bad time of the year.

When she came with the sandwiches she brought a wine-list too. The over-solicitous creature gave me no peace for the rest of the evening: 'Would you like your blankets warmed?' 'The bath's in there, if you want a bath . . .'

In the morning I hopped nervously out of bed and began dressing. I was freezing. Naturally, that damn sofa-bed had been much too short for me and I had slept badly. I rang. No one came. It must still be very early in the morning, I couldn't hear a sound from the streets, and when I was fully awake I realised that it was still not quite daylight.

I studied the room. It was the most elegant I had ever seen. With a sense of deepest foreboding I again rang, and then waited, up to my ankles in soft carpet. I was about to be stripped of every penny I had. Maybe I wouldn't even have enough to pay. In haste I began once again to count up how much I had. Then I hear footsteps outside and I stop.

But no one came. The footsteps were my imagination.

I started counting again, in a fearful state of uncertainty. Where was she now, that maid of yesterday, with her oppressive eagerness to be of service to me? Was the lazy creature still lying asleep somewhere, though it was now almost daylight?

At last she came, half-dressed, wearing just her shawl.

'Did you ring?'

'I would like the bill,' I said with as much composure as possible.

'The bill?' Well that wasn't so easy. Madame was still asleep, it was only three o'clock. The maid stared at me, utterly confused. What sort of look was that to give a person? Was it any business of hers if I chose to leave the hotel at such an early hour?

'I can't help that,' I said. 'I want my bill now.'

The maid left.

She was away an eternity. Compounding my unease was the thought that the room might be charged for by the hour, and that here I was wasting yet more of my money with all this useless waiting. I knew nothing about the way posh hotels are run and such a method of charging seemed highly likely to me. On top of that there was a notice above the hand-basin which said that any room not vacated by six o'clock in the evening would be charged for another day. Everything filled me with anxiety and spread confusion in my serious, literary head.

Finally the maid returned and knocked on the door:

Never, never will I forget fate's little joke that morning! Two kroner 70 øre—that was all! Nothing! A tip I might have given the maid to buy her hairpins with! I tossed a few kroner onto the table—and then one more. 'Keep the change, my friend!'

One had to show a certain amount of *savoir-faire*. Not to mention the fact that the maid deserved it, this rare and warm-hearted maid whom fate had deposited in a Drammen hotel to be the butt of any traveller's whim. They don't make women like that any more, the race has died out. And how solicitous she was of me once she realised that she was dealing with a wealthy man:

'I'll get the porter to carry your bag.'

'Certainly not! Certainly not!' I said, anxious to save her the bother. 'It's just a carpet-bag, an old carpet-bag. I always have to have it with me when I'm away lecturing on literature. It's a little peculiarity of mine.'

But my protests were in vain, the porter was ready and waiting for me outside. As I came walking towards him he stared at my bag as though transfixed. Remarkable, the look such a man can give a bag, as if he's just burning up with the desire to be carrying it.

'I'll carry that,' he said.

Surely I needed every penny I had left now? Was there any possibility of my coming into more money before giving my lecture? Thank you, I would carry the bag myself.

But the porter already had hold of it. That remarkably kind person didn't seem to find it any trouble at all. Payment seemed to be the last thing on his mind, and he carried it in such an innocent way, as though he was prepared to die for the owner of such a bag.

'Wait!' I called out and stopped. 'Where do you think you're going with that bag?'

He smiled.

'That's for you to decide,' he answered.

'Correct,' said I. 'That's for me to decide, not you.'

We had already passed one bed-and-breakfast place in a basement-café and it was my idea to enquire for a room there. I had to get rid of the porter as quickly as possible, so that I could sneak back to the basement without him knowing.

I gave him a 50-øre piece.

Still he held his hand out.

'I carried the bag for you yesterday too,' he said.

'That *is* for yesterday,' I said.

'And I've just carried it now too,' he said.

It was highway robbery.

'And this is for today,' I said, tossing another 50-øre piece into his palm. 'Now please get out of my sight.'

The porter went. But he looked back several times and kept his eye on me.

I made my way to a bench and sat down. It was rather chilly, but once the sun had risen it warmed up. I dozed off and must have slept for quite a while, for when I awoke the street was full of people and smoke was curling up from the chimneys. I walked back to the basement-café and made an arrangement with the woman there. Bed-and-breakfast 50 øre per night.

*   *   *

After the two-day wait was over I again walked out to Carlsen the lawyer's house in the country. Again he advised me to cancel the lecture, but I would on no account be talked out of it. In the meantime I had paid for an insertion in Arentsen's newspaper giving the date, place and topic of my lecture.

When I then tried to pay for the pavilion, which would have left me temporarily without funds, Carlsen, a remarkable man, said:

'There's no need to pay until after the lecture.'

I misunderstood him and took offence.

'Are you perhaps under the impression that I haven't got the eight kroner?'

'Goodness me no! But it's by no means certain you'll actually get the use of the pavilion, and if that happens then obviously there will be nothing to pay.'

'I have already advertised the lecture,' I told him.

He nodded.

'I saw that,' he answered. Shortly afterwards he said:

'Will you still speak if less than fifty people turn up?'

I found this question actually rather offensive, but after thinking it over I said that fifty would be a poor showing, but that yes I would still do it.

'But not for just ten?'

At this I burst out laughing.

'You will forgive me. There are limits.'

We spoke no more about it and I did not pay for the pavilion. Carlsen and I then began talking about literature. He rose in my estimation, and was clearly an interesting man, even though his views and opinions suffered by comparison with my own.

When we parted company he wished me a really good turn-out for the lecture that evening.

I returned to my basement in excellent spirits. The battleground was prepared—earlier in the day I had given a man 50 øre to walk round handing out my 500 cards, so now the whole town knew about the event.

My mood became strangely elevated, and as I contemplated the important task I was about to perform I became dissatisfied with my little basement home and its wretched occupants. Everyone wanted to know who I was and why I was living there. The landlady, the woman behind the counter, explained that I was a learned man who spent his whole day writing and studying and that people were not to bother me with questions. She was invaluable to me. The people who used the café were hungry working men and street porters in shirtsleeves who popped in to get themselves a cup of hot coffee or a lump of black pudding spread with butter and cheese. Sometimes they were unpleasant and abused the landlady because the waffles were stale or the eggs too small. When they found out I was going to lecture in the Park Pavilion itself they wanted to know how much tickets were. Some of them said they were interested in hearing me, but 50 øre was too much, and they began debating the ticket-price with me. I promised myself not to allow such people to upset me; they had absolutely no breeding at all.

There was a man in the room next to mine who spoke a horrible mixture of Swedish and Norwegian. The landlady referred to him as 'the director'. He always caused a stir when he breezed into the dining-room, not least because of his habit of dusting the seat of his chair with his handkerchief before sitting down. He was a real dandy, with an expensive way about him. I noticed that when he ordered a sandwich he was always most particular that it be served 'on fresh bread and with best butter'.

'Is it you who's giving the lecture?' he asked me.

'Yes he's the one,' answered the landlady.

'You're taking a big chance,' he said, continuing to address himself to me. 'You don't even advertise. Haven't you seen the way I advertise?'

It dawned on me who he was: the anti-spiritualist, the man with the apes and the wild beasts.

'I advertise with posters *this* big,' he went on. 'I stick them up all over the place, wherever there's room. Big writing on them. You must have seen them. I've got drawings of the beasts on them too.'

I pointed out that my lecture was on the subject of literature. Art, in a word. Intellectual matters.

'Doesn't make a damn bit of difference!' he scoffed. And then he compounded his insolence by saying that it would be a different matter if I worked for him. 'I need a man to introduce the animals and I would prefer a stranger who isn't known to the people here. If someone they know gets up the audience starts shouting 'Look, look, it's only Petterson, what does old Petterson know about wild beasts?'

I turned away in silent contempt, unwilling to dignify such shameless talk with a response.

'I'll pay you five kroner a night,' he continued. 'Think on it.'

At this I rose from my seat and left the room. I had no choice. Clearly the director was afraid of the competition; worried that I would steal his audience away from him he was looking to make some sort of deal with me, to buy me off. Never! I said to myself. Never will I allow myself to be seduced into betraying the world of art. Mine is the way of the ideal.

*   *   *

At seven o'clock I carefully brushed my clothes and set off for the Park Pavilion. I knew my lecture well and my head was ringing with the lofty and elegant phrases I would be using. I felt a powerful certainty that it would go down well and in my mind I could hear already the telegraph wires jangling with the news of my success.

It rained. The weather was perhaps not so kind as it might have been. But a public hungry for literature would not allow themselves to be put off by a drop of rain. And the streets were full of people, couples walking arm in arm beneath umbrellas. It struck me that they were all going in the opposite direction to me, which is to say, not in the direction of the Park Pavilion. Where did they think they were going? Hm, must be the plebs on their way to see the apes at the Workers' Hall.

The ticket-seller was at his post.

'Anyone here yet?' I asked.

'Not yet,' he answered. 'But there's a good half-hour to go.'

I went inside and took a walk round the massive auditorium, my footsteps echoing like hoof-beats. Ah God, if there were a full house sitting there now, row upon row of heads, men and women squashed together, all just waiting for the speaker! But not a soul!

I waited out the long half-hour. No one came. I wandered out and asked the ticket-seller what he made of the situation. He was cautious, but optimistic. In his opinion it wasn't lecturing weather, people didn't like going out when it was raining so heavily. Anyway, they would probably all turn up at the last minute.

And we waited.

At last a man came hurrying through the pouring rain, paid his 50 øre and went inside.

'Here they come,' said the ticket-seller, nodding his head. 'Drammen people have this terrible habit of turning up for things at the last minute.'

We waited. No one else came. Eventually the only spectator joined us outside.

'Beastly weather,' he said.

I recognised Carlsen the lawyer.

'I don't think you're going to get anyone this evening,' he said, 'It's pelting down!' Then, noticing my downcast expression, he added:

'I knew it when I saw the barometer. It sank much too quickly. That's the reason I advised you not to give your lecture.'

But the ticket-seller was still on my side.

'We should wait another half-hour,' he said. 'Bound to be at least 20 or 30 turn up at the very last moment.'

'I don't think so,' said the lawyer, buttoning up his coat. 'And while I remember,' he added, 'there is, naturally, nothing to pay for the hire of the pavilion.'

He doffed his hat, said goodbye and left.

The ticket-seller and I waited another half-hour and continued to discuss the situation. It was an embarrassing business and I felt thoroughly humiliated. On top of that the lawyer had gone off without getting his money back. I was all for going after him, but the ticket-seller advised against it.

'I'll keep it,' he said. 'That way you only owe me another 50 øre.'

But I gave him another krone. He'd stuck to his post and I wanted to show my appreciation. He thanked me warmly, we shook hands and off he went.

I wandered home, a beaten man. Numb with shame and disappointment I drifted through the streets scarcely knowing where my feet were taking me. To add to my distress I realised at a certain point that I no longer had the money for the train back to Kristiania.

The rain kept falling.

Presently I passed a large building. From the street I could see the lights of a box-office in the foyer. It was the Workers' Hall. Latecomers were still turning up, buying their tickets and disappearing through the great doors into the hall. I asked the ticket-seller how many were inside. The house was almost full.

That damned director. He'd beaten me in style.

I sneaked back to my lodgings and went quietly to bed, with nothing to eat and nothing to drink.

In the middle of the night there was a knock on the door and a man came in carrying a candle. It was the director.

'How did the lecture go?' he asked.

Under any other circumstances I would have thrown him out straightaway. Now, however, I was too crushed to put up any kind of front at all and I said merely that I had cancelled it.

He smiled.

'It wasn't the right weather for a lecture on serious literature,' I explained. He should have been able to see that for himself.

He was still smiling.

'The barometer just collapsed,' I said.

'I had standing-room only,' he replied. Then he stopped smiling, apologised for disturbing me and explained his errand.

It was a most curious errand: he had come once again to offer me work as the presenter of his beasts.

I was mortally offended and asked him, very firmly, kindly to leave me in peace.

Instead he sat down on my bed with the candle in his hand.

'We can at least discuss it,' he said. He explained that the local man he had hired to present the beasts had indeed been recognised by the audience. He himself—the director—had gone down extremely well with his exposure of the spiritualists' trickery; but his speaker, the man from Drammen, had ruined all his good work. 'Look, it's Bjørn Pedersen,' people shouted. 'Where d'you get the badger from, Bjørn?' And Bjørn Pedersen, keeping to the script, explained that it wasn't a badger at all but a hyena from the African bush that had already eaten three missionaries. Then the people booed and jeered because they thought he was trying to make fools of them. 'I don't understand it,' said the director. 'I blackened his face and put a wig on his head and still they recognised him.'

I couldn't see what concern all this was of mine and I turned over to face the wall.

'Think on it!' said the director before he left. 'I might stretch it to six kroner a night if you're good.'

Never would I be a party to such vulgarity! A man had his honour to consider.

*   *   *

The following day the director approached me and asked me to look over the speech about the beasts, correct the grammar, brush up the language here and there. He offered me two kroner.

In spite of all, I accepted. I was doing the man a favour really, and it was, after all, a service in the cause of literature. Moreover, I needed the two kroner. Before commencing, however, I warned him in the strongest possible terms not to mention my involvement to anyone.

I spent all day on it, reworking the speech from beginning to end, injecting life and humour into the descriptions, adorning it with similes, warming more and more to my task. It was a work of art in itself to be able to make so much out of a few wretched animals. Late in the evening, when I read it out to the director, he said he had never heard a speech like it in his life, it had made a remarkable impression on him. In recognition of this he paid me not two but three kroner.

This both moved and encouraged me, and to some extent restored my faith in my literary mission.

'If only I had someone good enough to deliver such a lecture,' he sighed. 'But where is such a man to be found in Drammen?'

I began thinking. It really would be a disaster if a speech like that were to fall into the hands of some Bjørn Pedersen or other to mutilate with his atrocious delivery. The thought was almost unendurable.

'I might, perhaps, on certain conditions, consent to deliver the lecture,' I said.

The director sat up.

'What conditions? I'll pay you seven kroner,' he said.

'That's fine. My main condition is that it must remain a secret between you and me who the speaker is.'

'I give you my word.'

'Because as I'm sure you'll understand,' I said, 'a man with my mission in life can hardly let it get about that he gives talks on wild beasts.'

No, he understood that.

'And of course, if it were not effectively my own composition from start to finish then I would not even contemplate doing it.'

No, he understood that too.

'In that case I am quite prepared to help you out.'

The director thanked me.

At seven o'clock we went together to the Workers' Hall for me to be shown the animals and given some basic instruction in how to deal with them.

There were two apes, a turtle, a bear, two wolf cubs and a badger.

There was nothing whatever in my 'presentation' about wolves and badgers, though it abounded with references to a certain species of hyena from the African bush, a rare pine marten, and a sable, both 'as mentioned in the Bible', and an enormous American grizzly. I had prepared an excellent joke about the turtle, that she was a real lady who would eat nothing but turtle soup.

'Where are the sable and the marten?' I asked.

'Here!' cried the director, pointing to the wolf cubs.

'And the hyena?'

He pointed decisively to the badger: 'Here is the hyena.'

I grew heated and angry. I said:

'This will not do at all. This is false pretences. I must believe in the truth of what I'm saying, with all my heart and soul.'

'Let's not fall out over a trifle like this,' said the director. He produced a bottle of brandy from somewhere and poured me a drink. To show that I had nothing personal against him, that it was just his dirty dealings I objected to, I accepted. We drank together.

'Please don't drop me in it,' he said. 'It's such a wonderful speech, and the beasts aren't that bad, not really that bad at all. Look at this great bear here. Give the speech, everything'll be all right.'

The first spectators were filing into the hall and the director was becoming more and more anxious. His fate was in my hands, and it would become me to use my power with discretion. Moreover, I realised that it would be impossible to make the necessary alterations to my speech in the short time remaining before the show. And I did not see how anyone could put as much into the description of a badger as into an account of the ways of the ferocious hyena. Clearly, any alterations would only weaken my work to a degree I found indefensible. I informed the director of this.

He understood completely, and poured me another drink.

The performance began in front of a full house. The director himself—the anti-spiritualist—astounded everyone with his tricks. He pulled a string of handkerchiefs out of his nose, produced the Jack of Clubs from the pocket of an old woman sitting near the back of the house, and made a table walk across the floor without touching it. Finally he dematerialised himself, disappearing through a trapdoor in the floor of the stage. The audience went wild, the applause was thunderous. Now it was the turn of the beasts. The director brought them on one at a time, and it was my task to describe them.

I realised at once that I could not hope to emulate the director's success; however, I did hope that the more discerning members of the public might appreciate my presentation. In this I was not disappointed.

Once the turtle was out of the way I had only land-dwelling animals to deal with, and in my speech I had linked them all with the story of Noah, who kept two of every kind of animal that was unable to live in the water. But things dragged a bit and the audience's good mood seemed to have deserted it. The marten and the sable didn't get the recognition they deserved, not even when I mentioned how many expensive furs from the backs of these animals the Queen of Sheba was wearing when she visited King Solomon. And then gradually things began to improve. Inspired by my biblical subject-matter, and the two glasses of brandy, my speech grew colourful, rich, passionate. I threw my script aside, I improvised, extemporised, and when I was done the whole house applauded and there were even a few cries of 'Bravo!'

'There's a brandy behind the curtain!' the director whispered to me.

I stepped back and located the glass. The bottle stood beside it. I sat down on a chair for a moment.

Meanwhile the director had brought out another animal and was waiting for me. I helped myself to another brandy and remained seated. The wait was obviously too much for the director, who presently began a presentation himself in his frightful mangle of a language. To my horror I realised that he was talking about the hyena; he even made a slip of the tongue and called it a badger. I rose indignantly and took the stage, gesturing for the director to step aside, and took over the presentation myself. The hyena was the climax of the whole show and I would have to surpass myself to rescue it now. I scoffed at the director, said he'd never seen a hyena in his life, and then swept into an account of the dissolute life of this savage beast. The brandies had their effect and my enthusiasm rose to dizzying heights. I could hear the passion and the fire in my own words as the hyena stood at the director's feet, blinking patiently with his little eyes. 'Hold him tight!' I shouted to the director. 'He's getting ready to pounce! He's after my guts! Keep your pistol cocked, he might break free!'

I must have alarmed the director himself. He pulled the hyena towards him with a jerk, the leash snapped, and the beast slipped between his legs. A great cry went up from the women and children out front and half the audience rose from their seats. For a moment the tension was unbearable. Then the hyena ran away from us with little tripping steps, across the stage and back into his little cage. The director slammed the door after him with a clang.

We all breathed out, and I concluded the presentation. This time we had been lucky, I said. After the show, this very evening, a heavy iron chain would be obtained for the monster. I bowed and stepped back.

The applause came like thunder. There were cries for the speaker, the speaker. I went on again and took another bow and if the truth be told I went down very well. The audience were still clapping as they went out of the door. Although there were some who were laughing.

The director was pleased and thanked me warmly for my support. He could certainly look forward to many more full houses.

A man was waiting for me outside as I left the hall. It was my ticket-seller from the Park Pavilion. He had heard the whole thing and was most enthusiastic and loud in his praise of my skills as a public speaker. On no account was I to give up the idea of lecturing in the pavilion, now was the time to advertise, now that people had heard me and knew what I could do. A repeat of the talk on the hyena, for example, would go down particularly well, especially if I brought the animal along with me.

*   *   *

But the following day that rascal of a director refused to pay me unless I gave an undertaking in writing to appear on his show the next evening. Otherwise I could sue him for it, he said. The cheat, the scoundrel! Eventually we reached a compromise under which he paid me five kroner. With the three he had already given me that made eight, which was enough to pay my fare back to Kristiania. He insisted on keeping my written speech, though I protested long about this, painfully aware of the abuse it would encounter. On the other hand it was undeniably his property and he had paid for it, so in the end I gave in. He was so inordinately appreciative of it.

'I've never heard a speech like it before,' he said. 'I remember yesterday, it gripped me the way no sermon ever has.'

'You see?' I said. 'That's the power literature has to move men's minds.'

These were my last words to him. In the afternoon I caught the train back to Kristiania.

JON TRO

At five o'clock on Christmas Eve I locked my door and went over to Quisling's. It was a cold day, and I knew Quisling had fuel for his stove; maybe he had a bite to eat as well. Quisling had no visible means of support, but he supported himself anyway and took each day as it came. He always managed to come up with something, for example about a week ago he acquired a pair of galoshes, though they were much too small for him.

I go in and I see Quisling, in the gloom over by the table.

'Go on then, sit down,' he said. That was a thing of his. He would never just say, 'Please, do sit down.'

'Merry Christmas,' I said. 'It's nice and warm here. I didn't bother starting a fire at my place today, it doesn't draw anyway so it's not worth it.'

Quisling didn't respond to this. He got up and fetched a bit of smoked ham and a fair-sized lump of bread. I sat staring off in another direction while this was going on, and when Quisling invited me to join him and even drew up a chair for me at the table I acted as though I was very surprised: Well now what on earth was this? Food in the house as well? Thanks very much, a bite to eat certainly wouldn't go amiss, especially food like that.

So I took a bite.

'Come on, don't muck about, get stuck into it,' said Quisling.

So I did as I was told, and I ate.

Quisling sat thinking for a while, then he got up, scratched his head and said:

'You ought to have a little something to drink with it, but I'm all out of . . . What say we go over to Jon Tro's?'

'No,' said I, feeling comfortable and satisfied. 'What do you want to go over there for? Well, if that's what you want . . .'

Yup, Quisling wanted to go over to Jon Tro's place. He fastened up his galoshes.

This Jon Tro was a queer bloke, a country boy, theology student, very practical with his hands. He was so tight with his money he could hardly bring himself to pay his rent. His living conditions were about as primitive as you could get, with no proper chairs and no curtains on the window. But let no man say when they saw Jon out walking that he lived any worse than anyone else. He was always well dressed, to my way of thinking. He even carried an umbrella when it rained.

'He just better be at home,' said Quisling as he knocked on the door.

Yes, he was home all right.

'Merry Christmas.' We made ourselves as comfortable as we could and began chatting away. I look round. The floor inclines steeply in the direction of the door, the ceiling slants, there's a window in it. On the wall hang a top hat and a straw hat, and apart from that there wasn't so much as even a picture on the walls. Just these two hats. There were almost no clothes on the bed either.

Suddenly Quisling says:

'You know Jon Tro, you're a very strange person. But I don't suppose it would be completely out of the question for you to lend me five kroner if I asked you for it, would it?'

'Just can't do it,' replied Jon. 'I'm not in a position to right now. I was expecting some money from home, but it hasn't arrived yet.'

'Because I'm expecting money too any day now,' Quisling continued. 'I just found out very recently. So you'd be sure to get it back.'

'Well no, yes, I'm sure. But no, unfortunately, I can't help you at the moment. I couldn't even put clean clothes on today—on Christmas Eve—because I can't pay the bill to get my washing back.' And to prove it he shows us he's still wearing his dirty clothes.

Pause.

'I see. So things are that tight for you too?' said Quisling. 'The two of us were hoping you might be able to help us out.'

Jon just shakes his head and smiles. I said nothing, I was feeling comfortable enough and not in need of anything. But I permitted

myself a little private laugh at this story about Quisling expecting money; where in the world would he be expecting money
from?

'Well, Christmas comes but once a year, Jon Tro, so you're just
going to have to help us out a bit this afternoon anyway,' says
Quisling straight out. 'Anything else would be unthinkable.'

'Who me?' Jon answers in alarm. 'How can I help you?'

Quisling points to the two hats hanging on the wall and says:

'Well if you haven't got any money let's pawn the top hat.'

'The top hat?' Jon gets to his feet. 'Come on, I'm not that daft.'

'The mean sod!' says Quisling to me, with a look of great astonishment on his face. 'He's got two hats and he won't lend us one of
them to help us out of a jam!'

'Okay you can take the straw hat.'

'Yeah the straw hat, thanks a lot. How much am I going to get
for a straw hat at this time of year?'

'No, no.'

Pause.

Quisling comes back to the top hat.

'I've never heard anything like it!' shouts Jon Tro. 'You expect
me to walk the streets with a straw hat on my head this Christmas?'

I still say nothing, I'm feeling so comfortable and warm inside
and pleased with the food I've eaten. But suddenly I have a vague
notion that it might be possible to attach earmuffs to the straw hat
to make it wearable in winter. I imagine them as red flannel earmuffs,
because just before that I was thinking about warm flannel shirts.

Meanwhile those two continued their discussion.

'While we're on the subject,' says Jon Tro, 'You're sitting there
in a brand-new pair of galoshes: why not pawn them?'

Quisling pulls off one of the galoshes and waves his foot in the
air. His shoe was full of holes, totally useless, we could all see that.

'I suppose you think I might be able to manage without the
galoshes?' he asks.

'No no. But for God's sake, is that my problem?'

Quisling stood up and reached out for the top hat on the wall. He
was quick, but Jon was quicker. He grabbed the hat, holding it well
away from himself so as not to dent it.

'Stir yourself,' shouts Quisling to me. 'Come on damn it, let's take the hat off him.'

I got up. Jon shouted threateningly:

'I'm warning you, if you damage this hat!'

So he had to let go of it, it was an easy matter for the two of us against him. Anyway, Jon's country-boy instincts told him that if we made a dent in the hat it wouldn't be worth much to either of us, so he soon let go of it.

Quisling was going to go out and pawn it and get something to eat with the money. 'Let's just hope the pawnbrokers aren't closed yet!' As he went out of the door he was still muttering: 'The mean sod. Money's practically waiting for me at the post office and still he . . .'

'Yeah, mean sod!' snarled Jon. And he opened the door and shouted down the stairs: 'Don't lose that ticket now, you hear?'

Jon Tro was very angry. The right thing would be for him just to get up and go, he said. But then it occurred to him that he ought at least to have his share of whatever was coming and so rescue at least some of the top hat. He began trying to work out how much Quisling would get for the hat. That calmed him down and his bitterness faded a bit and he asked me if I thought Quisling might get as much as six kroner. I was sitting on the floor again, my back against the wall, and I wasn't far off sleeping. Jon grew anxious again. Why hadn't Quisling come back? Where was he? He hadn't just taken the money and run off had he? And Jon opened the attic window in spite of the cold, and poked his head out so he could keep watch on the street. 'Let's hope he has brains enough to buy some smoked sausage!' he muttered.

Finally Quisling returned. No he hadn't bought any smoked sausage, he got two kroner for the hat and he spent it on cognac. Quisling plonked the bottle on the table.

'What kind of a top hat is that?' he sneered. 'Two kroner! Ha!'

'Where's the receipt?' Jon cried angrily. And once he got it he lit a candle and peered at it suspiciously, to make sure that really was all they'd got for the hat.

We sat at the table and had a drink. I drank a lot and wanted more. Jon Tro drank a fair bit too, as if he wanted to make sure he got most of it down himself. Quisling alone was careful never to fill his glass more than half-full.

'You two are knocking it back a bit aren't you?' he said.

The cognac had livened me up again and I couldn't let such a comment pass unanswered. I retorted:

'Envious, are you? Hear that, Jon Tro? He doesn't want us to drink so much!'

Quisling looked at me.

'What's the matter with *you*?' he said.

Jon cheered up perceptibly. He took another drink to stress the fact that the cognac was really his, which made him even more cheerful. He began singing. A few moments later he again raised the subject of smoked sausage. Quisling filled a glass and carried it over to me because I was sitting on the floor again; but I didn't take it.

'Don't tell me I've offended you, will you now,' said Quisling, looking at me closely.

I told him he needn't worry about me, I certainly wasn't going to drink up all his cognac. And if it was all the same to him I would just carry on sitting there and minding my own business. I could always leave if he wanted.

Pause. Quisling continued staring at me.

'If you were in your right state of mind I'd give you a clip round the ear, you know. But you're not in your right state of mind, you poor bugger.' He turned away from me.

'Maybe you think I'm drunk?' I shouted.

'Drunk? No, but for once your belly's full.'

I sat a while thinking this over while Jon carried on fussing with the cognac. He was pretty far gone by this time, humming and talking away to himself. 'Offended?' he said. 'Who's offended? Didn't you just say someone was offended?' He'd got smoked sausage on the brain and said in so many words that he'd never heard of Christmas without smoked sausage. Suddenly he suggested we all sing a song, and he and Quisling began with *The Sunset Smile*.

'Canon!' shouted Jon.

And they sang it again, in canon.

I listened, and even before they reached the end of the first verse

I was on my feet, in the grip of some powerful emotion, and I was holding Quisling's hand and muttering something or other.

'It's all right, it's all right, it doesn't matter,' said Quisling. And since he said it was all right I sat down again.

Jon started on a new song, some Swedish something about a Bianca. 'Listen, go and get some smoked sausage,' he said again.

'Give us the money then,' replied Quisling. 'I know you've got some, you don't fool me.'

Jon Tro's expression changed at once, he went over and sat on the edge of his bed and tried to sober up as best he could. The country boy in him woke up again, cautiously he felt his breast pocket and with the dull cunning of the drunken man he said:

'So. You know I've got money do you? And who told you that? You can search me if you like, I couldn't even pay to get my washing back today.'

'Yes of course,' said Quisling. 'It was only a joke. You're in the same boat as us.'

'Yes, you're right there, I'll tell you that.'

'No one would expect a man who lived in a dump like this to have money,' Quisling continued.

'Well I don't know about that . . .'

'No, come on now—a man whom even a pig wouldn't live with is naturally as dirt poor as the rest of us. Just riff-raff. There's no need to be ashamed of using a two-kroner top hat if you have to.'

'If I have to?' echoed Jon. 'Well now wait a minute . . .'

'Come on now that's the truth, isn't it? You wouldn't be having us on would you?'

Jon Tro leapt up from his chair, abandoned all his caution and gave full vent to his outrage. He slapped the table and called himself the lad from Tro, the Troa laddy. He pulled his wallet out of his breast pocket, thrust it under Quisling's nose and said:

'See this? I say, Do you see this?'

Quisling looked at it in great astonishment. He recoiled.

'That's the laddie from Tro for you,' said Jon. 'You didn't believe it, did you? You didn't think Jon had it in him, eh?'

'No,' said Quisling, hanging his head, beaten.

Jon got more and more worked up, relishing Quisling's discomfiture, piling on his superiority. He seemed to swell up, he stood on his tiptoes, shouted, even came over to me and waved the wallet in front of my nose.

'Ah, you can't threaten me with an empty wallet,' said Quisling cautiously.

'Empty? Look here, dope!' Jon began pulling out notes, waving fists full of notes in Quisling's face, chasing him round the room with his hands full of banknotes. 'Call that an empty wallet do you? Ha. Sorry he had to ask, it was because he was just a simpleton, only Jon Tro after all, the poor laddie from Tro, the Troa laddie without a penny in his pocket. Ha, ha, ha.'

He went on crowing, sat down, emptied the bottle, boasted some more. Quisling said:

'It's like I've always said. You're a strange bloke you, Jon Tro. What about those five kroner then? We've run out here and it's still Christmas Eve.'

'*However*,' said Jon, continuing his speech as if he hadn't heard Quisling, '*However*, I'm not showing you my money in order to lend it you. That's where you're making a big mistake.' But when Quisling again began hurling the worst kind of abuse at him Jon realised he would have to do something, so he interrupted Quisling and continued: 'Because as long as you're my guests you won't need to buy anything for the house. The laddie from Tro will see to that. It's all on me!'

'Bravo!' cried Quisling.

And that bravo made Jon Tro even prouder. He stood up, fumbled in his waistcoat pocket and took out a half-kroner piece which he bounced on the table in front of Quisling so hard that it pinged.

'For smoked sausage!' he cried.

Quisling was quite overcome, this was just too much.

'For smoked sausage? All of it? But in heaven's name man!' he exclaimed.

And Jon stood there stiff with pride and tried to figure out yet more ways of helping us. He turned very formal, even changed his manner of speaking as he grabbed Quisling by his buttonhole:

'I hereby authorise you to purchase on my behalf a long smoked sausage. Wait. Not another step. Here is five kroner, give me back the half. I hereby authorise you to buy on my behalf the two longest smoked sausages you can find and another bottle of cognac. Here is five kroner. If it is not sufficient you have only to ask, there is more here in my breast pocket.'

Quisling at last managed to pull himself free and hurried off. Jon shouted after him:

'Make sure you get the right change for the five kroner. There should be a lot of change.'

A few minutes passed, at least ten. Jon chattered incessantly and I grew sleepy just listening to him. Four times he sat down beside me on the floor and spoke to me; but he was so restless he had to get up again. He started singing again.

We heard footsteps on the stairs, slow footsteps. Jon smiled.

'Listen,' he said, 'he's well loaded down.' He grinned and waggled the tip of his tongue.

But Quisling wasn't well loaded down, he wasn't loaded down at all. By the time he got there all the shops were shut. Quisling cursed every shopkeeper in town.

Jon was the only one who seemed content. There was no doubt about it, he was secretly very happy indeed and at once demanded the return of his money. He swore at the shopkeepers too, but it wasn't *his* fault after all, was it? Hadn't he been quite willing to treat us? As a matter of fact, he'd been on the point of running after him with another five kroner to add to the treat. Money was no big thing for him . . .

The candle burnt down and it was getting late. Jon began to yawn and talked about going to bed. Quisling sat quietly, thinking. He always managed to come up with something. 'Well then,' he said to me, 'I guess we better go home, you and I. Go home and go to bed and try to forget it's Christmas.' And with that he turned to Jon Tro and bade him goodnight. The three of us should all have been together on such a night, of course, but Jon wouldn't dare come along now, would he?

Wouldn't he dare?

Surely he wouldn't dare walk along the street in his straw hat?

The laddie from Tro dared.

And Jon put on his straw hat and staggered down the stairs in front of us.

Down in the street Quisling set off in the direction of the cafés, with Jon's straw hat shimmering like a halo round his bobbing head. Now and then he had to hold onto it when the wind gusted. Quisling kept going until we came to the catacombs and he stopped there.

'No it's no good, Jon Tro,' he said. 'People are staring at you, they're saying you're a pantomime clown in your straw hat. There's no call for you to put up with that.'

Jon livened up again.

'Who says I'm a clown?' he shouted, and he was ready to have a go at anyone. He flared up again, walked unnecessarily close to the street-light outside the catacombs just so that people could get a really good look at his straw hat. He took it off for the sole purpose of swinging it, pushed it back onto his neck and said that he was sweating, it was too hot, and generally challenged anybody who dared look at the laddie from Tro.

And since Quisling had got him this far it wasn't all that difficult to get him into the catacombs, and Jon Tro broke into his five kroner in there.

It turned out that Quisling hadn't eaten all day, even though he'd given me a good meal . . .

SECRET SORROW

I've just met him for the fourth time. He follows me wherever I go, I can never feel safe from him, he appears right in front of me in the most out of the way places. Once I even met him in my room in Kristiania; he had got in before me and was standing there . . .

But let me begin at the beginning.

I met him for the first time in Copenhagen. It was Christmas 1879; I had a place in Klareboderne.

One day as I was sitting alone in my room—I remember very clearly that I was supposed to be copying out some music, and that it was causing me a great deal of trouble, since I was quite unable to read music—there was a knock on my door. Light and subdued, like a woman's knock. I shout: Come in! and a man enters.

A man of about thirty, pale, with a somewhat glowering expression, and narrow in the shoulder, remarkably narrow. He wore a glove on only one of his hands.

He removed his hat as soon as he entered and his large eyes remained fixed on me the entire time as he approached where I sat writing. He apologised for intruding like this; he'd seen me entering and leaving the lodging house a couple of times and it occurred to him that we were old acquaintances. Didn't I remember him from Helsinki, from the police-station in Helsinki?

I had never been to Helsinki, there must be some misunderstanding . . .

No? Then perhaps it was Malmö. The more he thought about it the more certain he was that it was in Malmö he had bumped into me.

But I hadn't been to Malmö either.

He mentioned a couple of other places, and each time I answered he said, 'Just wait now! I'm convinced I've met you before, I just can't recall where.' Finally he mentioned Kristiania, and I grudgingly conceded that we might possibly have come across one another there. He made me feel unsure of myself, and I could not rule out the possibility that I might once have met him in Kristiania.

'I don't have any particular news for you,' he said. 'It just occurred to me to drop in and say hello to a fellow-countryman and old acquaintance.'

We conversed briefly, on matters of no importance, I've completely forgotten what. All I remember is that he formulated himself in a curiously ambiguous way, as if he were really saying something quite different from what he actually said, and that in general he gave the impression of being a secretive man.

When he rose to leave he once again apologised for disturbing me. Among other things he said:

'I get bored. I can't think what to do any more. Sometimes I play a practical joke on the police, just to pass the time. But it's so easy I can hardly be bothered.'

He said this seriously, but I chose to treat it as a joke.

At the door he turned as though suddenly remembering something and invited me to go for a drive with him that evening, 'for old time's sake'. At first I said no—I really can't explain why—but a moment later I accepted his invitation. The last thing he said to me was that I mustn't take any money with me. One could never be too careful. I could leave my money with my landlord, he said. I didn't quite get it, but said yes anyway and promised to be outside The Horse at five o'clock.

Alone again I thought about the man and what he had said. I found it strange that he should have come to visit me. And what was all that about money? To begin with it all seemed very curious, but I soon forgot about it. When you're travelling you soon get to know people, strangers can become friends in less than an hour. I was at The Horse at the appointed time.

The weather was so mild and the streets so muddy that we had to use a carriage. We had the hood up and the windows closed.

We drove west through Copenhagen, past Ladegaarden, out along Rolighedsvei and past the waterworks. All that long way we hardly exchanged a word; anyway the carriage rumbled terribly. Once we had crossed Grøndals Bridge and were approaching Utterslev the stranger takes a piece of rope from his pocket and begins playing with it, all the while staring fixedly at me. It's dark in the carriage, but I can see perfectly well what he's doing. We're sitting on the same seat, but turned to face each another, watching each other. Suddenly he says:

'You're not scared, are you?'

At the same time he holds the rope up to my face.

I lied, answering with a quavering voice:

'No, what is there to be scared of?'

But I was shaking with fear and thought of pulling the bell at once and alerting the driver. It annoyed me to have that piece of rope dangling in front of my eyes, so I got up and moved to the front seat.

We drive on like this for a while. Shortly afterwards he turned his gaze away from me and slowly put the rope back in his pocket, as though he had changed his mind about something. Then suddenly he sits bolt upright in his seat, points out of the window as though in great alarm and says:

'Look! Over there!'

Instinctively I turned my head, and at the same moment felt an icy grip around my neck. The scoundrel stood half-upright in front of me with his cold fingers round my throat. I don't know if I screamed, I don't think I did. Suddenly it occurred to me that this person just wanted to scare me, or to tease me, I was convinced that he didn't want to throttle me. It made me angry and I pushed him back as hard as I could. He kept his grip. I felt behind me for the bell-pull, fumbled after it, found it at last and pulled. Still he kept hold of me. He heard clearly that the bell rang, yet he would not let go. We struggled together for some time. He cut me on the throat, just below my right ear, his effrontery knew no bounds, he gave me this wound with a nail or a screwdriver, which he twisted, and it hurt. Then at last I'm able to punch my way free, swinging out and hitting him with solid, brutal blows wherever I could. Then the cabby

opens the door, and for the first time I realised that the carriage had
stopped.

'Shall we turn back?' asked the driver.

In complete confusion I climbed out of the carriage. My travelling
companion remained sitting where he was, calm and collected.

'Yes,' he replied, 'Let's turn back.'

'I'm *walking* back,' I said. 'As far as I'm concerned you can drive
this chap to hell.'

'Walking?' repeated the driver. 'On foot?'

The stranger said nothing. Didn't even look at me. Now I got
really angry. I shouted to the driver to get going, jumped back into
the carriage and slammed the door shut. In my extreme anger I felt
remarkably, almost unnaturally, strong.

I pressed myself unnecessarily close to my fellow-passenger, took
up as much room as I could, squashed him into a corner. As I twisted
and turned in my seat I hit him several times with my elbows. He
accepted this, did not react. Not until we were once again in Copenhagen did he say, with a smile:

'Well, I presume you'll report me for this?'

I did not reply.

He put both his feet up on my hat, which I had removed and
placed on the seat opposite me so that I could sit upright in the
carriage. He brought his heels down hard on the crown and I heard
it crack. I became more and more convinced that his sole aim was
to frighten me. I felt an intense humiliation.

'But if you are going to report me,' he continued, 'you'd better
do it straightaway. I'll be long gone by the time anyone tries to
arrest me. I assure you, probably even before daybreak tomorrow
I'll be over in Skåne. You'll be wasting your time!' He continued
in this vein, about how he'd be gone in a very short while. Then
suddenly he said: 'Or maybe I can't be bothered. Maybe I'll have
the pleasure of greeting you again tomorrow, on Østergade?'

He didn't say it in a challenging, taunting way. His voice was
low, almost melancholy. My hat was gradually being squashed flat
under his feet.

I responded that I would have the honour of ignoring him completely, that I would pass by him as though he were thin air if I

should meet him again, and walk right over him if he should happen to block my path. I wouldn't waste my words even if they would get you hanged, I said. I despise you and I can't even be bothered to throw you out of the carriage window.

I couldn't have done that anyway, but all the same I said it, the way one says such things. And he accepted it.

Back at The Horse we both got out. I walked off—hatless—while he remained behind to pay the driver.

That was the first time I met him. I still have the mark on my throat he gave me that evening.

2

Some years later, maybe three or four, I was on a short visit to Germany and making the trip from Hamburg to Bremerhafen. The train wasn't due to leave for another ten minutes when I reached the platform, so I had good time. I walked along looking for a good seat and got almost as far as the engine. There a man waves to me from the window of a carriage and to my great surprise I recognise my 'old acquaintance' from the drive through Copenhagen, the man with the dark eyes. I recognised him at once.

I give a start, I feel at once extremely uncomfortable and walk straight past his compartment. But as I did so it occurred to me that I might be giving the impression I was afraid of him, and being now several years older anyway I was not disposed to pass up the chance of another encounter with this interesting person. So I turn round, still as though looking for a seat on the train, and stop in a casual and indifferent sort of way outside his compartment. I open the door and enter.

The compartment was empty, apart from him.

I squeezed past him on the way in and he drew his knees back to let me by. In doing so he looked up as though he hadn't seen me before; and yet I was convinced that he had been waving to me just a few minutes previously. I had even somewhat unwillingly touched my hat and nodded to him, but he made no response.

I sat down in the corner. I was irritated with myself for that little nod and steeled myself to offer him a show of the most sublime indifference. He didn't seem to have aged in the slightest since our last meeting, but his clothes were different. On that first occasion they had been smart, almost elegant; now they were much plainer, a light-coloured, hard-wearing travelling outfit. On the seat directly opposite him was a leather suitcase.

The bell rings and the train sets off.

I made myself comfortable and put my feet up on the seat. About quarter of an hour passed. I acted as though oblivious of my travelling companion. He seemed lost in thought.

Then he reaches into an inside pocket and pulls out an oilcloth bag that looks like some kind of first-aid kit. He opens it and begins examining a number of rusty iron tools which he takes out one by one. They were queer-looking things with hooks on, some flat, some round, some fine, a mixture of large and small. It was obvious to me that this was a collection of jemmies. Nor did he make any attempt to hide what they were. Indeed, he twisted and turned these implements in his hand as if he were already picking locks with them. He even tried to open his suitcase with a couple of them. It was as though he were deliberately trying to show me what the hooks were for. All this time I sat and watched.

Careful! I thought to myself. He's doing this deliberately to taunt you. There's something behind all this. He's leading you on, trying to tempt you in some way.

Ten minutes passed. He takes a small, shiny file from his breast pocket and begins cleaning the jemmies with it. And after he's cleaned each one he places it on the seat beside him. Note how I was sitting: with my legs up on his seat and stretched out towards him. My shoe was almost touching his coat. He sits there, scraping away.

Then, absentmindedly, as though lost in thought, he places one newly sharpened jemmy on my leg and starts on another. The man uses me as a work-surface. I sit there and allow it to happen. I didn't move. Sat waiting for him to do it again. And sure enough, he placed another jemmy on my leg, then another, and another. He treated me as though I were a cushion, as though I were part of the seat. By the time he was finished there was a row of some six of these little hooks ranged along my leg.

I stood up. Not suddenly, but quickly enough to make them all fall to the floor before he could prevent it. I had just one thought in mind: to return some of his profound contempt.

He didn't say anything when the jemmies fell. Just picked them up again in silence, one by one.

At that moment the conductor arrived. To my great surprise I observed that my travelling companion made not the slightest attempt, even now, to hide the hooks. All the time the conductor was present he left them on open display. Not until he had gone did he return the case and its contents to his pocket. It was almost as though he had been waiting for just such an opportunity to show off his dangerous tools.

We journey on for perhaps another half hour, we pass stations, stop, journey on, and still my travelling companion says nothing. Quite deliberately I conducted myself as though I were alone in the compartment. I put my feet up on the seat again, yawned noisily, sang now and then, all just to show him my awesome indifference. Yet none of it seemed to bother him. I lit a cigar and tossed the burning match onto his hand, just threw it away as heedlessly as if there were no one at all sitting there, and I saw it hit his hand. The only reaction was a slight twitching of the mouth as he drew back his lips slightly, almost as though he wanted to smile. Otherwise he sat quietly.

After we had journeyed a little further in this fashion he suddenly looked out of the train window as though he recognised the country-side, got to his feet quickly and picked up his suitcase by one of its straps. He stood like that for a few more minutes until the train came to a halt at a small station. Then he gives me an ironically deep bow, very deep, in complete silence, without looking at me, takes a couple of paces backwards, bows again, and with a broad smile turns and leaves the compartment. He hailed a porter to carry his baggage and walked off.

Throughout the entire journey he had neither spoken to me nor looked me in the face.

3

Years passed, three years, and I met him again in an obscure part of New York, in a gambling den. I was there before him and was sitting at the roulette table when he entered. An attendant offered to relieve him of his hat and coat but he merely shook his head and kept on both. Moments later he removed his hat and carried it in his hand. He turned his attention to the roulette table.

Space was made for him and he began to play. It seemed to me that he followed my bets with more interest than his own. I lost consistently, playing black and a double, black and a double, all the time, always losing. Maybe this was what interested him so much.

Suddenly he says to me straight across the table, in Norwegian:

'Don't you realise that you're being cheated?'

He ran the risk of others besides me understanding his words, and if there were any that did then he would be lucky to get away without spilling his blood. But he said it anyway, in a loud voice, looking directly at me as he spoke.

I pretended I hadn't heard him and carried on backing the same number and colour as before. And I lost just as heavily. I felt a burning and perverse obstinacy: if that person tried once more to involve himself in my affairs then I would speak to the croupier. I was angry and upset. There could no longer be any doubt that I was being cheated, I could see as much myself: the croupier had a key in his hand which he surreptitiously held close to the wheel whenever it was about to stop, and it had already occurred to me several bets ago that there might be a magnet in this key. But I chose to do nothing, just kept on playing and losing my little bets.

Then the stranger says to the croupier:

'Put that key in your pocket!'

His voice was cold and imperious and the croupier obeyed him at once, merely explaining that it was the key to the bank, he kept it in his hand for convenience. But he did as he was told, instantly. I found his obedience insulting and I became angry with him. I pushed my last ten chips onto the black, stood up and left without waiting to see what happened.

After that I did not meet my man again until last winter in Kristiania. I was living up on St Hans' Hill then, I had a fourth-floor room. As I returned from the dining-room after supper one day I found my secretive friend standing in the middle of my room. I had left the key in the keyhole and he had simply let himself in. All he does is hold out his hand and ask for 16 kroner — 16 kroner — then he thanks me, thanks me most humbly — twice — then heads for the door. He stops and says:

'My God, how stupid you are!'

He said it turned towards the door, in a tone of utter contempt.

My old bitterness revives and I take a couple of steps towards him. When I see that he is about to open the door and disappear I cannot stop myself from saying:

'Wait! You haven't stolen anything here, have you?'

I say this expressly to hurt him; I did not suspect him of having stolen anything, I merely wished to humiliate him.

He seemed not in the least embarrassed or angered by my words; he simply turned towards me and said, in surprise:

'Stolen?'

And with that he sat down in a chair, opened his coat and from his breast pocket took out a handful of papers, among which I saw a route-map and a small red wallet full of money, absolutely stuffed with notes, several hundred kroner. He held it out to me:

'And what would you have that I might find worth stealing?' he said, smiling.

He had trumped me again. He always trumped me, shamed me, condemned me to ignominy no matter what. He stood up and left and I did nothing, made no attempt to stop him leaving. I let him go. Only when I heard his footsteps on the staircase far below did I think to open the door and then bang it shut again so that it sounded through the whole house. That was all I did.

In his contempt for me he had simply left my 16 kroner behind. I found them on the chair he had been sitting on. And in my shame and anger I left them there for days before picking them up, hoping that he might come back and notice that I had neglected to reclaim them.

Later I heard that he had also visited my landlord and conducted himself in a bizarre fashion. My landlord, who was a police constable, would have nothing to do with him; in his opinion the man was insane. Among other things, the intruder had attempted to buy an antique Dutch coffee pot made of brass that was standing on the stove. He had practically refused to take no for an answer.

Such are the details of my several encounters with this most peculiar person. Recently I have learnt to think of him without rancour. He interests me greatly, and I look forward to meeting him again. I believe I understand now something of his nature and of the reasons for his absurd behaviour. Just a few months ago I met another person, a woman in her thirties, who told me something about herself that put me on the trail. She had once committed a crime which would have earned her several days on bread and water, and the incident continued to disturb her greatly. It was not conscience, nor contrition, but rather an inexplicable longing to be found out. For some time she had positively invited suspicion of herself, but to no avail. Her success in avoiding detection made her heedless and reckless; she wearied of not being unmasked even when she colluded in her own detection. She took steps to make her secret hard to keep. She exposed herself wilfully to arouse people's suspicions. But no matter what she did, no one ever suspected her, no one ever reported her.

The circumstances of her story made me think of my secretive friend, the man with the dark eyes. No doubt he hoped again and again that his behaviour would be enough to drive me to report him to the police. But in this he had failed.

A superior type of person, with a blemished and strangely twisted soul. A human being in psychic pain, suffering, perhaps, because a secret that might bring shame upon him was fated never to be revealed.

THE QUEEN OF SHEBA

1

You travel, wander about here and there, sometimes meeting people you've met before, suddenly, in unexpected places, so that from sheer surprise you forget to remove your hat and offer a greeting.

This happens to me frequently. Very frequently. Nothing to be done about it.

Something that happened to me in 1888 relates in a strange way to an experience I had earlier this year, in fact not much more than a week ago, during a short trip to Sweden. It's so simple, and puzzling. Everything seemed to happen so naturally. Perhaps it's not even worth relating at all. But I'll try as best I can.

The last time we met you asked me ... well, you remember yourself what you asked, I don't need to repeat it. But I answered on that occasion that it didn't seem to matter how hard I tried, something always seemed to get in the way and I would be rejected and shown the door. I'm about to demonstrate to you now that I was not lying, that I was telling you the truth. I have never come as close as I did this last time; and yet I was still—oh how sweetly— shown the door. There's nothing I can do about it.

In 1888 I came by a little money, I was supposed to travel somewhere or other, it was all very casual. I made my way to Sweden, on foot, following the railway line, the trains passing me day after day. I met many people, and they all greeted me, saying 'God be with you!' and I said 'God be with you' too, since I didn't know what else to say. By the time I reached Gothenburg my first pair of shoes were worn to pieces; but that's not what I am talking about.

The incident I am about to describe took place even before I reached Gothenburg. Let me ask you: when a woman glances at you from a window and later takes no notice of you at all, you ignore it, don't you? You don't get any ideas. You'd have to be a fool to get ideas after just one quick glance. But when the lady not only looks at you with the greatest interest but lets you have her room and even her own bed at a Swedish staging post—well, don't you think there's grounds for wondering what's on her mind, and allowing yourself to get a few ideas? I do, and I did, right up to the very end. Just last week it cost me a painful journey to Kalmar . . .

I had reached the Bärby staging post. It was late in the evening and I had been walking since morning so I made up my mind to stop for the day. I went inside and asked for food and lodging.

Yes I could have food all right but not lodging: every room was taken, the place was full.

I was speaking to a young girl whom I later found out was the daughter of the house. I look at her and act as though I don't understand that it's full. Is this maybe her way of trying to remind me that I'm a Norwegian, a political opponent?

'Lot of wagons here,' I say casually.

'Yes it's people on the way to market who're staying the night,' she answers. 'I don't think we've got a single vacant bed left.'

She goes out to order my food. When she returned she spoke again about how busy the place was. She said:

'You can either go on to the next station, to Ytterån, or back up the line a bit on the train. As I said, we're full up here.'

I forgave the naïve child, I had no desire to be unnecessarily sharp with her, but naturally I had no intention of leaving the place before morning. I was at a public staging post and it was my firm intention to get a bed there.

'Lovely weather,' I said.

'Yes,' she answered. 'So a walk on to Ytterån will be just the thing this evening. It isn't far, a good six-mile hike, that's all.'

I felt that the whole business was getting a bit out of hand and said, slowly and seriously:

'Naturally I am assuming you will provide me with a bed here tonight. I'm tired and I don't want to walk any more.'

'But all the beds are taken!' she answers.

'I can't help that.'

And slowly and gravely I lowered myself into a seat.

As it happens I felt slightly sorry for the girl, she didn't seem to be trying to cause me trouble just for the sake for it, she had an honest face and she was keeping her hatred of Norwegians well under control.

'Make up a bed for me wherever you like,' I said. 'Right here on the sofa will do fine.'

But it turned out that even the *sofa* was taken.

Now I started to feel a little anxious. I knew those Swedes and their good six miles; a good six miles was an infinity and would just about finish me off.

'For pity's sake, can't you see my shoes are completely worn out?' I cried. 'Surely you wouldn't drive people from your door with shoes like these?'

'Your shoes won't be any better tomorrow either, will they?' she answered with a smile.

She was right about that and I really couldn't think what to do next. Then the door flies open and another young girl rushes in.

She's laughing at something that has happened to her or that she's thinking about and she has her mouth open ready to tell the story. When she catches sight of me she doesn't seem the least self-conscious, just gives me a long, steady look and even a brief nod. Then she says quietly:

'What's the matter, Lotta?'

I can't hear what Lotta answers her, but I do know they're whispering about me. I sit there watching them, waiting and listening as though my fate were in the balance. They steal a glance at my shoes and I hear them laughing. The second of the two young ladies shakes her head and is about to leave.

When she reached the door she turned round suddenly as though something had just occurred to her and said:

'But I could sleep with you tonight Lotta, and then he could have my room.'

'No,' answers Lotta. 'Surely Miss, you can't mean that?'

'Oh but I do!'

Pause. Lotta thinks about it.

'Well, if you do Miss, then—' and turning to me she continues: 'The young lady wishes to hand over her room to you.'

I jump up, turn my toes outward and bow. I think I made a pretty good job of it. I also thanked the lady verbally, told her that she had shown me a munificence that was unparalleled in my life, and that her heart was as good as her eyes were lovely—dear lady! With that I bowed again, making yet again, I think, a good job of it.

Yes indeed, I performed the whole thing perfectly. She blushed and ran for the door laughing, with Lotta on her heels.

I sat there thinking it over. It was good; she had laughed, blushed and laughed. It couldn't have started better. God, how young she was, maybe 18, with high cheekbones and a dimple in her chin. No scarf round her neck, nothing round her neck, not even a neck-band on her dress, just a draw-string. And that heavy, dark look in her sweet face. Excellent, she had noticed me with interest.

An hour later I see her out in the yard; she's sitting up in one of the empty carriages and cracking a whip. How young she was, how full of energy, sitting up there quite alone humming to herself and cracking the whip as though she were driving along. It occurs to me to unhitch the team and pull the wagon myself and I raise my hat and am about to say something when she suddenly stands up, tall and proud like a queen on her throne, looks at me a moment and climbs down from the wagon. I shall never forget it. She had no real grounds for conducting herself like that, but she really did look magnificent the way she stood up and got down from the carriage. I put my hat back on and crept away, deflated and embarrassed. Damn this idea of pulling the wagon myself.

But on the other hand: what was up with her? Hadn't she just handed her room over to me? Then why this sudden coolness? It's just a game, I said to myself, she's just pretending, I know that trick, she wants to see me squirming, well that's okay, I'll squirm for her!

I sat down on the steps and lit my pipe. Market traders came and went around me. Now and then I heard from within the house the sound of corks being drawn and the clinking of glass. But I did not see the young lady again.

The only thing I had to read was a map of Sweden. I sit there smoking, annoyed with myself, and in the end I get the map out of my pocket and start reading it. Minutes pass, and Lotta appears at the door, offering to show me up to my room if I'm ready. It's ten, so I stand up and follow her. In the corridor we meet the young lady.

Something now occurs which I remember down to the least detail: the panelling in the corridor has just been painted, but I don't know this; I stand aside for the young lady as she comes towards us, and the damage is done. She screams:

'The paint . . . !'

But it's too late, the whole of my left shoulder has rubbed against the panel.

She looks at me in total dismay, then looks at Lotta and says:

'What shall we do about it?'

Those words exactly: What shall we do about it? And Lotta replies that the best thing to do about *it* is to rub it with something. Then she bursts out laughing.

We go out onto the steps again and Lotta finds something to rub me with.

'Please sit down,' she says, 'otherwise I can't reach up.'

So I sit down.

We begin to chat . . .

Believe it or not, by the time I parted company with the young lady that evening I had high hopes. We sat there chatting and laughing and gossiping about all sorts of things, we must have sat there gossiping for at least a quarter of an hour. So? Well no, I'm not making a big deal out of it either, all I'm saying is that I just don't think a young woman will spend a good fifteen minutes practically alone in conversation with a man unless she means something by it. And when we did at last part company she said goodnight twice; finally she opened the door just a fraction and said goodnight a third time before closing it. Then I heard the two of them laughing merrily away, yes indeed, we were all in an excellent humour.

I go into my room—*her* room. It was empty, an ordinary staging post room with bare, blue-painted walls and a small, low bed. On the table was a translation of Ingraham's *The Prince of the House of David*. I lay down and began reading. Still I hear laughter and giggling from the young girls' room. What a gorgeous young flirt! That dark look in her young face! And how lively her laughter was, despite that haughty demeanour!

I began thinking, and the thought of her glowed silent and powerful in my heart.

In the morning I awoke with something hard digging into my side, and discovered I had spent the night with *The Prince of the House of David*. Up and get dressed then, it's nine o'clock.

I go downstairs and get my breakfast. The young lady is nowhere to be seen. I wait half an hour and she doesn't show. Finally I ask Lotta in a circumspect way what has become of her.

'She's gone hasn't she,' answers Lotta.

Gone? Didn't she live there, at the staging post?

No, she was the young lady from the manor house. She left early this morning on the train, she had to go to Stockholm.

I am dumbfounded. She had of course left neither a letter nor even a note for me, and I was so dispirited I didn't even ask her name, nothing seemed to matter much any more. No, you should never put your trust in the loyalty of women.

I wander on to Gothenburg, dull of eye and sore at heart. Who would have thought it—she looked so proud, and so honest! But that was okay, I would take it like a man. Not a soul at the hotel should know of my suffering . . .

Now it was at just at this time that Julius Kronberg was exhibiting his great painting *The Queen of Sheba* in Gothenburg. Like everyone else I too went along to see it and I was really taken with it. The curious thing was that the Queen herself seemed to bear a remarkable resemblance to my young lady from the manor house—not when she was laughing and fooling around, but the way she was when she stood up in that empty carriage. God knows, I felt the pain of it all over again in my heart!

The painting gave me no peace, it reminded me too much of my lost happiness. One night it inspired me to write my celebrated article of appreciation, *The Queen of Sheba*, which appeared in *Dagbladet* on 9 December, 1888. In this I wrote the following on the subject of the Queen:

> She is a mature Ethiopian, 19 years old, seductively lovely, regal and womanly ... With her left hand she lifts the veil from her face as she gazes at the King. She is not dark, even her dark hair is almost wholly obscured by the silver diadem she wears; she looks like a European who has travelled in the Orient and been touched by the hot sun. But the darkness of her eyes reveals her real origins, a gaze at once heavy and fiery which causes the spectator to flinch. One will not forget these eyes, in far away places one will remember them, one will see them again in dreams ...

The stuff about the eyes is particularly good. Ask anyone, you can't write like that unless you feel something similar in your own heart. And from that day onwards my heart has always referred to that remarkable girl from the Bärby staging post as the Queen of Sheba.

2

I'm not finished with her, four years later she pops up again, it was only about a week ago.

I'm travelling from Copenhagen to Malmö, I'm supposed to meet someone there, someone who's expecting me: again, I'm telling this exactly the way it happened. My things are safely lodged at Kramers' and I've been shown my room. I leave to meet this someone who's expecting me, but first I want to take a short walk to the railway station to prepare myself for the meeting. I meet a man there and we start a conversation. Just as I'm standing there saying something to this man I see a face in the window of a train about to depart, the face is turned towards me, two eyes studying me—my God, it's the Queen of Sheba!

Instantly I leap on board the train and a few seconds later we're off.

It's fate. To see her again after the passage of four years, to hop

on board a departing train with all my luggage still at the hotel—
that's fate. Nothing you can do about it. I had even left my overcoat
hanging in the room, all I had with me as I jumped on board the
train was a shoulder bag.

I look round. I'm in a first-class carriage along with a couple of
other passengers. Fine, I sit down beside them and make myself
comfortable with a cigar and something to read. What was fate going
to do with me now? I would go where the Queen of Sheba went,
somehow I would force a meeting with her. Where she got off I
would get off too, my mission was to meet her. When the conductor
came and asked for tickets please, I didn't have one.

Then where was I going?

I couldn't be quite sure about that, but . . .

Okay then, I could pay as far as Arlöf, with a 40 øre surcharge.
At Arlöf I would need to buy another ticket.

I took the conductor's advice and paid the extra, with pleasure.

From Arlöf I bought a ticket on to Lund, maybe the Queen of
Sheba was visiting someone in Lund.

But she didn't get off at Lund.

Again I had to pay the conductor, this time to Lackalänga, with
another 40-øre surcharge—80 altogether so far. From Lackalänga I
bought a ticket to Hessleholm just to be on the safe side and with
that sat back, in a state of some anxiety over this complicated
journey.

The conversation between the other passengers began irritating
me. For God's sake, what did I care if there was an outbreak of
foot and mouth disease in Hamburg? My fellow-passengers were
apparently country folk, simple Swedish cattle-buyers, and for a good
45 minutes all they could talk about was this outbreak of foot and
mouth disease in Hamburg. As you might imagine, it was *absolutely
fascinating*. And on top of it all: wasn't there someone waiting for
me in Malmö? Let them wait.

But the Queen of Sheba didn't get off at Hessleholm either.

Now I'm furious. I pay the conductor to Balingslöf plus another
extra 40 øre—making a total surcharge of 1 kroner 20 øre—and
from Balingslöf with gritted teeth a ticket all the way to Stockholm.
By God this thing had now cost me no less than 118 kroner, cash.

But it was evident now that the Queen of Sheba was going to Stockholm, just as on that previous occasion four years ago.

We travel on for hours. I keep a watch out at every station but she doesn't get off. I see her in the carriage window and she watches me; one thing at least is for sure, she's lost none of her feeling for me, that much is obvious. But she seemed a touch shy and lowered her eyes each time I passed by her window. I didn't greet her, I forgot every time, and if she hadn't been stuck inside that box of a Ladies Only compartment I would have made my move long ago, reminded her that we were old acquaintances and that I had once even slept in her bed. I would have delighted her with the information that I had slept extremely well, slept right through until nine o'clock. How well the intervening four years had treated her. Now she was more womanly, more majestic than ever.

And hour after hour passed, and nothing happened except that around five o'clock we ran over a cow, we could hear the legs being crushed and had to stop briefly to check the rails before continuing. My two fellow-travellers were now conversing on the subject of steamships in the Øresund. Again, it was riveting stuff. What laughter, what laughter. Wasn't there someone waiting for me, waiting for me in . . .

Ah, to hell with that someone in Malmö.

Onward, ever onward, we pass Elmhult, Liatorp, Vislanda. At Vislanda the Queen of Sheba leaves her carriage, I don't lose sight of her for an instant; and now—yes, I thought so—here she comes back again. Fine. On we go.

We arrive at Alfvesta, change here for Kalmar.

Again the Queen of Sheba leaves her carriage. I watch to see if it's that again, but this time she transfers to the train to Kalmar. I wasn't prepared for this, it takes me completely by surprise and by the time I react I'm almost too late. I tumble head over heels onto the Kalmar train just as she's pulling out of the station.

A solitary man in the carriage, he doesn't even look up, he's reading. I sit down, start reading too. A couple of minutes later I hear:

'Tickets please!'

Another conductor.

'Ticket, right!' I say, and hand him my ticket.

'This is not valid,' he says. 'This is the Kalmar line.'

'Not valid?'

'Not on this line.'

'Well, it's not my fault if someone sells me an invalid ticket.'

'Where are you going?'

'Stockholm, of course,' I answer. 'Where else would I be going?'

'Yes, but this is the train for Kalmar, don't you understand, it's going to Kalmar,' he says irritably.

No I didn't know that, but was his pedantic response to such a minor misunderstanding really necessary?

No doubt it was motivated by the fact that I was a Norwegian, it was a politically motivated response. I would make a note of his name.

'Well then, what are we going to do?' I ask.

'What you'll have to do . . . where did you say you were going? You won't get to Stockholm on this train.'

'Fine, then I'll go to Kalmar, actually I meant to say Kalmar,' I answer. I've never really fancied Stockholm anyway, I can't say I'll be borrowing money to try and get there another time. So this wretched Queen of Sheba was headed for Kalmar, at least that put me out of my torment.

'Pay me as far as Gemla, plus a 40-øre surcharge,' says the conductor. 'At Gemla you'll have to buy another ticket.'

'But I've just paid 118 kroner,' I protested. All the same I paid, plus the 40 øre extra—making a grand total so far of 1 kroner 60 øre extra. But at Gemla my patience ran out, and I stormed up to the ticket office and shouted through the opening:

'How far can I get on this line?'

'How far? To Kalmar,' came the answer.

'No further? Not even a tiny bit further?'

'Impossible. After that you're in the Baltic.'

'Fine. Ticket to Kalmar!'

'What class?'

Ha, he asked me what class! Clearly the man didn't recognise me and hadn't read any of my books. I gave him the answer he deserved:

'First class.'

I paid and took my seat.

Night came and my unpleasant fellow-passenger had stretched out on his seat, eyes closed, in complete silence, without even a glance in my direction. How was I supposed to pass the time? I couldn't sleep, I was on my feet constantly, checking the doors, opening and closing the windows, freezing, yawning, keeping an eye out for the queen. Inwardly I began cursing her.

Finally, finally morning came. My fellow-passenger sat up and looked out of the window. Shortly afterwards, wide awake, he began reading again, still without looking at me. His book seemed to be endless. He annoyed me. I began singing and whistling to irritate him, but he declined to be irritated. I wished with all my heart I was back with the foot and mouth disease again rather than this unresponsive and stuck-up bastard.

Finally I couldn't stand him any more. I said:

'Excuse me, might I enquire, how far are you travelling?'

'Oh,' he said. 'Quite a way.'

That was all.

'We ran over a cow yesterday,' I said.

'I beg your pardon?'

'We ran over a cow yesterday.'

'Really?'

And he read on.

'Will you *sell* me that book?' I blurted out in desperation.

'This book? No.'

'No?'

'No.'

There the matter rested. He didn't even permit himself a sideways glance. In the face of such obstinacy I gave up. Actually it was all that damn queen's fault that I had been forced into the company of such a person, she really had caused me no end of bother. But all would be forgotten when I met her, and oh I'd tell her all the troubles I'd had, I'd tell her about my article in the paper, about the person waiting and waiting for me in Malmö, about my journey first on the Stockholm line and then on the Kalmar line—dear lady! I would make a really big impression on her again. And not the slightest hint of a reference to those øre surcharges and the 118 kroner.

And the train rolls on.

In my boredom I begin looking out of the window. The view is always and ever the same: trees, fields, plains, dancing houses, telegraph poles along the line and at every station the usual empty goods wagons. Each wagon was marked *Golfyta*. What was *Golfyta*? It was not a number, not a person. Maybe *Golfyta* was a great river in Skåne. Or a brand name. Or even a religious sect. Then I remembered: the *Golfyta* was a unit of weight. Unless I was very much mistaken there were 132 pounds in one *Golfyta*. But these were the old-fashioned pounds, so there would be nearer 133 of them to the *Golfyta* . . .

And the train rolled on.

How could that dumb idiot sit there in his seat hour after hour and just read? I could have read through a crummy little book like that three times in the time he took, but he was utterly shameless, puffed up with his own importance, podgy with learning. Finally his stupidity became utterly intolerable. I leaned forward, looked at him and said:

'I beg your pardon?'

He raised his eyes and gazed at me in astonishment.

'I'm sorry?' he said.

'I beg your pardon?'

He didn't understand it at all.

'What do you want?' he asked angrily.

'What do *I* want? What do *you* want?'

'Me? I don't want anything.'

'No. Neither do I.'

'I see. Then why are you speaking to me?'

'Me? Was I speaking to you?'

'I see,' he said, and turned away in anger.

After that we fell silent again.

And the hours pass, until finally the whistle blows for Kalmar.

Now for it. Now for the great battle! I stroke my chin, naturally I'm unshaven, as usual. A lack of foresight there, not having at stations along the line places where people could get themselves a shave in order to look half-decent for that important occasion. I wasn't demanding a permanent barber at every station, but surely

one at every fiftieth station wasn't an unreasonable demand? With
that I rested my case.

The train came to a halt.

I jump straight out and see the Queen of Sheba get out too. But
she's at once surrounded by so many people that it's impossible to
get close to her. There's even a young man who kisses her—the
brother, no doubt, he lives here, has a business here, he's the one
she's come to visit! A moment later a carriage pulls up, she climbs
in, two or three others join her and away they go.

I remain standing. Whisked away from under my very nose. Without a moment's hesitation. Fine, nothing to be done about it for the
time being. In fact, come to think of it, she's done me a favour,
given me time to get a shave and tidy myself up a bit before I present
myself. Now be sure to use your time wisely!

A porter approaches and offers to carry my luggage.

No, I didn't have any luggage.

No luggage *at all*?

No, no luggage *at all*, so now you know. Is that clear enough?

But I couldn't get rid of the man. He wanted to know if I was
travelling on.

No, not travelling on.

Then was I going to be staying here?

Maybe for a while. Was there a hotel nearby?

But what was I going to do here? Was I a secret agent? Some
kind of inspector?

Another person who didn't recognise me! No, I was not some
kind of inspector.

Then what was I?

'Good day!' I shouted into his face and left. Peerless insolence!
I could if necessary easily find a hotel on my own. In the meantime
I had to think up some occupation for myself, invent some purpose
for my being there; clearly when some wretch of a porter like
him was so inquisitive then the manager of a hotel was going to
be even worse. What in the eyes of God and Man was I going
to be doing in Kalmar? I would also need some credible excuse
for my presence there in order not to compromise the Queen of
Sheba.

So I set about thinking what to do in Kalmar. Even in the barber's chair I get no respite from the problem. Of one thing I was convinced: I could not show myself at the hotel until I had it worked out.

'Do you have a telephone?' I ask.

No the barber had no telephone.

'Then can you send a boy to the nearest hotel to book a room for me? I haven't had time myself, there are a few matters I must attend to first.'

'But of course.'

And off goes the boy.

I wander the streets, inspected the church, the harbour, walking quickly in case someone tried to stop me and ask what I was doing in Kalmar. Finally I reached the park, slumped down onto a bench and abandoned myself to my meditations. I was alone.

Kalmar—what was I doing in Kalmar? The name seemed familiar to me, I had read about it somewhere. What the hell was it, something political, some extraordinary assembly or other, some peace negotiation? I tried the Peace of Kalmar. The Kalmar Peace Agreement, wasn't that perhaps exactly what I had read about? Or was it the Kalmar Paragraph? But after due consideration it seemed to me that I really wasn't all that familiar with any Kalmar Paragraph. Suddenly I jump to my feet: Kalmar, that was it, the battle of Kalmar—like the battle of Kalvskindet, the battle of Wörth. Now I had it! And I head off in the direction of the hotel. Since it was the battle of Kalmar I would research the historical sites. That would be my business in town: *there* lay Niels Juels' ship, *there* it was that an enemy cannonball penetrated deep inland and ploughed up the dirt in a cabbage field. And it was *there* that Gustavus Adolphus fell on the deck of the man o' war. Kolbein the strong asked: 'What was that, so loud in its breaking?' And Einar answered: 'It was Norway, escaping your clutches . . . ,'

But reaching the hotel steps I made a cowardly about-turn and abandoned my whole battle theory. There had never been any battle of Kalmar, it was Copenhagen I was thinking of! Once again I set off wandering through the town. Things were not looking good for me.

I wandered for the remainder of the day, and neither food nor drink passed my lips. I was utterly exhausted. And it was too late to go into a bookshop and buy some books on the matter, all the bookshops were closed. In the end I accosted a man who was lighting lamps:

'Excuse me,' I asked politely, 'What historical event took place here in Kalmar?'

The man simply says: 'Took place?' and stares at me.

'Yes,' I say. 'I have this very clear impression that at some point a great event took place here in Kalmar. It's a matter of considerable historical importance, that's why I want to know.'

We stand there facing each other.

'Where do you live?' he asks.

'And I have come here for the sole purpose of studying it,' I continue. 'It's cost me quite a bit, I can assure you, in fact 1 krone and 60 øre in surcharges, not to mention the 118 kroner to which I make not even the slightest hint of a reference. Ask the conductor if you don't believe me.'

'Are you from Norway?'

'Yes I'm from Norway.'

'Are you a secret agent?'

This was exactly what I was trying to find out from the man myself, what I was, and tired as I was I was again obliged to move on as rapidly as possible. It was the queen's fault, just like everything else was her fault, and in mild fashion I suggested she go to hell for all the trouble she was making for me. Again I made my way to the park. No, now I could see no way out.

I stand there, sheltering close to a tree. People began passing by until I no longer thought it safe to stay there and once again dragged myself away. Three hours later I found myself outside the city, out in the country. I look around, I'm alone, and something massive appears before my eyes. I stand there staring at it. It looks like a mountain with a church on top. As I'm standing there a man walks by, so I stop him and ask him what kind of a mountain is that, I didn't know it from my geography though I did know a great many mountains.

'That's the castle,' he answered.

The castle. Kalmar Castle! That's what all this stuff going through my head had been about!

'The castle is inevitably, I suppose, in a ruined and poor condition by comparison with the days when it was the scene of great events?' I asked.

'Oh no, the caretaker keeps it in good repair,' answers the man.

'Who lives there at the moment? I mean: which king is it that's imprisoned in the south wing? The name is on the tip of my tongue.'

'It's packed with armour, swords and antiques, all kinds of ancient relics . . .'

There and then the idea comes to me: I have come to study the collection at the castle. If the man hadn't had a sack on his back I would have hugged him. I do remember that I asked after his wife and children before parting from him. By about midnight I was back at the hotel.

I roused the landlord and told him I was the one who had reserved the room. I'm here to study ancient relics, I told him briskly and angrily. And for all you know I might even have come here to *buy* some. *That* is what I do.

The landlord appeared to accept my explanation and showed me up to my room.

There follows a week of difficulties and wasted time, a whole week: the Queen of Sheba has not shown herself. Day after day I searched for her, looked high and low, tried cross-examining the postmaster, consulted a couple of policemen, searched every inch of the park during the promenading hour, every day studied the display gallery outside the photographers' to see if she might crop up there—all in vain. I hired two men to watch the station day and night in case she tried to slip away, and waited and waited for a resolution.

In the meantime I was also obliged to turn up at the castle every single day and study the collection of relics. I filled page after page with observations, counted the rust spots on the sabres and the battered old spurs, logged every damn date and inscription I came across on the lids of chests and on old paintings; why I even noted down a sack of feathers I found one day lying at the back of the ancient relics, which turned out to be the property of the caretaker.

Fuelled by bitterness and despair, my investigations were conducted to the sound of grinding teeth: having first begun this search for the Queen of Sheba I did not intend to abandon it halfway through, even if it meant becoming a fully fledged antiquary in the process.

I telegraphed to Copenhagen and had my mail forwarded and in general began preparing to spend the winter there. God only knew where it would all end, I had already been living six days at the hotel. On Sunday I paid four small boys to attend morning and evening service to see if she turned up; but no luck there either.

On Tuesday morning my mail finally arrived. That Tuesday nearly killed me. One letter was from the person who was waiting for me in Malmö: since I hadn't come by now then obviously I was never going to come—goodbye! I felt a pang deep in my heart. A second was from a friend informing me that *Morgenbladet* and some German newspaper were accusing me of plagiarism and could back it up with quotations. I felt a second pang deep in my heart. The third letter was a bill—I didn't read it, I couldn't bear any more, I slumped onto the sofa and sat staring straight ahead.

And still I had not drained my cup of sorrow.

There's a knock at the door.

'Enter!' I cry with hollow voice.

In comes the landlord, followed by an old woman. She's carrying a basket under her arm.

'Excuse us,' says the landlord, 'but you do buy antiques don't you?'

I stare at him.

'Antiques? Do I buy antiques?'

'Well you said so yourself.'

And so I was forced to confess my interest in antiques. Yes, that was quite right, I bought them too. Sorry I didn't quite follow, I was thinking of something else. Yes of course, I bought all manner of strange old things. Let's see what you've got!

And the woman uncovers her basket.

I clap my hands in delight and declare that I want the lot, every last piece. What an enchanting syringe! Into which ear of which king had that last been inserted? Well there was no hurry, I'd find out soon enough when I looked it up in my papers. How much did she want for that spoon made of horn? And those three charred Jaabæk pipes, I just had to have them at any price. Same goes for the pitchfork. How much for the lot?

The woman thinks about it.

'Give me ten kroner,' she says.

And I gave her the ten kroner, without haggling, gladly, just to get rid of her as quickly as possible. As soon as she had gone I made my way to the park to get some fresh air. The whole thing was getting completely out of hand!

A nanny and a small child sit down on the bench next to me, I glanced at them as a signal for them to be quiet. Shortly afterwards a couple passed by arm in arm, slowly walking along the gravel path. I notice them, I stir, sit bolt upright staring—it's the Queen of Sheba!

Finally, at long long last, the Queen of Sheba again!

There's a gentleman walking with her, the brother, the one who kissed her when she arrived. They walk arm in arm, speaking softly. I steel myself, now's the time, come what may. I would begin by reminding her that I had slept in her bed once, that should be enough to make her remember me, after that I would be into it, the brother would understand and walk on ahead a little . . .

I stepped forward.

Both looked at me in astonishment, and at that instant my introduction goes to pieces. I stammer: 'Miss . . . four years ago . . .' then fall silent.

'What does he want?' says the gentleman, looking at her. Then he turns to me and says the same thing: 'What do you want?' He says it rather condescendingly.

'I, er,' I answered, 'I just want permission to greet the young lady: is that any of your business? She and I are old acquaintances, I have even slept in her . . .'

The Queen interrupts me with a cry:

'Let us leave, let us leave!'

Okay so she doesn't want to know me, she denies me. In my indignation I follow the couple as they hurry away. Suddenly the gentleman turns round, sees that I'm following them and blocks the way. As it happens he didn't look all that bold, he was shaking visibly. The Queen carried on walking. Finally she broke into a run.

'What is you want, man?' he asks again.

'From you, nothing,' I say. 'It just occurred to me to say hello to the young lady, the woman you were walking with, I've met her before, and out of pure courtesy . . .'

'In the first place, it appears that the young lady doesn't want to see you again,' he answers. 'In the second place the young lady is married, she is in fact my wife. So there!'

'She is . . . what? . . . Is she your wife?'

'Yes she is my *wife*,' he bellowed. 'Now do you understand?'

His wife, his wife . . . What more is there to tell? I slumped down on a bench. This was the *coup de grâce*! I closed my eyes and let the chap go; what more business had I with him, now that the sun of my happiness was gone out? I continued sitting there for several hours, abandoning myself to the most abject grief.

Towards midday I made my way back to the hotel, paid my bill and sneaked unnoticed down to the railway station. After a good hour's wait my train arrived and I left the place, a beaten man, considerably lighter in pocket, and suffering the pangs of a pain that gnawed at me all the way home.

The basket full of antiques and relics which I had bought I left behind in Kalmar.

So you see, something always gets in the way. Personally speaking, I have *never* come as close as I did this last time, and yet still I failed. I can't see that it's a question of my not giving myself enough time. Or that I hesitate if travel seems to be involved; or that money is a problem, but all the same—it doesn't seem to help. It's fate.

Nothing to be done about it.

THE CALL OF LIFE

Down near the inner harbour in Copenhagen is a street called Vester-vold, a new and desolate boulevard. There are few houses, few gas lamps and almost no people. Even now that it's summer few people go walking there.

Well, last night something happened to me on that street.

I had already strolled up and down it a couple of times when a lady comes walking towards me. There's no one else around. The gas lights are lit but it's still quite dark and I can't see the lady's face. Just another child of the night, I thought as I passed her by.

At the end of the boulevard I turn and go back. The lady has turned too and I meet her again. I thought: she's waiting for someone, I want to see who she's waiting for. Again I walk past her.

Meeting her for a third time I touched my hat and spoke to her. 'Good evening.' Was she waiting for someone?

She was startled. No . . . in fact, yes, she was waiting for someone.

Did she mind if I kept her company until the person she was waiting for arrived?

No, she didn't mind, she thanked me. As a matter of fact, she said, she wasn't waiting for someone, she was just walking, it was so quiet here.

We strolled along side by side. We spoke of nothing in particular, and I offered her my arm.

'No thank you,' she said with a shake of the head.

It wasn't much fun to walk there. I couldn't see her in the dark. I struck a match and looked at my watch. I held the match up so I could see her too.

'Nine-thirty,' I said.

She shivered as if she were freezing. I took my chance and said:

'You're freezing; do you want to go somewhere and get a drink? The Tivoli? Or the National?'

'I can't very well go anywhere at the moment. You can see for yourself,' she replied.

And I noticed for the first time that she was wearing a long black veil.

I begged her pardon, blaming the dark. And the way in which she accepted my apology convinced me that she was not some common streetwalker.

'Take my arm,' I said again. 'It'll warm you a bit.'

She took my arm.

We wandered up and down a few times. She asked me to check the time again.

'It's ten,' I said. 'Where do you live?'

'On Gamle Kongevei.'

I stopped her.

'May I walk you to your door?'

'Hardly,' she answered. 'You can't do that . . . You live on Brede-gade, don't you?'

'How did you know that?' I asked in surprise.

'I know who you are,' she answered.

Pause. We walk arm in arm down the lighted streets. She walked quickly, the long veil floating behind her. She said:

'We'd better hurry.'

At her door in Gamle Kongevei she turned towards me as though to thank me for escorting her. I opened the door for her, and she entered slowly. I leaned my shoulder gently against the door and followed her in. Once inside she seized my hand. Neither of us said a word.

We climbed a few stairs and stopped on the second floor. She unlocked the door to her apartment herself, unlocked a second door, took me by the hand and led me in. This was presumably a drawing-room; I could hear a clock ticking on the wall. Once inside the door the lady stopped a moment, then suddenly she threw her arms around me and kissed me feverishly on the lips. Full on the lips.

'Sit down,' she said. 'Here, on the sofa. I'll turn on a light.'

And she turned on a light.

Surprised, but curious, I looked around. I found myself in a large, extremely well-furnished drawing-room. There were doors open into other rooms leading off it. I found it hard to understand what kind of person this lady was. I said:

'This is beautiful. Do you live here?'

'Yes, this is my home,' she answered.

'Your home? Are you the daughter of the house?'

She laughed and answered:

'Oh no. I'm an old woman. See for yourself.'

And she removed her coat and her veil.

'Now you can see!' she said. And again she threw her arms around me, abruptly, in the grip of some uncontrollable urge.

She might have been 22, 23 years old. There was a ring on her right hand, so she might really have been a married woman. Pretty? No, she was freckled and had almost no eyebrows. But there was a striking vitality about her, and her mouth was strangely beautiful.

I wanted to ask her her name, and where her husband was, if she had one. I wanted to know whose house I was in; but each time I opened my mouth she threw herself at me and forbade me to be inquisitive.

'My name is Ellen,' she said. 'Can I get you something to drink? All I have to do is ring. But you must just go into the bedroom over there for a moment or two.'

I went into the bedroom. It was partially lit by the lamp in the drawing-room and I could see two beds in there. Ellen rang and asked for wine, and I heard a maid bring it and leave again. Shortly afterwards Ellen followed me into the bedroom. She remained standing a moment by the door. I took a step towards her, she gave a little cry and came forward to meet me . . .

This was last night . . .

What happened next? Just be patient—there's more.

It was turning light when I woke up this morning, daylight creeping in on both sides of the blind. Ellen was awake too. She sighed and smiled at me. Her arms were white and velvety, her breast high. I whispered to her and she closed my mouth with hers, mute with tenderness. The daylight grew brighter and brighter.

Two hours later I was up. Ellen is up too, getting dressed, putting on her shoes. And now something happens, a nightmarish thing which still makes me flinch when I recall it. I'm standing by the wash-basin. Ellen goes off to do something in the next room and as she opens the door I turn and see into it. A draught of cold air from the open windows meets me, and in the centre of the room I see a table with a corpse stretched out on it. A corpse, clad in white, lying in a coffin. Grey-bearded. The corpse of a man. Beneath the sheet his thin knees protrude like two angry fists, and his face is yellow and terrible. I see all this clearly, in full daylight. I turn away and say nothing.

When Ellen returned I was dressed and ready to leave. I could hardly respond to her embrace. She put on some outdoor clothes, saying she would see me to the street door, and we went down together. Still I said nothing. In the doorway she pressed herself up against the wall so as not to be seen and whispered:

'Goodbye for now.'

'Until tomorrow?' I said, experimentally.

'No, not tomorrow.'

'Why not tomorrow?'

'Hush, love. I'm going to a funeral tomorrow. One of my relatives is dead. So—now you know.'

'Then the day after?'

'Yes, the day after tomorrow. Here in the entrance. I'll meet you. Goodbye.'

I walked off . . .

Who was she? And the corpse? The grotesque comedy of those bunched fists and the drooping corners of its mouth! She's expecting me again the day after tomorrow. Should I go?

I go straight to the Café Bernina and ask to see the street directory. I look up Gamle Kongevei such and such a number. Good—there's the name. I wait a little while longer for the morning papers to arrive and I skim through them looking for the Births and Deaths. Good—there's her announcement, at the top of the list in bold type: 'At the age of 53 my husband died today after a protracted illness.' The announcement was dated the day before yesterday.

For a long while I sit there thinking about it. A man marries a woman 30 years younger than himself. He contracts a lingering illness until finally one day he dies.

And the young widow breathes out.

LADYKILLER

A group of young people were rowing towards the island. One of them, a well-built young gentleman, stood up and recited a verse. You could hear him from the shore. All the ladies listened to him, except the youngest, a lively woman with fair hair and flaring nostrils who was more interested in the handsome young man who was rowing the boat. She smiled at him behind the others' backs.

This made the gentleman unhappy and he read his poems more loudly. His face coloured.

Suddenly he falls silent. He turns towards the inattentive beauty on the seat behind him and says:

'You're quite right, my poems are no good. But I tell stories too, perhaps I'm better at that. I'll show you once we're ashore.'

And all the ladies clapped their hands in anticipation of what he might tell from his travels, because he had had so many adventures. But the one who hadn't bothered to listen to his poems didn't seem any more interested now.

'What do you want?' he asked in his despair.

'What do I want? I don't understand you,' she answered in surprise. 'My name is Andrea. There's nothing wrong with me, I'm just happy that I was able to come along on this outing.'

And she looked as though she really meant what she said, the little flirt.

After landing they unpacked the wine, filled their glasses and drank. But it seemed that Andrea and their oarsman had to go off looking for seagulls' eggs somewhere far beyond the low growth of brush, for now and then the sound of their laughter was carried on the wind down to the company.

'Somebody tell them!' came the cry.

'Get everyone here,' said the man, 'get Andrea too.' And he climbed up onto a rock himself and shouted Andrea in his warm, calling voice.

And Andrea came. She stood and looked quizzically at him.

'Young lady,' he said so that all could hear him. 'It's you I'm telling the story for. Not just because of your beauty, but because of the sweetness of your youth. It intoxicates me, it drives me out of my mind. Look at your arms, at the blood beneath your skin. I promise you, I want to tell this story just for you.'

But Andrea looked terribly embarrassed and ill at ease as she sat down.

Then he told his story.

He continued for half an hour. That voice never failed, he seemed possessed by some sweet, wild spirit, and the story he told was of a companion of his who had lived through the strangest adventures.

'Am I boring you?' he asked.

'No no,' shouted all the ladies and gentlemen.

And Andrea didn't answer.

He asked:

'Why don't you answer? I'm doing this for you. Listen, all I have left now to tell you about this man is that he was not a happy man. Everything went his way, he won all these small victories and he triumphed in his bold adventuring; but then one day he found himself caught up in a great and eternal love. And there he lost.'

'Bravo!' said Andrea with downcast eyes. 'Tell that story.'

But the ladykiller was confused by her assurance. Her coolness unnerved him and he strove manfully to get the upper hand over her. The other ladies sat back and watched, for more than one of them knew his fickle ways. If he chose one today he would choose another tomorrow, when the sun lit up a different view in his heart.

Andrea repeated:

'Tell that story!'

'Why should I?' he answered. 'Your coldness makes me shiver. Ladies and gentleman, I think it is already evening.'

They rowed home. On the trip back he gave the oarsman a hefty slap on the cheek and took the oars himself. He saw nothing, heard nothing, just rowed like a bear.

Ashore Andrea walked suddenly alongside him. He grabbed her by the arm and spoke to her, deathly pale and trembling:

'Don't torture me any more, I can't take it. Make your decision now. Never have I loved as I love you; tell me now, shall I live or shall I die?'

'Live!' she cried jubilantly. 'I have loved you from the first moment I saw you. Why do you think I have tortured you today? It has been a worse torture for me, I have never suffered as I have suffered today.' And she looked at him with great marvelling eyes and called him her prince and her god . . .

For a few days he enjoyed perfect happiness. The victory had been sweet and he savoured it as on previous occasions. Then his old unhappiness began gnawing away at him again, he was bored, weary from the struggle, the old curse. He sneaked off from his home, left, travelled to the next town, didn't send any messages, didn't return.

2

Two days earlier he had arrived at this tourist hotel, a quiet place with few guests. The town was blessedly dull, nothing happened there, and his heart felt easy and rested.

Then one afternoon he meets a lady on the stairs. She was coming down, he was going up, and he took off his hat and greeted her as she passed. She disappeared into the garden. The owner informed him that she had just arrived and was accompanied by her father.

A long green dress, a large black hat and a riding crop—that was what had detained him on the stairs. She had hardly looked at him, just the brief, sidelong glance; then gathered up her dress in one hand and passed him by.

He went after her into the garden. It was seven o'clock, dew had begun to settle.

'There's a dew,' he said straight out and went up to her.

She looked in some surprise at the importunate gentleman.

He pointed to her shoes.

She turned and was about to leave.

'I beg your pardon,' he said, 'I really didn't come down here to talk to you; but there is a heavy dew, the paths and the grass are already wet. That's what I wanted to tell you, in case you're a stranger here.'

'Yes thank you, I can see that there's a dew.'

'I greeted you on the stairs,' he continued. 'That was me. The way you looked at me, it did something to me.'

She said:

'What do you want?'

His heart beat like a hammer, he lost all composure and blurted out:

'Look, take whatever you want, I'll give you everything I own if you think I'm after something from you. I only want to stand in front of you and look at you, because you must know yourself that you're remarkably beautiful.'

'I've never heard such cheek,' she said coldly.

'Then please forgive me!' he muttered, abandoning all hope.

She turned her eyes away from him and looked down at the flowerbed, turning her back on him. Attempting to remedy the effect of his conduct on her he said:

'The roses you're looking at make a swishing sound, isn't that strange. Suppose they talk to each other, and that swishing sound is their language. If you listen maybe they're saying something.'

She was walking away.

'Shouldn't I have said that either?' he asked in dismay.

'They aren't roses, they're poppies,' she answered.

'All right poppies,' he said. 'Don't you think the swishing sound from their heads might be their way of speaking to one another?'

She had gone. As he was finishing his sentence he heard the latch go on the garden gate.

Fine.

In a curious and disturbed state he found a bench and sat down. The woman's striking beauty had made a great impact on him. When the dinner bell rang he rose and made his way to the dining-room in a state of high excitement. What if she came in and sat down just *there*? What if he said hello to her?

She came. She still carried the riding crop in her hand. Her father was with her, a handsome old man, looked like an officer.

Now to get this thing just right. Bow and sit down right opposite the two of them. I'll do it now, he said to himself. And he did it.

The beauty blushed furiously! Father and daughter were discussing their journey the next day, and the old man leaned across his table and asked something about the route, the roads, the hotels. And that poor ladykiller who had never before thought about routes and roads pulled himself together and gave them some expert advice. At the end of the meal he went over to their table and introduced himself. Excellent, excellent—they both knew his name.

In the corridor he at once detained the officer's daughter and said:

'Just one word, Miss: don't leave tomorrow. Stay. I'll show you the sights—the waterfall, the shipyards. Tomorrow night I will throw myself at your feet and I will thank you.'

The beauty didn't walk on immediately, she listened to him patiently.

Then he added:

'My life is in your hands.'

She smiled.

'To prevent any misunderstanding I must inform you that I am travelling to my fiancé and I shall be leaving tomorrow,' she said.

'No,' he cried, and stamped his foot. And he took hold of her hand, crushed it, kissed it.

She pulled herself free, lifted her riding crop and brought it down hissing across his face. He controlled himself and stood up straight. A ribbon of blood flowed down his left cheek.

She observed him a moment and lowered the riding crop.

'You hit me,' he said. 'But it doesn't matter. Do it again, make me happy again.'

But with head bowed and her eyes on the floor she fled, up the stairs and back to her room . . .

She didn't leave the next day. She saw the sights, the waterfall, the shipyards. How changed was the world, how her heart was filled with a most delicious madness. No, she said, she would never make that sad journey south to be with a man she no longer loved—but her father insisted on it. Oh but she would return, she would come back soon. And she gave the ladykiller her hand.

'I'm coming with you,' he said. 'I'll follow you—tomorrow. Until we meet again, my only love!'

3

There now followed—as on every previous occasion—a brief period of time, a few hours of indescribable ecstasy in which he saw and heard nothing but his beloved. At intervals of a few hours she telegraphed him and wrote a letter, two letters on scented notepaper. He read her lovely words with the most intense pleasure, and walked around like one who carried a fresh bouquet of flowers inside him.

The hours flew by. Why did he not follow her? In his enraptured state he forgot to leave the hotel and begin his journey. Two days later he was still there, not having the heart to go from these enchanting letters which continued to arrive. But, just as a matter of interest, why were there so many of them? The first ones were the most loving. Of course, each one was like a rose unto his heart; but they were beginning to lose their scarcity value.

One evening he left a letter from his beloved unopened until the following morning. Imagine that, he did not open it at once with trembling fingers, but at his leisure, the following morning. Afterwards he got dressed and went downstairs.

In the dining-room he met a lady wearing travelling clothes. She and her companion had just arrived, she was an artist, young, on her first trip, full of laughter, warm, spontaneous, fun-loving. She was chaperoned by her mother.

He greeted her. She smiled and nodded back. Her smile was red. Today, at last, he had intended to set off; but he did not set off. Was it fate? At the first opportunity he put his services at the disposal of the young artist, would show her the sights, lead her by the hand. They arranged for him to take her to the shipyards.

He arrived an hour too early. It was raining, and he waited there like a hero. It doesn't matter, he said to himself, I am as happy as a god because I am getting wet and weary for her sake.

He stood there for two hours. Finally her mother came. She brought a message from her daughter asking him to excuse her, she couldn't come, she had been obliged to visit some friends in the town. And the old mother never asked if he had been waiting long, if he was wet, if he had caught cold.

He went home. Wandered about in that dull hotel, in the grip of unendurable impatience. What a long time to be spending with one's friends! What on earth sort of business could an artist have with friends that would take such an eternity?

It grew late, night came, he had to go to bed without seeing her. Sleep was impossible so he lit the two lamps and let them burn. How heavy and dark his head felt, how his eyes stared with dazed intensity at the pattern of the paper on the wall.

He heard the main door open, waited a few moments, then leapt out of bed and got dressed. He had ascertained where the artist's room was and made his way there. She was there, he could heard her moving about inside. Shortly afterwards her bare arm appeared round the door with her shoes, then the door was closed again and the key turned in the lock. Good night in there, sleep well tonight you precious one! Kneeling down he kissed the two small shoes, like a clown, a madman. Then he promised himself to make an end of it in the morning, to declare himself to her, victory or death.

But in the morning the lady and her mother had left. He enquired what route she had taken and heard that she was travelling north to the next town.

That same morning the officer's daughter had written: 'Come south! All is in bloom down here!'

Without further ado he set off north.

THE LADY FROM THE TIVOLI

It was this summer, at the Paris Choir's concert at the Tivoli Gardens. I had taken a walk up Castle Hill; at the top I turned and headed in the direction of the Tivoli.

A large crowd of people had gathered outside to listen to the singing of the Paris Choir and I joined them.

I met a friend and we spoke together. The singing inside began and was wafted out to us in faint, jolting bursts. Suddenly I felt uneasy, gripped by some unpleasant, edgy feeling. Involuntarily I moved to one side and began responding to my friend's words in a meaningless, random way. For a minute or two after that I felt quite calm, until once again that same inexplicable feeling of unease overcame me. At the same moment my friend said to me:

'Who is that lady looking at you?'

I turned round. A lady was standing directly behind me and my gaze met a pair of the most remarkable eyes, blue, heavy-lidded, unblinking eyes.

'Don't know her,' I answered and turned away.

I was in a state of extreme agitation. These eyes continued to watch me, I could feel them burning into my neck. There was something metallic about them, pressing into me from behind like rods of cold steel.

It became impossible for me, in my nervous state, to tolerate this stare. After turning round once more to assure myself that I really did not know the lady I left and walked on.

A few days later I was sitting with an acquaintance, a young lieutenant, on a bench directly opposite the university clock. It was the promenading hour and we sat watching the people walking back and forth. Then amongst the crowd I see two cold, hooded eyes directed towards us and recognise at once the young lady from the

Tivoli. She continued to fix us with her gaze as she walked by. The lieutenant was curious and asked if I knew who she was.

'Haven't a clue,' I answered.

'Well she must know one of us,' he said and got to his feet. 'It could well be me.'

The lady meanwhile had sat down on the next bench. We made a move in her direction, and I gave a tug on the lieutenant's coat so that we both in fact passed her by.

'Don't mess about!' he said. 'Of course we're going to say hello to her.'

'All right then,' I said. I went back with him.

He greeted her and told her his name. Might he have permission to join her there on the bench? And without more ado he sat down.

He spoke to her and she replied in a friendly, if distracted manner. Before too long he'd got hold of her parasol which he sat and toyed with. I stood and watched the entire time. I felt a little embarrassed and didn't quite know what to do. A small boy passed by carrying a basket of flowers. The lieutenant, who always knew exactly what to do, immediately called the boy over and bought a dozen roses from him. Might he have permission to fasten one to the lady's chest? After a half-refusal she allowed him to do so. The lieutenant was a handsome man and I was not a bit surprised that she allowed him such a liberty.

'But look it's spoiled!' she cries suddenly. She pulls the rose out of her buttonhole and stares at it a moment in fear. As she tossed it away from her down the street she said in a low voice: '*It's like a child's corpse.*'

I paid no particular attention to these words; but I observed all her movements closely.

At the lieutenant's suggestion we took a walk up to Castle Park. On the way the lady began for no particular reason to talk about a child she had seen, who was now buried. We said nothing to this. Shortly afterwards she began talking about Gaustad, about how dreadful it must be to be locked up there *when one wasn't insane*.

'Yes,' the lieutenant said, 'but that doesn't happen nowadays.'

'Oh yes, it happened to the mother of that child,' replied the lady.

The lieutenant began to laugh. 'Well I'll be damned!' he said.

She had spoken in a pleasing voice and her language was that of a cultivated lady; I thought she might be a little too highly strung; perhaps even a touch hysterical, something which that sickly light in her eyes seemed to confirm. Apart from that I couldn't see that there was anything wrong with her. But I was experiencing difficulty in keeping up with her many sudden changes of subject, it disorientated me, she bored me so I stopped and said goodbye. As I left I saw the two of them carrying on into the park, I don't know what happened after that, I didn't look back.

*   *   *

A week passed. One evening as I was making my way down Karl Johan I met the lady from the Tivoli again. As we approached one another we both spontaneously began to walk more slowly and before I had time to change my mind I found myself walking beside her.

We spoke of nothing in particular as we wandered slowly down the pavement. She told me her name—the name of a well-known family—and asked for mine. Before I could answer she rested her hand on my arm and said:

'Oh no never mind; I know it anyway.'

'Yes,' said I, 'my friend the lieutenant is always helpful in matters like that. May I ask, what name did he give for me?'

But her thoughts were already elsewhere. She pointed towards the Tivoli and said: 'Look!'

A man was riding a bicycle up and down in the air through a field of burning torches. The Man on the Corkscrew.

'Shall we go over there?' I asked.

'Let's find a bench,' answered the lady.

She led the way, we crossed Drammensveien and went into the park where she chose the darkest spot she could find. We sat down.

I at once tried to start a conversation, but to no avail. She stopped me with a small, pleading gesture: would I be so kind as to say nothing at all for a few moments? My pleasure, I thought, and kept quiet. For a whole uninterrupted half-hour I kept quiet. The lady sat motionless. In the darkness I could see the whites of her eyes, and the whole time she kept glancing over at me. In the end I grew half-afraid of this penetrating, mad look and was on the point of leaving; but I forced myself to stay and instead just put my hand inside my jacket in search of my watch.

'It's ten o'clock,' I said.

No answer. Her eyes remained fixed on me. Suddenly, without any preliminary, she says:

'Would you have the courage to dig a child's corpse up from a grave?'

Now I felt really uneasy. It was becoming increasingly obvious to me that the woman was mad. At the same time I felt deeply curious and did not want to leave her. I looked at her and said:

'A child's corpse? Yes, why not? I could certainly give you a hand with that.'

'Because it was buried alive,' she says, 'and I must see it again.'

'Yes of course,' I answered, 'we must dig up your child.'

I watched her closely. She was at once on her guard.

'Why do you say it was my child?' she asked. 'I didn't say that, I'm only saying that I know the mother. Now: I'll tell you the whole story.'

And this person, who was otherwise incapable of carrying on a single intelligible conversation, now began telling a long story about this child, a strange story that made the most profound impression on me. She spoke spontaneously, openly, urgently; there were no gaps in her story, no faults in her grammar, so that at the very least I no longer felt there was something wrong with her mind.

A young lady—she was not saying that the young lady was herself—had some time ago got to know a young man whom she presently became very fond of and finally engaged to. They were together a great deal, openly in the street, and also clandestinely, in private; they came together at a certain hour, he to her place, she to his room, or they met in the shadows, behind this very bench upon which we were now sitting. And of course it all went wrong and one fine day they realised at home what condition she was in. The family doctor was called—the lady mentioned his name, one of our best-known general practitioners—and on his advice the girl was sent to a country town. Here she was boarded with the local midwife.

Time passed, the child was born. Oddly enough, the Kristiania family doctor was also in town at the time, and the young mother was still lying weak in bed when she was given the news that her child was dead. Stillborn? No, it survived for a few days.

But in point of fact the child was not dead. Throughout, the mother was refused permission to see the child. Finally, on the day of the burial, it was brought to her in a coffin. 'And I'm telling you, it was not dead then, it was alive, it had blood in its cheeks and once or twice the fingers on the left hand moved.' Despite the mother's protesting cries the child was removed and buried. The whole thing was arranged by the doctor and the midwife.

Time passed, the mother got back on her feet again and—still unwell—returned home to the capital. Here she openly confessed to a couple of her friends the purpose of her visit to the country town and, preoccupied as she was with her child, she made no attempt to hide her fear that the child had been buried alive. And the girl grieved and suffered. At home they disapproved of her, even her fiancé had run off and was nowhere to be found.

One day a carriage stands waiting outside her parents' house; she was to be taken for a drive. She got in, off they went, and the cabby drove her to—Gaustad. The family doctor appeared again. Why had she been taken to a lunatic asylum? Had she really gone mad? Or were people afraid she might begin talking a little too loudly about the child?

Time passed. They made use of her in Gaustad, getting her to play the piano for the insane. In the meantime they could find nothing wrong with her there, except possibly an exaggerated sense of her own impotence, a certain weakness of the will. Ha, they asked her to try to exercise her willpower, make herself hard. That was funny, eh, them toughening her up themselves, so that one day she would be strong enough to expose the crime against her child! Then she was released. And she grieved and suffered; she couldn't find a single person willing to help her in this business—'That is, unless you will?' she said to me.

The lady's account struck me as highly novelettish; yet I felt convinced that she believed the story herself. The whole thing was too well, too passionately told to be merely invention, and it seemed to me there might be a kernel of truth in the story, that, for example, she had really had this child. In her illness she had perhaps been too weak to accept the child's death and in a feverish moment had conceived this notion, that it had been killed. I said:

'Is the child buried here?'

'No it was buried at the place where I lay sick,' she answered.

'Ah then it was your child?' I said quickly.

She made no response, merely looked at me out the corner of her eye, her expression suddenly wary and suspicious.

'It goes without saying that I'll help you all I can,' I said calmly. 'When shall we start?'

'Tomorrow,' she said brightly, 'you dear man, tomorrow!'

'Fine!' I said.

And we arranged to meet at seven the following evening, when the train was scheduled to leave.

I waited for her at the station, determined to keep my word. The clock turned seven and she didn't come. The train left and I waited on. I waited until eight o'clock. Still no sign of the lady. Finally, as I was on the point of going home she turned up, almost running down the street towards me. And in the hearing of all of those present, without a greeting, with no preamble she says loudly and clearly:

'You must realise I was lying to you yesterday. You do understand, don't you? The whole thing was a joke.'

'Of course,' I replied, somewhat embarrassed on her behalf. 'Of course I realise that.'

'Yes of course,' she said. 'But you might have taken it seriously, in which case God help me!'

'Why would that make you say God help me?'

'No, come on!' she said and pulled my arm. 'Please, don't let us say any more about it.'

'Whatever you like,' I answered.

We walked up Rosenkrantzgaten in the direction of the Tivoli, crossed Drammensveien and again headed off into the park, the lady leading the way the whole time. We sat on the same bench as before and again spoke of nothing in particular. Her thought processes were as usual strikingly desultory, but also very interesting. She even laughed a couple of times and hummed a snatch of some tune now and then.

At ten o'clock she stood up and asked me to accompany her. More for a joke than anything else I offered her my arm. She looked at me.

'Oh I daren't!' she answered seriously.

We walked in the direction of the Tivoli and stood listening to the cacophony. Then the Man on the Corkscrew again began his aerial riding. My lady was at first very afraid for him, and she gripped my arm tightly as though it was she herself who was in danger of falling down; then she started to enjoy it. What if he were to slide off it? What if the poor cyclist fell and landed up to his knees in someone's beer mug on one of the tables? The fantasy made her laugh till she cried.

Still in excellent humour we made our way home; again she hummed that fragment of song. In a dark street, by a house with a little black iron staircase, she abruptly stopped and stood staring ahead in fear. I stopped too. She pointed to the bottom step and said hoarsely:

'That's exactly the same size as the little coffin.'

Now I grew really annoyed. I shrugged my shoulders and said:

'Aha, here we go again!'

She looked at me. And slowly, quite slowly her eyes began to fill with tears. In the light from the ground-floor windows of the house I saw that her lips were trembling. She folded her hands forlornly. A moment later she took a step forward and said:

'You dear, kind person, please be patient with me!'

'Of course,' I answered again. And we walked on. Outside her door she impulsively held my hand as she was saying goodnight.

Several weeks now passed during which I saw nothing of the strange lady. I was annoyed with myself for being so credulous and grew more and more convinced that she had been amusing herself at my expense. Fine! I thought. Well, to hell with her from now on.

So I'm sitting in the theatre one evening watching *The League of Youth*. In the second act I feel suddenly overcome by a strange unease, something outside me acting on my nerves, the same unpleasant sensation as I had that time outside the Tivoli during the concert by the Paris Choir. I turn round quickly. Sure enough, there she is, staring at me with that same burning gaze.

I slumped down, squirmed in my seat, tried to follow Daniel Heire with all my might. But the whole evening through I had the unpleasant sensation of being drilled from behind by the gaze of these metallic, unblinking eyes. I got up and left before the end of the play.

*   *   *

For a couple of months I was out of town. By the time I returned I had quite forgotten the lady from the Tivoli, I hadn't even thought of her once. She vanished from my consciousness as suddenly as she had appeared.

One evening during the recent period of foggy weather I spent walking back and forth between the soup kitchen and the Elephant Apothecary. I noticed how people bumped into each other in the fog. After I had been walking this stretch for about quarter of an hour I thought to myself: Now I'll go one last time to the apothecary, then I'll go home. It was eleven o'clock. So I walked again to the apothecary. In the light from the nearest lamp I see someone coming towards me. I veer a little to one side, the other person does the same. To avoid a collision I jump the other way, to the left—and see now two eyes staring at me through the fog.

'The lady from the Tivoli,' I whispered, transfixed.

She came right up to me with her rigid stare. Her face was strangely distorted. She carried a muff in one hand. She looked at me a moment.

'It was *my* child!' she said urgently. Then she turned and disappeared into the fog.

REVOLUTION ON THE STREETS

One morning in the summer of 1894 I was woken by the Danish
writer Sven Lange who came into my room in the Rue de Vaugirard
in Paris and said that a revolution had just broken out in the city.

'Revolution?'

'The students have taken matters into their own hands and are
rioting in the streets.'

I was sleepy and angry and said:

'Turn a firehose on them, swill them off the streets.'

But Sven Lange took offence at this, because he sided with the
students. He turned and left in silence.

The 'matter' the students had taken into their own hands was this:

The society or association known as 'The Four Fine Arts' had
arranged to hold a ball at the Moulin Rouge. The four ladies who
were to represent the four fine arts at this ball all appeared more or
less naked, wearing nothing more than a silk ribbon around their
waists. Now the Parisian police are tolerant and put up with most
things; but on this occasion they raided the place. The ball was
stopped and the establishment closed.

The artists lodged a formal protest about this. Students throughout
the Latin Quarter sided with the artists and entered their protest too.

A couple of days later a small group of policemen were patrolling
down Boulevard St Michel. Sitting outside one of the many pavement
cafés are some students who shout a few insults at the patrol as it
goes by. The Parisian police are tolerant and put up with most things,
but at this one of the constables gets angry, picks up a heavy stone
matchstick-holder from a table outside a boulevard café and tosses
it in the direction of the troublemakers. His aim, however, is atrocious. The holder goes through the window of the bar and hits on
the head a student who just happens to be sitting there. The innocent
victim dies on the spot.

It was after this that the students took the 'matter' in hand . . .

After Sven Lange left I got up and went out. Tumult in the streets, crowds of people, police on horseback, police on foot. I made my way through them, reached my restaurant, ate breakfast, lit my cigarette and left to go home again. When I emerged from the restaurant there were even more people and even greater tumult. To keep order foot soldiers and mounted soldiers of the national guard had been called in. When these were first sighted along Boulevard St Germain they were greeted with booing and stone-throwing by the people. The horses reared, snorted, stumbled. The crowd broke up the asphalt on the streets and began using it as ammunition.

A man asked me indignantly if I thought this was any time to be smoking. I had no idea this was such a dangerous thing to be doing. Moreover I understood little or no French, so in one sense I could be excused. But the man shouted, with wild gestures:

'Revolution! Revolution!'

So I threw away the cigarette.

Now it was no longer just the students and artists who were in action. The Parisian mob with all its tens of thousands had streamed up, the beggars, the layabouts, all the human detritus. They came from every quarter of the city, popped up from every side street and merged with the crowd. More than one honest man lost his watch.

I drifted with the stream. The crossroad between Boulevards St Michel and St Germain formed a focus for the rioting and proved difficult to control. For a long time people did as they pleased. An omnibus crossed the bridge from the other bank of the Seine; when it stopped at Place St Michel a man emerged from the mob, approached it, removed his hat and said:

'Ladies and Gentlemen, please be so kind as to disembark.'

And the passengers disembarked.

Then the horses were unhitched and to fierce jubilation the omnibus was overturned in the road. The next omnibus met the same fate. Passing tram cars were also stopped and overturned and soon there was a high barricade that stretched across the road from pavement to pavement. The flow of traffic ceased. Those who tried to continue their journey could find no way through but were swept off course by the tide of people and driven far away up into side streets, and even through closed doors and into houses.

I found myself swept back almost to my starting point at the restaurant, and then further and further away again, until I came to a high black iron railing round a museum. Here I dug my heels in. I nearly had the arms pulled off me but I held fast. Suddenly there was the sound of a shot, two shots. Panic gripped the mob. Howling wildly they rushed down the side streets. The police seized the chance to chase after the horde, riding them down in several directions, slashing away with their sabres.

At that moment one had the sensation of war.

Fortunately for me I had retained my place by the iron railing, where there was now a good deal more room. Some straggler came tearing towards me, wild with fear. He was holding in his hand his calling card, which he pressed into my hand, pleading for his life, presumably in the belief that I might kill him. On the card it said 'Dr Hjohannes'. He stood before me, trembling from head to foot. He explained that he was an Armenian doing some research in Paris; in his everyday life he was a doctor in Constantinople. I spared his life, I didn't take it. I remember him well, especially his distraught face with its thin, sparse beard, and the large gaps between the teeth in his upper jaw, though none of them appeared to be missing.

It was rumoured that the shots came from a shoe shop, or more accurately from the workshop above it. It was 'Italian' workers who had been shooting at the police—naturally, it was the Italians who got all the blame. Now the mob found its courage again and once again it streamed onto the boulevard. At the rallying point of the cordon mounted police tried to block it off from any further influx of people from other parts of Paris. But as soon as the crowd got wise to this they began smashing the windows in the newspaper kiosks, stoning the glass round the gas lights and pulling up the iron railings protecting the chestnut trees along the boulevard, all this to give the police something else to think about besides isolating the quarter. When this had no result their aim then became to frighten the rearing police horses as much as possible, and to this end the barricade of overturned omnibuses was set on fire. The tearing up of the asphalt for use as missiles continued, and since this was heavy work, and the supply could scarcely match the demand, they turned to other sources. The protective iron railings round the chestnut trees were broken up into smaller pieces, as were handrails and stair rails, and soon it was the turn of my own lovely iron railing. People threw things, shouted, destroyed, fled, came back.

Hours passed in this fashion.

The forces of law and order were reinforced by troops from Versailles. A shock passed through the crowd. The crowd had been happy to mock and do what they could to hinder the police and the national guard; but when the troops showed themselves the people shouted: 'Long live the army! Long live the army!' And the officers touched their caps in response to the welcome. But the moment the officers and soldiers had ridden by the business with the police, the windows and the railings started up again, and things continued as before.

Evening came.

Now the students were howling:

'Let's spit on Lozé!'

Lozé was the prefect of police. And a huge procession formed with the intention of marching to police headquarters in order to 'spit on' Lozé. The procession set off. The thousands who remained behind continued to chant abuse.

As there didn't seem to be much else left to gawp at for the day I made my way back to my restaurant, ate, and finally, after a long, long detour, reached home.

But days passed and the unrest continued. The moment one left one's room and went down into the street one saw remarkable sights and heard remarkable sounds. One evening I again decided to go to my restaurant for my meal. It was raining slightly and I took my umbrella with me. About halfway there I was stopped by a group of men engaged in dismantling a temporary barricade erected to stop passers-by from falling down a hole in the road. The barricade was made of timber and planks. In a firm voice I was requested to assist in the work of demolition, I looked like a big strong chap who knew how to make use of himself. I knew there was no point in trying to get out of it so I answered that I would be delighted to help. So we started pulling and breaking. It was no good. There were maybe 50 of us, but we weren't pulling in rhythm so we made no impression on the barricade. At that point it occurred to me bawl out a work song, a Norwegian stone-breaker's work song. That did it. Pretty soon the planks began to split and soon afterwards the whole barricade was down. We all cheered like mad.

I was about to continue on my way to the restaurant when a dubious-looking passer-by picks up my umbrella, which I had set to one side, and walks off with it, saying it was his. I called witnesses from among my comrades at the barricade to prove that the umbrella was mine, I had it with me when I arrived.

'That may be so,' replied the man. 'But isn't there a revolution going on?'

And at that my witnesses fell silent, conceding that the man was right.

I was not of the same mind, however, and I took the umbrella back by force. As this wasn't possible without the two of us rolling about in the street together, the man began to shout for help. He complained to the others that I had attacked him, to which I responded:

'Fair enough. But isn't there a revolution going on?'

And with that I took my umbrella and left . . .

In the evenings when my work for the day was done I usually went out and watched the rioting from a safe distance. The streets were very dark, practically all the gas lights were smashed and the quarter was lit chiefly by the lighting from shops whose owners didn't dare to turn it all off for fear of looting. The national guard rode along the pavements, their great horses looked like monsters in the half-light, and one heard incessantly the tramping of horseshoes on asphalt, and the shouting of some gang or other in the side streets.

The students meanwhile, realising the proportions that the whole thing had assumed, issued a proclamation disclaiming responsibility for all crimes committed and all acts of vandalism. It was now no longer the students protesting against the behaviour of the police at the ball at the Moulin Rouge, but the Parisian mob, and the students were advising everyone to stay indoors. Numerous copies of the proclamation were printed and displayed on trees along the boulevard.

But the good advice naturally no longer had the slightest effect.

It was the *police* the mob wanted to get their hands on. The marching in processions to police headquarters to 'spit on' Lozé continued, the police were stoned and shot at on every possible occasion, and one poor constable crossing a bridge over the Seine with an order was grabbed by a gang of men and thrown into the river. His body surfaced the following day, way downstream from Nôtre Dame, and was taken to the mortuary.

One evening there was an incident on Boulevard St Michel that attracted considerable attention. A constable found himself isolated on the pavement in the middle of a mob. One gentleman pulls a long duelling pistol from his pocket and shoots the constable. At the sound of the shot the police rushed the crowd, some hasty interrogations were conducted and a few people arrested. But the guilty party was not found. After firing his pistol the murderer retreated into the crowd, the crowd closed in behind him and he was gone for good. But witnesses reported that the gentleman was an officer in the Légion d'Honneur. They seemed also to know who he was, though they were unwilling to hand him over—a gentleman whose name was known all over Paris, all over France, indeed over much of the civilised world. And this particular evening the man had experienced a wish to kill someone: the Frenchman's murdering, revolutionary instinct had quickened and flared in him . . .

One evening I was commandeered to break up asphalt. I was walking quietly up a street where I saw a group of people busy at something. As I came closer I was called over, handed a pick and set to work. A company of guards was positioned not far away in order to close off a street, and as far as I could gather the idea of breaking up the asphalt was to stone the guards and force a way into the street. It was an ignominious, slavish sort of work to be doing and I regretted bitterly that I had not taken a different direction in my walk. But there was nothing to be done about it and I broke the asphalt. Nor was I alone, several picks were in use and men took the work in turns. The mob stood about boasting what they would do to the guards: Those guards were really in for it, there wouldn't be many of them left standing!

Suddenly we heard the command:

'Charge bayonets!'

We looked up.

The same voice again:

'Advance with bayonets!'

And the company of guards marched directly towards us.

We threw down our picks in terror and ran. God how we ran! We left all our ammunition behind, all our precious asphalt, and we fled. Now my long legs came into their own and I ran like a hare— indeed, though I say it myself, I've yet to meet a man who's as good at running away as I am. I remember well how I ran a little Frenchman straight into a wall, and how he fell over, rolling and howling. Naturally I was well ahead of most of my companions in flight, and when those at the very front finally stopped I profited from the general confusion to slip away from all that slaving in the asphalt fields.

Nor did I ever go back . . .

Within a couple of weeks the trouble in the streets eased off, and within three weeks Paris was as orderly as it had been before. But for some time the vandalised streets bore witness to the ravages of the latest French revolution. The rioters did achieve something with their efforts: the prefect of police, the 'spat upon' Lozé, had to resign.

FATHER AND SON:
A GAMBLING STORY

1

Last autumn I made a long trip south, very far south, arriving early one morning by river-boat at a small country town called D—, a strange place, little known, little visited. Besides a score or so of houses there is a church, a post office and a flagpole. The place is known to insiders, to adventurers and gamblers, to aristocrats and tramps, when for a few summer months each year it comes alive and a lot of money changes hands in a lot of shady corners.

It was market time and people from the outlying districts had come to town. They wore clothes of silk and hide, with belts and scarves decorated with jewellery, all according to how rich they were. Surrounding the church was a row of booths belonging to traders. One—the blue one—belonged to Pavo from Sinvara.

Close to the church, between the flagpole and the post office, lay the hotel. Its upper storey was painted blue. That was where the gamblers gambled away their money.

I heard it said in the hotel that Pavo was sure to be along that evening. I asked who Pavo was, a question that showed I was a stranger in town, for everyone there knew Pavo. He was the man who had broken the bank three times, his father owned the biggest estate for miles around and at the festival last spring Pavo had gambled away everything he owned. Every child knew Pavo, all the country girls talked about him when they met in the evenings to gossip at the water pump, and the pious said a prayer for him whenever his name was mentioned. In short, he was a gambler and a black sheep, a great man fallen on hard times, an ex-Croesus: Pavo from Sinvara. The town's disgrace, and the town's pride.

As for the booth, his mother had bought it for him and started him up in business hoping he would change his ways. It might have worked out if only Pavo had been serious about it; but that very same week the perverse boy had gone and painted his booth casino blue, showing that he hadn't changed at all. He still gambled too. Everything he earned over the counter he put on the spin of the wheel, and more often than not when he left the casino he had less in his pocket than when he came in. His booth was popular and he sold well; neither farmers nor townspeople would pass him by; everybody wanted to do business with Pavo from Sinvara. And his mother kept him well supplied with goods, his booth was always stocked to the roof.

He was expected that evening. The whole town was waiting for him.

2

The church clock struck, I heard five ringing clangs that mingled in with the general noise from the market. The hotel porter knocks on my door. He seemed very excited.

'Guess what?' he said. 'The master of Sinvara is coming too.'

I hadn't asked for this piece of information and I told the porter that the gentleman in question had nothing to do with me. Who was he? Why was he coming? The porter shrugged his shoulders and explained that the master of Sinvara was not only the most important and the wealthiest man in the whole district but a friend of Prince Yariw, and father to Pavo himself. That's who he was. And probably the whole purpose of his trip was to see what was happening about his son. He wanted to see for himself this damned roulette wheel that was ruining his boy and causing his wife so much heartache.

'This information doesn't interest me,' I said. 'What I asked for was my tea. Good day.'

And the porter left . . .

At six o'clock there was a great commotion in the hotel as the master arrived. He was with his son, Pavo in bright clothes, the father wearing dark. He looked serious and purposeful. The church bells rang, for as soon as he arrived he had promised to give the church a large sum of money, enough to ensure its survival even if hard times came again. He had also promised a new flag for the flagpole, something that caused great excitement in the town. Servants were given the rest of the day off and everyone was out on the street, including the mayor, who was wearing a brand-new uniform.

The master of Sinvara was a dignified-looking man, a little over sixty, rather stout, with a pallid complexion from his indoor life. But his moustaches were waxed and his eyes young, and his nose was snub and lively. It was well known that he was a friend of Prince Yariw and the holder of two high distinctions, but he seldom used them because even when not wearing them his bearing inspired respect. Whenever he spoke to someone they would remove their hat and answer politely.

After he had drunk a glass of water and wine he looked round at the crowd of curious onlookers who had followed him over to the hotel and he gave something to each one of them. He even called a little child forward from the crowd and with his own hand gave her a gold coin. Actually she wasn't all that little, she must have been nearer sixteen or seventeen years old.

All of a sudden he says:

'Where's the casino? I want to see it.'

Pavo, delighted by his father's whim, leads him up the stairs. The crowd follows.

On entering, his presence occasions the greatest interest. All the wheels are in use and there's plenty of action from the gamblers. A brooding gentleman whom the waiters call 'prince' graciously makes room for his equal, the great master of Sinvara.

The croupier calls:

'Thirteen, black.'

He scoops up almost all the money and piles of silver, big gold coins and notes all disappear into the metal drawer set into the table. More money appears and is pushed onto the table, as calmly and quietly as though nothing had happened. Yet number thirteen had really raked it in for the bank that time. Still no one says anything, the wheel spins, the roulette ball whirls round, slows, stops: thirteen again!

'Thirteen!' the croupier shouts once more, and rakes in most of the money.

These two games have made a small fortune in gold for the bank. Still the money appears. The prince tosses a fistful of notes onto the table without even counting them. No one speaks, there's silence all around. One of the waiters brushes into an empty wine glass on a table, knocks it over and a pure, crystalline ringing mingles with the lazy jolting of the roulette ball round the wheel.

'Explain the game to me,' says the master of Sinvara.

And Pavo, who knows the game inside out, tells him all about it. The great man is much preoccupied by the prince, whom he claims is ruining himself. As though it were his own money that were at stake he shifts uneasily back and forth in his chair.

The prince isn't ruining himself at all, replies Pavo. He bets only with the day's winnings. He *knows* the game.

And that was evidently true enough. The prince had won a lot. A waiter stood in constant attendance beside him, ready to hand him water, pick up his handkerchief when he dropped it, do anything at all for him, all in hopes of a fat tip when the game was over.

Next to him stands a tall, pale man, a swarthy Romanian, who is playing as if his life depended on it. On the last two spins he's lost heavily on thirteen. He stands half-hidden behind the master of Sinvara and has to reach over his shoulder each time to place his bet. His arm shakes.

'This young man is lost,' says the master.

Pavo, the son, nods: 'Lost.'

'Ask him to stop,' the father continued. 'Tell him from me. Wait, I'll do it myself.'

The son informs him that it isn't done to offer advice. Forlornly he adds that it isn't done either for the two of them just to sit there and watch.

His father looks at him in surprise. He doesn't realise that in his heart Pavo is already longing to join the game.

'But there are a great many others here who aren't playing either,' he protests.

Pavo lies and tells him that these are players awaiting their turn. So, with great dignity, the master of Sinvara gets out his wallet.

'Then play,' he says. 'Play a little. Show me what to do. But keep it small, nothing risky.'

Then almost at once he takes his son by the arm and demands to be told about the mysterious number thirteen. 'Why does thirteen win each time? Surely the croupier's cheating? Tell him.'

He is on the point of returning his wallet to his pocket when suddenly he has second thoughts. He counts out a few notes, shoves them over to Pavo and says:

'Put it on thirteen.'

Pavo protests:

'Thirteen has already won twice in succession.'

His father nods and replies firmly:

'Go on. Put it on thirteen.'

Pavo changes a note, tosses a gold coin down on thirteen, smiling tolerantly at such foolishness.

'Lost!' says his father. 'And again. Make it double.'

Pavo no longer protests. This is just too funny. Places are changed around the table. Again and again he doubles the stake and everybody wants to see this remarkable player, the master of Sinvara. He is himself already engrossed in the game, bright eyes following the hopping ball as he moves restlessly in his seat. He clenches his podgy hand; on the one finger are two costly rings.

When the croupier called twenty-three and not thirteen he exclaimed:

'Right then! Thirteen again. Make it a hundred.'

'But . . .'

'Make it a hundred.'

And Pavo places the bet. The wheel spins and the ball hops in the opposite direction, twenty or thirty times over each number, searching through every chance combination of black and red, ransacking the whole system, sniffing at each number then stopping.

'Thirteen!' calls the croupier.

'See, Pavo? What did I tell you?' says the master of Sinvara. And he puffed out his chest and spoke loud enough for the bystanders to hear. 'And again. Another hundred on thirteen.'

'You can't be serious, Father. Thirteen might not come up again for the rest of the evening.'

'Put a hundred on thirteen.'

'Why throw your money away?'

The master of Sinvara grew impatient and made a gesture as though to take the money himself from his son. Then he controlled himself and said:

'My boy, what if my plan were to break the bank? If for a certain reason I wished to destroy this horrible roulette game? Put a hundred on thirteen.'

And Pavo placed the bet again. He exchanged a smile with the croupier, and the Romanian laughed out loud. The baccarat game on the neighbouring table was at a standstill, everyone was watching the goings-on round the roulette wheel.

'Thirteen!'

'What did I tell you!' shouted the master of Sinvara. 'Here's the money. How much should there be? Count it up.'

Pavo was thoroughly dismayed.

'There's three and a half thousand,' he said wanly. 'Altogether you've won nearly five thousand.'

'Good. Now you play. Let me see how you get on. Bet on red.'

Pavo bet on red and lost.

His father nodded and smiled at the spectators.

'So that's the way you play! Don't you see what it leads to? They tell me you've broken the bank three times. That was well done. But why did you lose it all again? Back evens.'

'How much?'

'As much as you like. Six hundred.'

'Six hundred is too much.'

'I'm sitting here thinking it should be even more. I think I will. Put twelve hundred on evens.'

Evens lost.

Then the master of Sinvara shook his podgy finger at his son and said roughly:

'Go away, Pavo. We've lost twelve hundred here because of you. Get out of here. I'm telling you.'

And Pavo left. I followed him out. He was laughing, laughing like a madman. Had I ever seen play like that? He sits there and purely and simply because he's stupid he wins thousands. May God preserve and protect him! What a notion that was, to want to play roulette!

Pavo spoke to everyone he met and amid great laughter told them what the old man was up to.

Later that evening I heard that the master of Sinvara had lost nine thousand before he left the casino.

3

It was ten o'clock. I was sitting out on the hotel balcony smoking with Iljitsj, the Russian. Suddenly the hotel porter shouts up to us that the master of Sinvara had just sent for his son. I was on the point of rebuking him for interrupting us, but the Russian stopped me. His curiosity was aroused.

'Watch now,' he said, 'and let's see what happens. Sending for Pavo this late at night.'

We sat on a while, smoking in silence. Pavo arrives, and his father is there to greet him even before he enters the hotel.

'Listen,' he says, 'I've lost nine thousand at this damned roulette. I went to bed, but I couldn't sleep. This money is on my mind, it's exactly the sum I've promised the church. I must win it back. I'll get no peace until I have that money in my hand again. I must go back to the casino.'

Pavo is speechless. A compulsive gambler himself, Pavo is struck dumb with astonishment. He says nothing.

'Don't just stand there like that!' exclaims the father. 'The game goes on until well after midnight, that gives us hours. Let's not waste any more time.'

And away they go again.

'Come on,' says the Russian to me. 'Let's go. Something's bound to happen.'

The gaming was wilder now. As always, with the approach of midnight, the stakes get higher and higher. The prince is still sitting in the same seat, brooding and calm, gambling, winning. There was maybe twenty thousand on the table in front of him. He makes three separate bets each time, is in complete control, lays his money down in handfuls, sometimes without even counting it. Nothing disturbs him, not even the palely furious Romanian who after three-quarters of an hour of small wins has begun to lose again. His money lies loose before him and each free moment he gets he tries to count up how much it is, arranging it in piles of a thousand so that he can tell at a glance exactly how much he has. But he's too nervous, his hands are shaking, plus he has to keep his eye on the wheel all the time, and in the end he abandons the attempt to count it. How stupid he is. He backs four numbers, sticking to these four numbers, holding on to them like a stubborn child. Maybe he's ready to leave the table without even the shirt on his back rather than give up his chance of winning. And all the time he increases his stake.

The prince glanced over at the door as father and son entered once more, and made room for them beside him. Then he continued playing, cold, dark, cool as ice. It was obvious that he was held in great respect by the other players.

'Pavo,' says the master of Sinvara, 'just play the way you usually play. Here's the money. Red's your lucky colour isn't it, play red then.'

Pavo has a word with the man next to him, an old soldier with one arm, who informs him that red has won the last seven times in succession. So Pavo puts his money on black.

'Twenty-five, red,' announces the croupier as he rakes in the money.

'Bad beginning, Pavo, but just follow your nose,' says the master of Sinvara, disappointed. 'How often do I have to tell you? D'you think I'm made of money? Play red.'

But red lost. Finally, after eight reds, it was black's turn. The Romanian had a win that almost put him back on his feet again. Furious with his own bad luck, driven to recklessness, he had this time tossed down the house maximum on his four numbers; shored up by his own stubbornness for a moment it was as though he didn't care whether he won or lost. When the ball stopped on one of his numbers from sheer force of habit he signalled to the waiter behind the prince's chair and without a word handed him a note. Then once again, with trembling hands, he placed his bet.

'Pavo,' says the father once more, 'you lost again. Your luck just isn't with you. I'm letting you eat your way through my money and I'm doing it for your sake. Tonight I'm going to reform you. Do you understand me, Pavo?'

And the chastened Pavo understands him only too well. He knows that his father is already intoxicated by the game, that even when he loses he feels the thrill of playing. He's going through all the agonies of the gambler, and when the stakes are high his blood stops flowing and he can hear the sound of his own breathing. Pavo knows the story only too well.

Suddenly he looks preoccupied, and his concentration goes. The croupier draws his attention to the fact that he—the most practised of players—is betting against himself, and it makes him wonder about Pavo. And I notice too that on several occasions Pavo makes a gesture in the direction of the bets he has already made, as though to claim the money back before the ball stops. Is he seeing sense, backing away from trouble?

But the Russian leads me off to a sofa at the end of the room and begins to talk about Pavo. Hadn't I noticed the way he changed his style of play? Ah that Pavo was a clever devil, he had real insight. The Russian pointed over towards father and son and said:

'Of the two of them the son is the most in control. Pavo has already noticed that his father has gambling fever and he's trying to get him to ease off. It's really very funny, he's trying to stop the old boy. It's wonderful, isn't it? He can't be indifferent to the fact that his old man is headed for ruin.'

We sit there on the sofa. Something unusual is happening over on one of the roulette tables, and everyone swarms round the master of Sinvara and his son. Again the baccarat is at a standstill, and even the three hill-farmers in their great grey capes and metal belts and the old market traders who have been gambling by the door for jugs of wine in a game of their own get up and join the throng. We go over too.

'Just watch now!' says the Russian. He was very tense.

Again the master of Sinvara had begun to back thirteen. In his excitement he took control of the money himself and placed his own bets. His fat hands fumbled among the notes, trembling, seeking, grabbing at the grubby paper, working to count it, to arrange it in piles. His two rings shine out brightly in the pit of dirty paper. He says nothing, and Pavo sits in brooding silence beside him.

'Thirteen!' announces the croupier.

A jolt passes through the master of Sinvara. Pavo sits there gawping like an idiot. What luck he was having with this senseless system! Now there was a big hole in the bank. Calmly the croupier counts up the money. Nothing can surprise this man any more, he's seen luck's every trick and whim and the wildest ploys of desperate men. For a moment the prince looks completely bewildered. Then he gathers up all his money, separating the coin from the notes, and stuffs it down into his pockets. He orders a glass of wine which he downs in one, then he gets to his feet and ends his gambling for the day. On the way out he hands out notes left and right to any waiter standing in his way.

But the master of Sinvara punches his son on the shoulder and gives him a fevered look.

'You see? You see? And you think you're going to teach me how to play? I'm in a class of my own here.'

And before the astonished spectators he gives a short, loud laugh. Ecstatic at his own good luck he throws another bet down on number thirteen.

'Leave them there, I said just leave the money there. Thirteen is a remarkable number.'

But the croupier rakes his money in with the rake. He does it almost unwillingly. Probably he would have liked to see thirteen come up yet again to encourage the wealthy customer who, sooner or later, come what may, will fall into his clutches anyway.

After four failed attempts with thirteen the master of Sinvara loses his patience. He turns excitably to his son:

'I tell you Pavo, I'm not playing thirteen any more. I've lost enough on that stupid number.'

His irritation grows and grows. A waiter with squeaky shoes is asked to leave the room, and he gave a filthy look to the Romanian when he held up play by forgetting to claim his winnings. The master of Sinvara was also growing tired of all the people standing around watching. Couldn't they find something else to do? Something useful? He beckoned the child, the young girl, to come forward, and said:

'Aren't you the one I gave the gold coin to?'

The girl blushed and curtsied deeply.

'Yes sir,' she answered.

'Why don't you just go, my little friend?'

Her little red mouth began to move, but she stayed silent and lowered her eyes. The master of Sinvara looked more closely at her and handed her another gold coin.

'Here, take this. Come to me when the game is over. After midnight.'

Her whole face brightened and she curtsied again as a mark of respect. Smiling at everyone in the crowd, she left.

The master of Sinvara turned his attention back to the game.

'Now there are flies on the window,' he said. 'So many distractions. Someone get them out.'

His money ran down rapidly. Now luck was with the Romanian. The master of Sinvara didn't like it at all.

'Look,' he said to Pavo, 'this lousy handful of notes is all I have left. But I'm not giving up, I'll lose the lot. Right, here's a thousand on red. Maybe red's my lucky colour.'

Red won.

He said: 'It just could be that red really is lucky. I'll try again. This is an experiment.'

Red lost.

At that the master of Sinvara lost all vestiges of self-control.

'Leave!' he shouted at his son beside him. 'You're a jinx. You're spoiling everything for me. I must have my revenge, get my money back.' —And then, remembering the part he was supposed to be playing, he added: 'Now you see here what I'm doing for you. Let this be a lesson to you.'

'I've learnt my lesson,' Pavo mutters.

'Be quiet. No you haven't. You'll be back. I'm doing all this for you, do you hear? Now get out.'

And Pavo stood up and left.

4

It was getting on for 12 o'clock. One after another men leave the
roulette table, until only the Romanian and the one-armed military
man remain. The white-bearded old soldier played with an extreme,
brutal caution, keeping his stake low and winning. He won consistently, but his luck didn't affect his caution.

The master of Sinvara went about matters in a completely different
way. At the slightest sign of good luck he became foolhardy. At the
time at which Pavo left he probably still had just over a thousand.
With his next two bets he won another six hundred, which he at
once staked and lost. People began to feel sorry for him. The prince
had returned to the room as a spectator and personally took a large
glass of wine over to him.

'Your luck's run out,' said the prince. 'Call it a day.'

The prince gave his advice audibly. The master of Sinvara did
not reply. He merely looked up, thinking about the game, and emptied
the wine-glass in silence.

And then it seemed as though his luck had turned, and he won
three times in a row.

'That's the way to play!' he says brightly and warmly to the old
soldier. He never even heard him, preoccupied as he was with his
own game and his repetitive little wager. The Romanian notices that
the master of Sinvara is in a strangely agitated state. He exchanges
a look with the croupier and rakes in his winnings. He too quits.

The master of Sinvara is by now almost broke. All he has left are
a couple of hundred, every last cent of which he bets on black. Black
loses. Deathly pale, he looks round in despair.

'Damn the colour black!' he rages.

Then he seems to reconsider. The croupier watches him closely,
mechanically paying out the old soldier his little wager whether he
wins or not. The master of Sinvara remains sitting quite still, as
though deep in thought. Why didn't he just leave? One by one he
pulls off his two rings and hands them across the wheel to the
croupier. The croupier glances at them and calmly places them in
the metal drawer in the table alongside several other items of jewellery. He hands the master of Sinvara three thousand in gold coin.

No one says a word. For a whole minute the master holds the thick packages in his hand. He trembles uncontrollably. Suddenly he makes a violent motion, half-rises from his chair and one by one places the three packages on black. The coin clinks dully inside the paper rolls.

The ball goes round, whirls round light and soundless, lingers over one number, then another, then stops.

Red!

The master of Sinvara leaps up. He puts both hands to his head and shouts, cries out loud. Then he leaves the table.

5

In the morning that gossip of a hotel porter informed me that the master of Sinvara had lost 54,000 at the roulette table the previous evening. As for Pavo, he had gone back to his booth. He—the porter— had met him at the water pump, bare-headed and talking or preaching to himself—and when Pavo was in the right mood there was no priest who could preach like him. 'Flee from all corruption!' he heard him cry several times. 'Turn your back on the Tempter! Show him your finger and he takes your heart. Are you already lost that one such as I—a wretched soul such as I—must give you warning?' Pavo's speech had been powerful and persuasive, and in the porter's opinion he was rehearsing what to say to his father when he met him.

That fox of a porter sniffed out every bit of news that was to be had.

'You're leaving today,' he said to me.

I had said nothing about it at the hotel, hadn't asked for my bill. 'How do you know that?' I asked.

'I don't know it,' he answered. 'But you've given instructions at the post office for your letters to be sent on. Also you've booked a carriage to take you down to the boat at five.'

He even knew that! I had a feeling that this sharp-eyed man was spying on me and I felt an extreme distaste for him. I grew angry and found I couldn't stand the insolent look on his face. When he looked at me with his white eyes I felt frozen through, as though I were standing in a draught.

'Get away from me, you dog!' I said.

He didn't move. Not an inch. His hands were behind his back.

What was he up to? What was he doing with his hands behind his back? Was he planning something?

'What you just said then is very hurtful,' he says. He says nothing more, but looks me straight in the face. I walk behind him to find out what he's up to. He isn't holding anything, just has his fingers clasped. He's twisting them. I stand in front of him again, his shoulders are shaking and his eyes begin to water. I regret having shouted at him and am about to apologise in some way when suddenly he lunges towards me. Something curious is glinting in his hand, a ridiculous-looking key with two long teeth. He raises it and strikes me on my right arm, on the wrist. The crude blow draws blood and my hand drops. His insolence astounds me and I stand there speechless, unable to move. Once again he places his hands behind his back. A few moments later I again walk past him and head for the door.

'You think I'm going to hit you again, but you mustn't think that. God forbid,' he says.

I open the door with my left hand and reply, as I show him out: 'Bring me my bill.'

The porter bows deeply and leaves. Once the door closes on him I hear him utter a loud sob . . .

I did not leave that day. My hand hurt too much and I felt unfit to travel. There were two deep punctures on my wrist, little blue holes of bruised meat. The veins were swollen right up to my elbow. What a crude and disgraceful thing to do! The porter seemed to regret it immediately and brought me spirits to cleanse the wound and a bandage. No one could have been more solicitous of me after that. On his own initiative he insisted on quiet in the neighbouring rooms after I had gone to bed for the night. And at about one o'clock in the morning, when a crowd of drunken farmers started singing outside my windows, he ran out in a fury and moved them on, telling them they were disturbing the rest of a distinguished gentleman who was unwell, a prince whose wrist had been smashed.

The following day I rang twice, but no one came. Ill and irritable as I was I gave the bell a third, hefty pull. Finally I saw him approaching along the street. He had been out. When he came to my room I said:

'I have been ringing for the last 15 minutes. I'll be happy to double your tip if that seems to be the trouble. Now bring me some tea.'

I could see how much my words hurt him. He didn't answer, but hurried off to get the tea. Instantly I was moved by his patience and his humility. Like a young woman, I thought to myself, perhaps he has never in all his life heard a kind word and now here I am making it even worse for him. I decided to make amends immediately. When he returned I said:

'Forget it! I'll never say anything like that to you again. I'm afraid I'm not feeling very well today.'

My friendly words seemed to make him very happy. He answered:

'I had to leave you. I assure you, I had a very necessary errand in town.'

But then, encouraged by my friendliness, he reverted to being the gossip again, full of tales and ready to divulge all manner of things he'd ferreted out about the hotel guests.

'I must tell you, the master of Sinvara has just sent a man home to fetch more money, a lot more money. Pavo thinks he's going to ruin himself at the tables. He still hasn't got his rings back yet.'

'Well is that so,' I said.

'And that young girl from yesterday spent the night with him. She's from the mountains, she's probably never dreamt of such an honour. Even her father could hardly believe it.'

Towards supper-time I was again sitting out on the balcony watching the traffic down in the market-place. My arm was in a sling. The Russian was lounging on a bench beside me reading a book. Suddenly he looked up and asked if I knew that the master of Sinvara had sent home for more money. He'd also had a meeting with Pavo earlier in the day and Pavo had given him a lecture, some of which he said he was prepared to agree with. But his father wouldn't be told what to do and insisted that at the very least he was going to win back the money he'd lost. Did anyone really think he'd hand over the sum of 63,000 in gold coin to that bunch of gangsters? Wrong. Moreover he didn't intend to continue for the sole purpose of recouping his losses, and those good people who pitied him when he lost his rings should know that he could still give any one of them a ring for each finger and not even notice the difference.

'It's true,' said the Russian. 'He's already enough of a gambler not to worry primarily about his losses. It's the sweetness of it that attracts him now, the tension, the torture, the wild jolting of the blood.'

And Pavo? What did Pavo say?

'Flee from all corruption!' That's what he said. 'Be upstanding, man! Let me be your example.' Pavo had spoken at length, in a voice filled with emotion. Now and then he'd actually pointed up at the sky. It was priceless, to see the cunning young reprobate feigning a virtue he'd already lost long ago. The cheek of it, giving his own father a lecture like this. He'd protested that he was gambling for his sake, that he wanted to save his son from this vice and to that end would spare nothing. That made Pavo angry: he had always preserved his self-respect, but his father had gambled away his rings, pawned his jewels in front of everyone. He—Pavo—had kept his dignity. He had never borrowed on his booth, he had left that out of it, kept his business affairs quite separate. Finally Pavo threatened the old man with Prince Yariw.

'Be quiet!' said his father. 'I have promised myself to show you the consequences of your irresponsible ways and that is what I am doing. Goodbye, Pavo.'

And Pavo had to leave. But on leaving his father he went directly to the casino.

'Don't you believe that it really is his father's intention to get Pavo back on the right track in this strange way?' I asked the Russian. He shook his head.

'Maybe. But it's not working. Anyway, the father's as hooked as the son is now.'

By now everyone was talking about the master of Sinvara and his gambling. He didn't care a damn about that, he maintained, and he carried his head even higher than before and looked to be in excellent humour. Now and then he deigned to share a joke with a bystander: 'I see you're looking at my hands,' he might say. 'Yes yes, I'm much poorer now, I've even had to pawn my rings, ha ha ha.'

Since he had no money he didn't go back into the casino, but he got the hotel porter to tell him the spin of the wheel, who was winning, who was losing, how big the stakes were and who was taking the biggest risks. The following day the Russian told me that the master of Sinvara had prayed to God for good luck for three hours; as soon as he won back the lost money he would stop. He made this promise to God in a loud voice, and even shed a few tears. The Russian got all this from the hotel porter, who had been spying through the keyhole.

6

Three days passed. My hand wasn't hurting any more and I had made up my mind to travel that evening. I went into town to arrange a few matters, and had my passport stamped at the police station. On the way back I passed Pavo's booth. Finally, against my own will, I had begun to be interested in this man and his father. Everyone was talking about them, they were the subject of every conversation in the hotel, and in the end it had become impossible not to go around thinking about them just like everyone else, and to ask each day for the latest news of the master.

I went into Pavo's booth. The previous evening he had won a considerable sum at baccarat. He had cleaned out a stranger, let him have a couple of hundred back and turned to the roulette. His luck held and he took the bank for a small fortune.

'Can you imagine,' said Pavo to me the moment I stepped inside, 'Can you imagine, the master of Sinvara, my father, has just been here and tried to borrow money! He wanted to get his rings back. I wouldn't dream of doing anything so stupid. My father is a good man, and it hurt me to have to turn him down, but I did it for his own good. A son has to do what he can to uphold the family honour. My father must learn to realise the consequences of his own foolishness. I think I did the right thing. Don't you?'

I found myself rather repelled by him. His matchless good fortune of the previous day had filled his pockets but made him smug. As he spoke he lowered his brow, hid it as though it were branded, and when he looked up his eyes brimmed with lies. But his neck was beautiful, and his mouth delicate and red.

'Don't you think so?' he repeated.

'This is none of my business,' I answered.

He was offended. 'Well then,' he muttered, 'that means you don't understand good sense when you hear it spoken.'

He raised his shoulders, paced back and forth behind his counter. Then he stopped and said:

'Well, what can I do for you, now that you've had the misfortune to come in here?'

I mentioned a few things off the top of my head, things I had no real need of. When I had them I left.

No sooner had I reached the hotel than the porter came rushing up and told me that the master of Sinvara's man had returned with his money. Now he was just waiting for the casino to open so he could start playing again. Pavo didn't know anything about it—and he didn't want him to. The messenger had been paid expressly not to run across to Pavo with the news.

Five o'clock.

The moment the casino opened the master of Sinvara went in. He was extremely agitated, gestured strangely with his hands as though affirming something or swearing something.

The prince and the old soldier were there, but not the Romanian. A couple of strangers had also begun playing. The first thing the master of Sinvara did was redeem his rings.

He said to the croupier, without looking at him: 'This evening I'll be betting at the house limits.' His expression was cold, aristocratic.

'May your lucky star shine down on you!' said the croupier, and bowed.

The game began.

The master of Sinvara looked very determined. He backed red three times in succession and won. Then he put his own money in his pocket and thereafter played only with his winnings. He tries thirteen a couple of times but loses. The change in luck bothers him and he backs red a few more times and wins. By now he has a considerable sum on the table in front of him. He plays spontaneously, doesn't hesitate, and not to waste time he has his next bet ready even before the ball has come to rest. He doesn't check the amount either, but plays in a kind of trance. His eye sees a black square on the table and he places a big bet on this square.

Black wins. Now he wins all the time. This black becomes a goldmine oozing money and he exploits it. Suddenly he controls himself, stops a moment, draws breath. The wheel spins, but the master of Sinvara forgets to lay his bet, he's still drawing deep breaths. His little girl enters the room and walks towards him, smiling and flushed. He sees her and waves her away.

'See that,' he says. 'You come in and I forget to place my bet.' A moment later he beckons her to approach again. The ball has stopped on red. His luck that time was to forget to put money on the black. He puts one of his costly rings in the young girl's hand and whispers something to her. And the girl blushes all over and crosses her arms around her own neck as she runs from the room.

But the master of Sinvara plays on, recklessly, mechanically. He takes several handfuls of gold in tall piles and lays them on red. Instantly a powerful uncertainty strikes him and he half-reaches out to take the money back. He controls himself and lets the bet stand.

The ball stops.

Red!

'Red!' echoes the master of Sinvara. And he smiles triumphantly at the spectators and says loudly: 'Red again. Well, I had a feeling it would be.'

From that moment on he loses control. Ten o'clock comes around and more players arrive, the nightly regulars who don't really get going until it's late. The Romanian was among them. I forgot my journey and didn't leave my place, following the master of Sinvara's doings in a state of utmost tension. He seemed not to notice all the new people now crowded round him at the table. His luck hypnotises him and he operates with large bets on several numbers simultaneously. On a sudden whim he picks up a handful of gold and bets the house limit on twenty-five. Three others follow his example. Whispers all around, everyone waiting.

Thirteen.

Lost. The Romanian shows his teeth in anger. The master of Sinvara has another whim. Half-rising from his chair he stakes the limit on zero. No one follows him this time, the desperate move scares everyone off.

Zero!

In the tumult that then arose I could hear the terrible cursing of the Romanian. Moments later Pavo came through the door, followed by the hotel porter who had told him the news anyway. Pavo went straight over to his father's chair. Without a word he took him by the shoulders and began shaking him.

He looked up, recognised his son, and surrendered at once. He realised that here resistance was useless, that anyway he was in much too deep.

'How angry you are, Pavo,' was all he said. Mechanically he gathers in his winnings, begins collecting up his money and filling his pockets with it, notes and coins forced in any old how. He picks up the last wad of notes in his hand, rises and follows Pavo.

The croupier watches angrily as the two of them leave. The game collapsed . . .

Later at the hotel the news was that the master of Sinvara had not only recouped the losses from his previous visits to the roulette table but had even come out in front by something like six or seven hundred. His good fortune made me very happy for him. No one played more honestly than him, and henceforth he would presumably keep well away from the roulette table.

7

Next evening I was all set to leave. My things had been taken down to the quay, my bill paid, everything was in order. I stick a note in the hotel porter's hand and say goodbye. His big white eyes blink and he begins to cry. The poor devil even kissed my hand.

'Guess what,' he says at once, drying his eyes, 'the master of Sinvara is travelling on the same boat as you. He's promised Pavo he's going home.' And this encyclopaedic person pursues me to the finish with his tales: Pavo had given his father another lecture. When the threat to tell Prince Yariw didn't get anywhere he had shown him a dud little pistol with which he intended to shoot himself in order to rescue his father's honour. At this the father gave up. Nor was he particularly anxious to lose Prince Yariw's friendship. Moreover he had sworn to God by all that's holy that he would stop playing once he won back all the money he'd lost. In a word: the master of Sinvara was indeed going home.

'Goodbye!' said the hotel porter. 'You'll see him down by the boat.'

It was five o'clock.

Just as the casino was opening I set off down to the quay. A cargo of raffia mats was being loaded on board. A few minutes later the master of Sinvara arrived with his man, both of them dressed to travel. There were a great many people present, but no Pavo. I asked an old man where he was:

'Why hasn't he come to see his father off?'

'Pavo is proud,' replied a young girl who had just arrived. 'He won't recognise a father who gambles away his rings. That's Pavo for you.'

The master of Sinvara's little girl was there too. She stood off to one side, with head bowed. The man she was looking at didn't even glance at her once.

I walked up and down the quay a couple of times, put my luggage through customs and checked as my things were carried on board, and then went aboard myself. The master of Sinvara's old manservant was there, but I saw no sign of the master himself. I looked around for the young girl, but there was no sign of her either.

The last mats were lowered into the hold and the last passenger boarded the boat. Suddenly everyone is asking what has become of the master of Sinvara who was supposed to be travelling with them. Where was he? His old servant is in quite a state. Where in the world can his master be? The boat stayed where it was, for there was no question of leaving without the great man. Everyone on board joins in the search for him, they look for him on the quayside, in hidden corners, they ask everywhere for news of him and no one knows. Had he fallen overboard? Or had he jumped overboard and gone to his death in silence? Suddenly I have a hunch, a quite unreasonable notion. I ask the skipper to wait five minutes and I might be able to bring news of the missing person.

I jump ashore, hurry back to the hotel, race up the steps to the blue room on the top floor. Holding my breath I open the door and peer inside.

First I see the master of Sinvara's little girl. She's got her healthy pink flush back and she looks radiant. And on the chair in front of her, sitting at the roulette table again, is the master of Sinvara.

A GHOST

Several years of my childhood were spent with my uncle at a rectory in Nordland. It was a hard time for me, with a lot of work, a lot of beatings and seldom if ever a little free time for play and recreation. My uncle was so strict with me that in the end the only pleasure I had was to steal away and be on my own somewhere. On the rare occasions when I had no duties to perform I would go up into the forest, or else to the graveyard, where I wandered between the crosses and the gravestones, dreaming and thinking, talking out loud to myself.

The rectory was beautifully situated on the banks of a tidal river, the Glimma, a broad, rocky river which thundered and roared by day and night, night and day. At a certain time of the day it ran south, at another north, all according to whether the tide was ebbing or flowing; but whichever way it was flowing it always sang its wild, rushing song, and winter or summer it flowed with the same urgent speed.

The church and graveyard were situated on a hill. The church was an old cruciform church made of wood, and the graveyard wasn't cultivated, there were no trees and never any flowers on the graves; but up under the stone wall grew the ripest raspberries, big juicy berries that sucked up the nourishing mould from the dead. I knew each grave and every inscription, and saw how crosses that were erected would begin to tilt with the passage of time and finally collapse one stormy night.

But if there were no flowers over the graves there was, in the summer, a sumptuous carpet of grass that covered the whole cemetery. It was so high and so rough, and many times I sat listening to the sighing of the wind through this hard grass which grew up to the height of my waist. And in the middle of this soughing the weather-vane up on the church steeple might swing round with a rusty metallic creaking that sounded across the whole parish. It was as though this one piece of iron were gnashing its teeth at another.

I had many a conversation with the gravedigger while he was about his work. He was a serious man who rarely smiled, but he was very friendly to me and sometimes when he was standing tossing up dirt from a grave he might warn me to get out of the way because he had here on his spade a great thigh-bone or some grinning skull.

Often I found bones on the graves and tufts of hair from the corpses which I put back under the ground again as the gravedigger had taught me. I was so used to this that I felt no unease when I came across such human remains. There was a vault under one end of the church with bones lying around all over it and I sat there many times whittling something or made pictures on the floor using the crumbling bones.

Then one day I found a tooth in the graveyard.

It was a front tooth, brilliant white and strong. Without really thinking about it I put it in my pocket. I would make something out of it, some figure or other, and use it to decorate one of the strange things I used to carve in wood. I took the tooth home with me.

It was autumn and dark early. I had a few chores to do first so it was an hour or two before I went over to the servants' quarters to work on the tooth. The moon had risen; it was a half-moon.

There was no light in the servants' quarters and I was quite alone. I didn't dare simply to go ahead and light the lamp before the farm-hands arrived, but I knew once I got a good draught going I could manage well enough by the glow from the draw-hole in the woodburning stove, so I went out to the shed for wood.

The shed was in darkness.

As I fumble about in search of wood I feel a light touch, like a finger on my head.

I turned swiftly round but saw no one.

I flailed around with my arms but caught nothing.

I asked was there anyone there, but got no answer.

I was bareheaded, and as I touched my head with my hand I felt something icy cold and at once took my hand away. That was curious! I thought. I touched my hair again, but the cold thing was gone.

I thought:

Something cold has fallen from the roof and hit me on the head.
I wonder what it could have been?

I gathered up an armful of wood and returned to the servants'
quarters, lit the stove and waited until the light from the draw-hole
began to glow.

Then I took out the tooth and the file.

There was a knock at the window.

I looked up. Outside the window, with his face pressed against
the glass, stood a man. He was a stranger, I didn't know him, and
yet I knew everyone in the parish. He had a full red beard, a knotted
red scarf round his neck and a sou'wester on his head. I didn't think
about this at the time, because it only occurred to me later: but how
could I have seen the head so clearly in the dark? And from a part
of the house on which the half-moon wasn't even shining? I saw
the face with horrifying clarity. It was pale, almost white, and the
eyes stared straight at me.

A minute passes.

Then the man begins to laugh.

It wasn't audible, shaking laughter; but the mouth opened wide
and the eyes continued to stare as before, and the man was laughing.

I dropped what I had in my hands and a chill passed through me
from head to foot. In the hideous gaping, laughing face outside the
window I see suddenly a black space in the jaw—he has a tooth
missing.

I sat staring straight in front of me in terror. Another minute
passes. The face took on colour. It turned deep green, then deep red.
The smile remained fixed. I did not lose my presence of mind, I
continued to notice everything around me. The fire was glowing
brightly from the draw-hole and cast a small gleam right over onto
the opposite wall where there were some steps. From the room next
door I could hear a clock ticking on the wall. So aware was I that
I even noticed that the sou'wester the man had on was faded black
on the crown but that the brim was coloured green.

Then the man lowered his head slowly down the window, slowly
down, further and further until finally he was beneath the window.
It was as though he had slipped down into the earth. I did not see
him again.

I was in a terrified state and had begun shaking. I searched the floor for the tooth, at the same time hardly daring to take my eyes from the window in case the face should show itself again.

When I found the tooth I would have returned it to the graveyard immediately except that I didn't dare. I sat there, still alone, unable to move. I hear steps out in the yard and imagine it's one of the maids clacking by in her clogs; but I didn't dare to call out to her, and the steps went by. An eternity passes. The fire in the stove begins to die down. It seemed as if no one would come to rescue me.

Finally I grit my teeth and get up. Opening the door I walk backwards from the servants' quarters, keeping my eye fixed on the window where I had seen the man standing. Once I was out of the yard I ran over to the stables to get one of the lads to come with me over to the graveyard.

But the lads weren't in the stables.

However, being out in the open air had made me bolder and I decided to go alone to the graveyard. That way I wouldn't have to tell anyone what had happened and perhaps get in trouble with my uncle for the story.

So I made my way alone up the hill. I had the tooth wrapped in my handkerchief.

By the cemetery gate my courage deserted me and I stopped. I hear the endless rushing of the Glimma. Apart from that, silence. There was no door at the cemetery gate, just an archway you walked under. I stand nervously on one side of this arch and stick my head carefully through to see if I dare go any further.

At once I sink to my knees.

Beyond the gate, standing among the graves, was the man with the sou'wester again. His face was still white as he turned towards me. He was pointing forwards, on into the graveyard.

I took this to be an order, but didn't dare to obey. I remained there a long time, just looking at the man. I pleaded with him, and he stood unmoving and silent.

Then something happened which gave me my courage back again. I heard one of the farm-workers whistling as he busied himself with something down in the stables. This sign of life nearby helped me to get to my feet again. Gradually the man began to distance himself from me, not walking, but gliding across the graves, still pointing forwards. I stepped through the gate, the man waved me on. I walked a few paces and then stopped, unable to go on. My hand trembling, I took the white tooth out of the handkerchief and threw it as hard as I could into the graveyard. At that instant the weather-vane swung round on the church steeple and I felt the screeching grate inside my bones. I hurtled out of the gate, down the hill and home. When I came into the kitchen they said my face was as white as snow . . .

Many years have passed since then, but I remember everything. I see myself kneeling by the cemetery gate and I see the red-bearded man.

I couldn't even guess what age he might have been. Twenty perhaps, but he could as easily have been forty. Since this was not the last time I saw him I did think about this at a later date; but it is impossible for me to say how old he was . . .

Many evenings, many nights he reappeared to me. He showed himself, laughed with those gaping jaws with the tooth missing, then disappeared. It had snowed and it was no longer possible for me to go up to the cemetery and put the tooth back under the ground. And throughout that winter, though less and less frequently, he continued to appear. My terror of him grew less intense, but he made my days unhappy, desperately unhappy. Often I would comfort myself with the thought that I could put an end to all my misery by throwing myself into the Glimma when she was rising.

Then came spring and the man disappeared completely.

Completely? No, not completely, but for the whole of the summer. Next winter he was there again. Just the once, then he stayed away for a long time. Three years after my first encounter with him I left Nordland and stayed away for a year. By the time I returned I had been confirmed, and was in my own eyes a full-grown man. I no longer lived with my uncle in the rectory but at home, with my mother and father.

One autumn evening, not long after I had gone to bed, I felt a cold hand on my forehead. I opened my eyes and saw the man in front of me. He was sitting on my bed watching me. I wasn't sleeping alone in the room but shared it with two of my brothers. I didn't scare them, however. When I felt that cold pressure on my forehead I waved my arm and said:

'No, go away!'

From their beds my brothers asked who I was talking to.

When the man had been sitting there for a while he began to rock his upper body back and forth. As he did so he seemed to grow taller and taller, until finally he was swaying almost up by the ceiling. And since he was unable to get much further he stood up, walked with soundless steps away from my bed and disappeared over by the stove. I followed him with my eyes the entire time . . .

Never before had he come so close to me as that. I saw right into his eyes. The expression was dead and empty, he was looking at me and yet past me, through me, deep into another world. The eyes were grey. His face never moved and he did not laugh. When I shoved his hand away from my forehead and said, 'No, go away!' he took his hand away slowly. During the minutes that he was sitting on the edge of my bed he never blinked once . . .

A few months later it was winter again and I was again away from home, living with a merchant, W——, working in his shop and his office. Here I met the man for the last time:

I go up to my room one evening, light the lamp and undress. As usual I leave my shoes out for the maid and I have them in my hand and open the door.

He stands there in the corridor, right in front of me, the red-bearded man.

I know there are people in the rooms next to mine so I'm not afraid. I say out loud: 'Are you here again?'

Then he opened his wide mouth and began to laugh. The effect no longer terrified me, and as I looked more closely I saw that the missing tooth was now in place.

Someone had perhaps pushed it back into the ground. Or maybe over the course of the years it had crumbled into dust and been reunited with the dust from which it had been parted. God knows.

The man closed his mouth again as I stood in the doorway, turned and walked down the stairs and disappeared.

That was the last time I saw him. And many are the years of Our Lord that have passed since then . . .

This man, this red-bearded emissary from the land of the dead, brought me indescribable distress in my childhood. He hurt me. I have had other visions since then, other encounters with the inexplicable; but nothing has had such a powerful effect on me as him.

And perhaps after all it wasn't just harm he did me. This has often struck me. It seems to me he was one of the first reasons I had to learn to grit my teeth and make myself hard. In later life I have sometimes needed to be able to do that.

A WOMAN'S TRIUMPH

I was a conductor on a tram-car in Chicago. My first job was on the Halstead line, the line that goes from the middle of town all the way down to the cattle-market. Those of us working the nightshift never felt particularly safe on that line because of all the dubious types who used it. We weren't allowed to shoot and kill people, in case the company was held responsible and made to pay compensation; as for me, I never carried a revolver anyway, I just trusted to luck. But in any case it's rare that a man is completely unarmed, and there was always the crank for the brake which could be removed in an instant and would make a very handy weapon. Even then, I only had to use it once.

In 1886 I worked every night over the Christmas period without anything special happening. A gang of Irishmen got on at the cattle-market and filled up the car, they were drunk and had bottles with them and began to sing loudly and were reluctant to pay, even though we'd already set off. They said they had been paying the company five cents every morning and night and now it was Christmas and they weren't going to pay. It seemed a reasonable enough attitude to take, but I daren't let them off because of the company spies who travelled about checking on the honesty of the conductors. A policeman boarded. He stood for a few minutes, passed some remark about Christmas and the weather and then got off again because we were so full. I knew quite well that it would only have taken a couple of words in his ear and all of them would have had to pay their five cents; but I said nothing. 'Why didn't you report us?' someone asked. I answered that I didn't think it was necessary, since I knew I was dealing with gentlemen. At this some of them burst out laughing at me; but one or two others sided with me and they paid for the rest.

By next Christmas I was working on the Cottage line. Here things were very different. Now I had a train of two and sometimes three wagons, operated by an underground electric cable. The public in this part of town were gentry and I had to collect my five cents with gloves on. But nothing exciting ever happened, and one soon got bored with seeing and hearing these people from the big houses.

And yet something odd did happen that Christmas of 1887.

On Christmas Eve morning I drove the tram downtown; I was working the dayshift at the time. A gentleman gets on and begins talking to me. When I had to pass inside through the wagons he waited until I came back to my place on the platform at the rear and again began talking to me. He was about thirty, pale, with a moustache, very well dressed, but not wearing an overcoat in spite of the cold.

'I just dashed out in my indoor clothes,' he said. 'I want to give my wife a surprise.'

'Christmas present,' I observed.

'Correct!' he answered with a smile.

But it was a curious smile, more of a grimace, a contortion of the mouth.

'How much do you earn?' he asked.

This is not an unusual question in Yankeeland and I told him what I earned.

'How would you like to earn an extra ten dollars?' he asked.

I said, 'Yes.'

He took out his wallet and without further preamble handed me the money. He said he had faith in me.

'What do you want me to do?' I asked.

He asked to see my timetable. Then he said:

'You're working eight hours today?'

'Yes.'

'On one of your trips I want you to do me a little favour. Right here on the corner of Monroe Street we pass over a shaft that leads down to the underground cable. There's a cover over that shaft and I'm going to lift it off and get down inside it.'

'Do you want to kill yourself?'

'No, but that's the way I want it to look.'

'Ah.'

'You're to stop your tram and drag me up out of the hole, even though I'll be resisting you.'

'I'll manage that.'

'Thanks. And by the way, I'm not mad, if that's what you're thinking. This is for the benefit of my wife, I want her to think I'm trying to kill myself.'

'So your wife will be on my tram at the same time?'

'Yes. She'll be riding in the Grip.'

I was surprised. The Grip was where the driver stood. It was an open wagon with no sides and on a winter's day was a cold place to be. Few travelled there.

'She'll be riding in the Grip,' the man repeated. 'She says so in a letter to her lover, that she'll be riding there today and she's going to give him a signal that she's coming to him. I've read the letter.'

'All right. But I must warn you, be quick about lifting the cover off the shaft and getting down into the hole, or we'll have another tram on top of us. There are only three minutes between them.'

'I know all that,' answered the man. 'The cover will be loosened before I get there. In fact it's already loose now.'

'One more thing: how can you know which tram your wife will be on?'

'I'll be informed by telephone. I've got people watching her. She'll be wearing a brown leather coat, you'll recognise her easily, she's very pretty. If she faints, get her into the chemist's shop on the corner of Monroe Street.'

'Have you spoken to the driver too?'

'Yes,' said the man. 'And I've paid the driver the same as you. But I don't want the two of you joking about this. I don't even want you to mention it to each other.'

'No.'

'Go forward to the Grip when you're approaching Monroe Street and keep a sharp lookout. When you see my head sticking out of the shaft give the order to brake and the tram will come to a halt. The driver will help you to overpower me and pull me up out of the shaft, even though I will be struggling and protesting that I want to die.'

I thought the whole thing over for a moment, then said:

'It occurs to me you could have saved your money and not let anyone in on your plan. You could have just climbed down into the shaft.'

'But Good Lord!' the man exclaimed. 'The driver wouldn't see me! You wouldn't see me! Nobody would see me!'

'You're right.'

We discussed one or two other things, and he travelled with us all the way to the terminus, and then back with us when we turned the tram round.

At the corner of Monroe Street he said:

'There's the chemist's shop where I want you to take my wife if she faints.'

Then he got off.

I was ten dollars richer! God be praised, life still had its good days! All through that cold winter I'd been wearing a layer of newspaper over my chest and my back. I made embarrassing crackling noises every time I moved, something which my workmates found highly amusing. Now there would be money for among other things a fine, close-fitting leather waistcoat. Next time my mates prodded me to hear me crackle I wouldn't have to put up with it.

I make two, I make three trips to town; nothing happened. Leaving Cottage station for the fourth time a young lady boarded and sat up front in the Grip. She was wearing brown leather. When I went forward to collect her fare she looked me full in the face. She was very young and very beautiful, her eyes so innocent and so blue. Poor thing, I thought to myself, you're in for a terrible shock today. You've committed a little sin and now you're going to get your punishment. But I'm looking forward to carrying you into the chemist's.

We rolled on into town.

From my place at the back I saw the driver begin talking to the woman. What could he be saying to her? In any case he wasn't supposed to talk to passengers while the tram was in motion. Then to my great surprise I saw the lady move to a seat even closer to him. He stood there listening intently as he drove on.

We carry on into town, stopping to pick up passengers, stopping, letting them off again. We approach Monroe Street. I think: this eccentric young man has chosen his spot wisely. The corner at Monroe Street is a quiet place and he isn't likely to be disturbed as he climbs down into the shaft. I think of how I've sometimes seen company engineers down in that shaft doing repair work when something's gone wrong; but if anyone tried to stand up when a tram came by he would quite simply end up several inches shorter than he was before. The grab connecting the Grip to the cable would rip his head off.

Monroe was the next stop. I walked forward to the Grip.

Neither the driver nor the lady were speaking any more. The last thing I saw was the driver nodding, as though agreeing to something, and then he looked straight ahead and drove on at full speed. My driver was Big Pat, the Irishman.

'Slack here a bit!' I called out to him, meaning slow down a bit, for on the tracks ahead of us I saw something dark sticking up that might have been a human head.

I looked at the lady too. Her eyes were fastened to the same spot and she was holding on tightly to her seat. She's already afraid there might be an accident! I thought to myself. What will she be like when she sees it's her own husband that's trying to do away with himself!

But Big Pat didn't slow down a bit. I shouted to him that there was someone down in the shaft, but it made no difference. We could see the head clearly now, that young madman standing there with his face towards us. I put my whistle to my lips and blew a loud stop-signal. Pat drove on at the same speed. In a few seconds there was going to be an accident. I rang the bell, leapt forward and grabbed hold of the brake. But it was too late, and the tram went screeching across the shaft before it came to a halt.

I jumped down. I was bewildered. All I could remember was that I was supposed to grapple with a man who would try to fight back. Then, in confusion, I climbed straight back onto the Grip again. The driver was in the same confused state too, he kept on asking meaninglessly if there had been someone down in the shaft, and why hadn't he been able to stop. The young lady exclaimed: 'Horrible! Horrible!' Her face was deathly pale and she still clutched tightly at her seat. But she didn't faint, and a few moments later she got down and went on her way.

A crowd of people had gathered. We found the victim's head under the rear carriage, and the rest of him still in the shaft. The grab had caught him under the chin and taken the head with it. We lifted him out of the way and handed the body over to a constable. The constable noted down a lot of names, and many of the passengers could testify that I had whistled, rung the bell and finally grabbed the brake. In addition we, as employees, would have to make our own report to the company.

Big Pat asked for the loan of my knife. I misunderstood, and said that there had been enough accidents for one day. At that he smiled, showed me a gun he was carrying and said he wasn't intending to do anything stupid with the knife, he had quite another use for it. I gave it to him, and he bade me goodbye, saying he couldn't possibly carry on after what had happened. He was sorry, but I would have to take the tram down to the terminus myself; they would give me another driver there. He gave me a few instructions in how to drive it. I'd have to let him keep the knife, he said—he was going to find somewhere quiet and cut the buttons off his uniform jacket.

Away he went.

There was nothing else for it, I would have to drive on to the terminus myself. Several trams were now lined up behind me and waiting to get on. And because I'd had a little practice with the machine the rest of the journey passed without incident . . .

*   *   *

One evening when I had a day off between Christmas and New Year I was wandering the streets. Passing the railway station I went in for a moment to see all the bustle and activity there. I made my way to the end of one platform and stood watching a train that was about to depart. Suddenly I hear my name, a man smiling down from one of the carriages and calling my name. It was Big Pat. It took me a few moments to recognise him, because he was so well dressed and had shaved off his beard.

I greeted him in return.

'Ssh, not so loud! What happened in the end, about that business?'

'We were questioned,' I answered. 'They're looking for you.'

Pat said:

'I'm going out west. What's to stay here for? Seven, eight dollars a week and it costs you four just to live. I'm going to get some land, going to be a farmer. I've got the money you know. Come with me if you like and we'll buy a fruit farm out 'Frisco way.'

'Can't do it,' I answered.

'While I remember, here's your knife. Thanks for the loan. No, you know, there's no future driving trams. I was at it for three years and never got the chance to get away until now.'

The train whistle blew.

'Well, so long then,' said Pat. 'By the way, how much did you get from that man we ran over?'

'Ten dollars.'

'Me too. He paid well—but not as well as the wife.'

'The wife?'

'The young lady, yes. I made a little deal with her. A thousand or two was no hindrance when it was a matter of getting rid of her husband. It's her money that's giving me the chance of a better life.'

ON THE PRAIRIE

During the summer of 1887 I worked on a section of Dalrumple's huge farm in the Red River Valley, in America. As well as me there were two other Norwegians, a Swede, ten or twelve Irishmen and a few Americans. In all there were about twenty men working our little section—just a fraction of the workforce of hundreds on that farm.

The prairie was green-gold and endless as the sea. Not a building to be seen apart from our own stables and bunkhouse in the middle of the prairie. No trees grew there, no bushes, only wheat and grass as far as the eye could see. There were no flowers either, just occasionally in among the wheat you might come across the yellow tassels of wild mustard, the prairie's only flower. They were forbidden; when we found them we pulled them up by the root, took them home and dried and burnt them.

No birds in flight either, no other sign of life but the rippling of the wheat in the wind, and the only sound the endless singing of a million grasshoppers—the prairie's only song.

We thirsted for shade. When the chuckwagon came out to us at midday we lay on our stomachs beneath it so that we could eat our food in shadow. The sun was merciless. We wore hat, shirt, trousers and shoes, nothing else, and nothing less either, or else we would have been burnt up. If, for example, you wore a hole in your shirt while working the sun would burn through it and leave a blister on your skin.

During the harvesting we had a working day up to 16 hours long. Ten cutting machines worked in a line behind each other in the same field day after day. When one square was cut flat we turned into the next one and cut that flat too. On and on like that, always on, with ten men walking behind to stack the wheat. And high on his horse, watching over us, the foreman, a revolver in his pocket and an eye in every finger-tip. He rode his two horses to exhaustion every day. If something happened, if a machine broke down, for example, the foreman would be on the spot at once and repair the damage or order it to be sent home. Often he might be far away when something happened, and since there were no roads he had to ride the whole day through the thick wheat while his horses foamed with sweat.

September and October wore on. The heat of the day was still punishing, but the nights turned bitterly cold. Often we froze. Nor did we get anything like enough sleep; we might be roused at three in the morning while it was still dark. By the time we'd fed the horses and ourselves and ridden the long way out to our place of work it would be daylight and we could see the task that lay ahead of us. Then we set fire to a haystack to heat up the oil we used for greasing the machines, and took a little warmth from it ourselves. But it only lasted a few minutes, and then it was back up on the machines.

We didn't keep the sabbath, the day of rest, Sunday was the same as Monday. But when it rained there was nothing for us to do and we lay in. We gambled, talked to each other, slept.

There was one Irishman who to begin with puzzled me greatly: God knows what he used to be in his previous life. When it rained he always lay on his bunk and read the novels he had with him. He was a big, handsome man about 36 years old and he spoke beautiful English. He spoke German too.

This man arrived at the farm wearing a silk shirt and in fact he always wore a silk shirt to work in. When one wore out he took out a new one. He wasn't much of a worker, his 'touch' wasn't good, he was a little clumsy. All the same he was an unusual man.

Evans was his name.

There was nothing special about the two Norwegians. One of them, from Hadeland, ran off because he couldn't take the work. The other held out—but then he was a Valdres man.

While the threshing was going on we all tried to get a place as far as possible from the steam-engine; from every corner and blade of the thing came a great billowing cloud of dust, sand and chaff. For a few days I was right in the middle of this storm, until I asked the foreman to put me on something else—which he did. He gave me an excellent place out in the field loading bales onto the wagons. He never forgot a favour I did him right at the beginning.

It happened like this:

My jacket was a uniform jacket with shiny buttons that I had with me from my time as a conductor on the trams in Chicago. The foreman liked this jacket with its lovely buttons; he was like a child when it came to fancy things, and out here in the desert you didn't get fancy things. I told him one day he could have the jacket. He offered to pay for it, asked me to name my price. When I told him he could simply have it he said that he owed me a favour. After the harvest was over he gave me another jacket, a good one, when he saw I had no jacket to travel in.

I remember one episode from the time when I was doing this work as what they call a bundle-pitcher.

The Swede was stacking. He was wearing big boots, with the trousers tucked in the tops. We started loading. He worked at a ferocious speed and I had my work cut out keeping him supplied with bundles. He kept at it, harder and faster, and in the end it started getting on my nerves and I began working as fast as I could too.

Each wheat shock consisted of eight sheaves and the usual thing was to pitch one sheaf onto the rack at a time; now I took four. I drowned the Swede in sheaves, I flattened him with sheaves. Then in one of these great loads I was tossing up it turned out there was a snake, and it slithered down into one of his boots. The first I know of it is when I hear a shriek of terror and see the Swede hurl himself down from the load with this dappled snake dangling from one of his boots. But it didn't bite, and on hitting the ground it wriggled out of the boot and disappeared like lightning over the field. We set off after it with our pitchforks but we couldn't find it. The two mules pulling the wagon stood shivering in their traces.

I can still hear the Swede's shout and see him flying through the air as he threw himself off that wagon.

After that we agreed that he would work at a more reasonable pace, and I would send him just one sheaf at a time . . .

So we'd ploughed and sowed, mowed and gathered in the hay, mowed and threshed the wheat—and now our work was at an end and it was time for us to be paid off. Light of heart, our pockets full of money, a 20-strong gang of us wandered down to the nearest prairie town to find a train to take us back east. The foreman came too, to have a last drink with us. He was wearing the jacket with the shiny buttons.

People who have never been with a gang of prairie workers having a farewell party will find it hard to comprehend just how much drinking takes place on such occasions. Every man buys a round, straightaway that's 20 glasses for each man. But if you think it stops there you're wrong, for some among us at once demand five rounds. And God help any saloon-keeper who protests that this is unreasonable, if he does he's liable to find himself thrown out of his own bar. A group of migrant workers like this mows down everything that gets in its way. As early as the fifth glass it elects itself lord of the town and from that moment on its rule is absolute. The local police are powerless. They join the gang and even drink with it. And for the next two days and nights there's nothing but drinking, gambling, brawling and shouting.

We workers were kindness itself towards each other. Mutual love had often been in short supply during the long summer, but now at parting all the old grudges were forgotten. And the more we drank the bigger our hearts grew, we treated each other until we just about dropped, and threw our arms around each other with emotion. The cook, a humpbacked little runt of a man with a high-pitched voice and no beard, confided to me between hiccups that he too was a Norwegian and that the reason he hadn't mentioned it earlier was because of the way Yankees looked down on Norwegians. Often he'd heard me and the man from Valdres talking about him at mealtimes and he'd understood every word; but now was a time for forgiving and forgetting, because we were such great guys. Oh you bet, he was 'born of the sons of good old Norway', he was *born* in Iowa on 22 Julai (*July*), 1845'.* So we must stay good friends and *partners* as long as the Norwegian language flowed from our lips. Cook and I embraced each other; our friendship would never die. All the workers embraced each other. We squashed each other flat with our sinewy arms and we danced each other round and round.

* In English in original.

We used to say to each other: what are you going to have to drink now? There's nothing here that's too good for you! Then we'd go behind the bar ourselves in search of the finest of the fine. We pulled down strange bottles from way up on the top shelves, bottles with beautiful labels that were there chiefly for show but whose contents we best of friends treated each other to, and drank, and paid the earth for.

Evans was probably the worst when it came to calling for rounds. His last silk shirt was in a sorry state by now, sun and rain had dulled its bright colours and the sleeves were in tatters. But Evans himself stood there tall and proud, calling imperiously for more rounds. He owned the place, in fact he owned the world. The rest of us usually paid about three dollars for our rounds, but when Evans called for a round it cost six dollars a time, for there was nothing in that dump of a place good enough for the men he had with him, he said. That was when we had to haul down those strange bottles from the top shelves to find something that would cost enough . . .

Brimming over with friendship Evans took me to one side and tried to persuade me to go with him to the Wisconsin forests for the winter and chop cordwood. Once he'd kitted himself out with some new shirts, a pair of trousers and a few new novels he would be making his way back to the forests, he said, and stay there till the spring. And come spring he would head for the prairie again. That was his life. For 12 years he'd been dividing his life between the prairie and the forest, and he'd got so used to it that now it just happened by itself.

But when I asked him what it was that had started him off living this way he didn't answer, the way drunk people often do, with a long and pathetic account of all that had gone wrong, but with just one word: 'circumstances'.

'Such as?' I asked.

'Circumstances!' he repeated. And he wouldn't be drawn any further.

Later in the evening I saw him in an annexe to the bar where they were shooting crap. Evans had lost. He was pretty drunk and didn't much care about money. When I came in he showed me the few notes he had left and said:

'I've still got money, see here.'

Some were telling him to quit. One of his countrymen, an Irishman named O'Brien, hinted that he should use the money to buy a railway ticket. Evans took offence at this.

'No, you lend me the ticket money,' he said.

O'Brien refused point-blank and left the room.

Now Evans was irritated. He put all his money on one throw of the dice and lost. He took it calmly. Lighting a cigar he smiled and said to me:

'Will you lend me some travel money?'

By now I was a little confused from a last swig of one of these fancy bottles from up on the top shelves, and I unbuttoned my jacket and handed Evans my wallet and all its contents. I did it to show him how ready I was to lend him the travel money, and I left it to him to take what he needed. He looked at me, and he looked at the wallet. Some curious emotion flickered through him. He opened the wallet and saw that it contained all my money. When he turned his head towards me I simply nodded.

He misunderstood this. He thought I meant he could help himself to the lot.

'Thank you!' he said.

And to my horror he commenced playing with my money.

My first thought was to stop him; but I held back. First let him spend his ticket money any way he likes, I thought; when he's lost a fair amount I'll take the rest back.

But Evans didn't lose any more. All at once he seemed to have sobered up and now he played decisively and rapidly. The confidence shown him in front of so many of his comrades had transformed him. He sat up straight and silent on the whisky barrel that served as his seat, he bet, and he won. If he lost he doubled his stake the next time. He lost up to three times in a row and doubled his bet each time, raking in his winnings on the final throw. Then he bet a whole five dollars and said that if he won now he would quit.

He lost.

And he carried on playing.

After an hour had passed he handed my wallet back to me with the money in it. He had kept a careful account throughout the game.

By now he had a thick wad of notes himself. He played on. Then suddenly he staked everything he had. A murmur passed round the room.

Evans said:

'Win or lose, I quit after this.'

He won.

Evans stood up.

'I'll take my winnings, please,' he said. 'Tomorrow,' answered the banker. 'I don't have it tonight. I'll get it for you tomorrow.'

'Fine, tomorrow then . . .'

As we were leaving a group of men came in, carrying between them a mutilated body. It was the Irishman O'Brien, the same man who had refused to lend Evans his train fare. He had just been run over by a wheat train; both his legs had been severed, one of them high up on the thigh. He was already dead. In the darkness he had walked straight under the train wheels. The body was placed on the floor and covered up . . .

We found places to sleep where best we could; some lay down right there on the floor of the saloon itself. The man from Valdres and I found a hayloft somewhere in town.

In the morning Evans came walking down the street.

'Did you get your money from the banker?' asked the man from Valdres.

'Not yet,' answered Evans. 'I've been out in the field and dug a hole for our comrade.'

We buried O'Brien some ways outside of town, in a box we found outside a house. Since the body was cut so short it meant the box was big enough for him. We didn't sing nor say any prayers; but everyone turned up and stood in silence for a moment, hat in hand.

So then that ceremony was over . . .

But when Evans went to get his money it turned out that that sneak of a banker had run off. Evans took it calmly, just like he took everything else. It seemed hardly to matter to him. He still had plenty of money anyway, enough for his train ticket, his shirts, his trousers and his novels, all he needed for the winter.

We stayed in town until the evening of the following day. We carried on as before and drank the bar dry. Many of the workers were flat broke when they left the place, and since they couldn't pay for a train ticket they sneaked on board the freight wagons and buried themselves in the wheat. But it didn't work out for that little humpbacked cook, the Norwegian from Iowa. He was lucky and managed to get under the wheat without being seen, but once there he couldn't keep quiet and in his drunkenness began to sing dirty songs in his high-pitched voice. He was caught and thrown out, and when they emptied the little runt's pockets he had plenty enough money to pay for tickets for all of us, the bastard!

We spread to the four winds. The man from Valdres bought himself a little shooting gallery in a town in Minnesota and the cook headed west to the Pacific coast. But for sure Evans is still roaming around in his silk shirts and handing out the money. Every summer he's on the prairie harvesting wheat and every winter in the Wisconsin forests chopping cordwood. That's his life.

A life maybe as good as any other.

ZACHÆUS

1

The deepest peace reigns over the prairie. For miles, as far as the eye can see, there is not a house, not a tree, nothing but wheat and green grass. Far, far away, tiny as flies, horses and men can be seen working—the harvesters, sitting on their machines and mowing the grass down in furrows. The only sound is the singing of the grasshoppers; and when the wind is in the right direction, just very occasionally, the sharp buzzing of the threshing-machines over on the horizon. At times the sound seems remarkably close.

This is Billybonny Farm. It lies quite alone, without neighbours, without any connection with the world, and the nearest little prairie town is several days away on foot. From a distance the farmhouses look like a couple of tiny skerries in the endless sea of wheat. The farm is unoccupied in the winter; but from spring until late October over 70 men work there. There are three men in the kitchen, the cook and his two helpers, and 20 mules in the stables as well as numerous horses, but no women; not a single woman on Billybonny Farm.

The sun burns down at 102 degrees Fahrenheit, sky and earth stand quivering in the heat, and there is no breath of wind to cool the air. The sun looks like a morass of fire.

Everything is quite still over at the farm buildings too. From the large, shingled shed that is used as a kitchen and dining-room you can hear the voices and footsteps of the cook and his helpers as they go about their work. They burn grass in the huge stoves and the smoke that belches from the chimney is mixed with sparks and flames. When the food is ready it is carried out in zinc tubs and lifted up onto the wagons. The mules are hitched up and the three men drive out onto the prairie with it.

The cook is a huge Irishman, 40 years old, grey-haired, with a military bearing. He goes half-naked, with his shirt open, and his chest is like a barrel. Everyone calls him Polly because he looks like a parrot.

Polly has been a soldier at one of the forts down in the South. He is a literary man, and owns a song book as well as a copy of an old newspaper. He won't allow anyone else to touch these treasures; he keeps them on a shelf in the kitchen so as to have them to hand in idle moments. He makes good and regular use of them.

But Zachæus, his wretched fellow-countryman, who is almost blind and uses glasses, once took the newspaper to read. It was no good offering Zachæus an ordinary book, where the small print just danced in a mist for him; but he took a great pleasure in reading the cook's newspaper and lingering over the big lettering of the advertisements. But the cook missed his treasure at once, he went to Zachæus in his bunk and grabbed the paper back. A violent and entertaining argument between the two men ensued.

The cook called Zachæus a blackhearted robber and a son of a bitch. He snapped his fingers under his nose and asked if he'd ever seen a soldier, or even knew how a fort was laid out? No, I thought not. Then in that case he'd better watch it by God, just watch it. Shut your trap. How much did he earn a month? Did *he* own property in Washington and had *his* cow calved just yesterday?

Zachæus didn't respond to any of this; what he did was accuse the cook of serving the food up half-cooked, and bread pudding that had flies in it. 'Go to hell and take your newspaper with you!' He— Zachæus—was an honest man and would have put the paper back once he'd read it. 'Don't stand there and spit on my floor, you dirty pig!'

And Zachæus's blind eyes stood out like hard steel balls in his raging face.

But from that day onwards there was a hostility between these two men . . .

The chuckwagons spread out across the prairie, each one carrying enough for 25 men. Men come running from every quarter, grab a little food and lie down under the wagons and the mules to find a little shade while they eat. Within ten minutes all the food has gone, the foreman is already in his saddle ordering the men back to work and the chuckwagons are heading back for the farm.

But while the kitchen hands wash and clean the cups and pots after the meal Polly sits out in the shade at the back of the house and for the thousandth time reads the songs and the soldiers' ballads from the precious book he brought with him from the fort in the South. Then Polly is a soldier again.

2

In the evening, shortly after dusk, seven haywagons roll slowly home from the prairie carrying the workforce. Most wash their hands out in the yard before going in for the evening meal. Some comb their hair as well. There are all nations, all races, young and old, immigrants from Europe and native-born American wanderers, every last one of them some kind of villain living out his derailed existence.

The more affluent among them carry revolvers in their back pockets. Usually the food is eaten quickly, with conversation kept to a minimum. Everyone respects the foreman, who eats with the men and is responsible for discipline. After the meal the men go straight to their rest . . .

But one evening it so happened that Zachæus wanted to wash his shirt. It had become stiff with sweat and chafed him during the day, with the sun burning down on his back.

It was dark, everyone was resting. From the great bunkhouse came the sounds of a muted conversation before the fall of night.

Zachæus went over to the kitchen wall to where several containers of rainwater stood. This was the cook's water. He collected it carefully whenever it rained, because the water on Billybonny Farm was too hard to wash in.

Zachæus took one of the containers, removed his shirt and started to wash it. It was a quiet, cold evening and he was shivering; but the shirt had to be washed. He whistled a bit to keep his spirits up.

Suddenly the cook opens the kitchen door. He holds a lamp in his hand and a broad beam of light falls on Zachæus.

'Aha!' said the cook.

He put the lamp down on the step, went straight up to Zachæus and said:

'Who gave you that water?'

'I took it,' answered Zachæus.

'That's my water,' shouted Polly. 'You've taken it, you slave, you liar, you thief, you son of a bitch.'

Zachæus didn't respond to any of this, he only began repeating his accusations about the flies in the pudding.

The row these two were making attracted men over from the bunkhouse, they gathered around in groups, shivering and listening to the exchanges with the greatest interest.

Polly shouted to them:

'What do you make of this little bastard? My own water!'

'Take your water,' said Zachæus, and tipped the container over. 'I'm finished with it.'

The cook bunched his fist under his nose and said:

'See this?'

'Yes,' answered Zachæus.

'Want a taste of it?'

'Just you dare.'

There came the sounds of blows being traded. The onlookers howled their pleasure and approval.

But Zachæus didn't last long. The short-sighted, skinny Irishman fought like a cornered rat, but his reach was too short to do any damage to the cook. Finally he staggered three or four steps across the yard and went down.

The cook turned to the onlookers.

'All right, he's down now. Let him lie there, where a soldier put him.'

'I think he's dead,' says one voice.

The cook shrugs his shoulders.

'That's fine by me!' he says contemptuously. And he feels like some great invincible conqueror in front of these people. He tosses his head and sets about consolidating the effect. He goes all literary.

'I don't care a damn about him,' he says, 'Let him lie there. Who does he think he is, Daniel Webster? Comes here trying to teach me how to cook puddings! Me, who's cooked for generals! Is it colonel-in-charge of the prairie he thinks he is?'

And everybody had to admire Polly's speech.

Then Zachæus gets to his feet again and says angrily, defiantly:

'Come on then, you rabbit!'

People howled with pleasure; but the cook smiled tolerantly and answered:

'Rubbish. I might just as well fight with this lamp.'

And he took his lamp with him and slowly and with dignity went back in.

It was dark in the yard as the men made their way back to the bunkhouse. Zachæus picked up his shirt, wrung it out carefully and put it on. Then he sloped off after the others to find his bunk and get some rest.

3

The following day Zachæus was on his knees in the grass out on the prairie oiling his machine. The sun was just as strong today and behind the glasses his eyes were swimming in sweat. Suddenly the horses jerk forward a couple of paces, something scared them, or maybe it was an insect bite. Zachæus lets out a shriek and jumps high into the air. Shortly afterwards he begins to swing his left hand through the air and starts walking rapidly up and down, up and down.

A man driving the hayraker not far off stops and asks:

'What's the trouble?'

Zachæus answers:

'Come here a moment and help me.'

When the man arrives Zachæus shows him his bloodied hand and says:

'One of my fingers has come off; it happened just now. Help me look for the finger, I can't see it.'

The man searches for the finger and finds it in the grass. There were two joints of it. It was beginning to wizen already and looked like a tiny corpse.

Zachæus looks at the finger in his hand, seems to recognise it and says:

'Yes that's it all right. Wait, hold it for me a minute.'

Zachæus pulls his shirt out of his trousers and tears two strips off it. He makes a bandage for his hand with one and wraps his finger in the other and then puts it in his pocket. He thanks the other man for his help and gets back up onto his machine.

He held out almost until the afternoon break. When the foreman heard about the accident he gave him a severe telling-off and sent him back to the farmhouse immediately.

The first thing Zachæus did was to hide the severed finger. He had no spirits, so he poured engine oil into a bottle, dropped the finger into it and corked it up tight as he could. He hid the bottle in his bunk, under the straw mattress.

He was off work for a week. He had terrible pains in his hand and had to hold it quite still all day and all night. The infection went to his head, he developed a fever in his body, his suffering was almost intolerable. He had never experienced enforced idleness before, not even on that occasion years ago, when the blasting shot went off and damaged his sight.

What made his situation even worse was that Polly the cook in person brought his food to him in bed each day, and made the most of his chance to torment the sick man. The two enemies had many a spat during this time, and on more than one occasion Zachæus had to turn to the wall and grit his teeth in silence because he could do nothing against the giant.

And the pain-filled days came and went, dragged by at an unendurable crawl. As soon as he was able Zachæus began sitting up in his bunk, and in the heat of the daytime he left the door open to the prairie and the sky. Often he sat with his mouth open listening out for the sound of the threshers in the far distance, and then he would speak out loud to his horses as though they were there in front of him.

And that wicked Polly, that devious Polly could not leave him in peace. He would close the door, pretending that there was a draught, a terrible draught, saying that Zachæus must be careful not to expose himself to any draughts. Then Zachæus would crawl from his bed in a rage and hurl a boot or a stool after the cook, and it was always his heartfelt desire to make a cripple of Polly for the rest of his days.

But he never succeeded, his sight was too poor for him to aim properly and so he never hit him.

On the seventh day he declared his intention of eating his evening meal in the kitchen. The cook said that any such visit would be most unwelcome, and so that was that. Today, like every other day, Zachæus would have to eat his food in bed. He sat there, utterly forlorn, numb with boredom. Then he heard the cook and his helpers set out with the chuckwagons, singing and shouting, just to torment him, and he knew that the kitchen was empty.

Zachæus climbs out of his bunk, staggers across to the kitchen and looks round. The book and the newspaper are in their usual place. He grabs the paper and staggers back to his bunk. Then he wipes his glasses and begins to read, with great pleasure, the large lettering of the advertisements.

An hour passes—two—time passed so quickly now. Finally Zachæus heard the chuckwagons return and he heard the cook's voice as he ordered the others to get started on washing up the cups and plates.

Zachæus knew that now the newspaper would be missed, that this was the moment at which the cook always went to his library. He debated with himself a moment, then wedged the paper under his mattress. Moments later he pulled it out again and put it next to his skin. Never again would he part with it.

A minute passes.

Heavy footsteps approach the bunkhouse. Zachæus lies there staring at the ceiling.

Polly comes in.

'All right, have you got my newspaper?' he asks, standing in the middle of the floor.

'No,' answers Zachæus.

'You have got it!' growls the cook. He takes a step nearer.

Zachæus sits up.

'I do not have your newspaper. Go to hell!' he says furiously.

With that the cook pulls the sick man onto the floor and begins to search through his bunk. He turned the straw mattress over and shook the thin blanket several times, but he didn't find what he was looking for.

'You've got it,' he kept on saying. And even when he had to leave, and was out in the yard, he turned and said it again:

'You stole it. Just you wait, my fine friend!'

Zachæus laughed a loud, cruel laugh and said:

'All right you bastard, so I took it—I *needed* it, don't you know!'

At that the cook's parrot-face turned blood-red and an ominous expression entered his eyes. He stared back at Zachæus:

'Just wait!' he muttered.

4

Next day the weather was foul, the rain poured down and drummed against the walls of the buildings like showers of hail. By early morning the cook's water buckets were already full. The entire work-force was at home, some patching the wheat sacks ready for winter, others mending broken-down machinery and tools, and sharpening the blades on the threshing-machines.

When the dinner bell rang Zachæus got up from his bunk and made ready to follow the others to the dining-room. But at the door he found Polly waiting for him, carrying his food. Zachæus protested that from now on he would eat with the others, his hand was better and his fever gone. The cook retorted that if he wouldn't eat the food he was brought then he wouldn't get any. He tossed the tin plate onto Zachæus' bunk and said:

'Maybe you think it isn't good enough for you?'

Zachæus gave in and went back to his bunk. Best if he took the food he was given.

'What sort of pig swill is it today then?' he growled as he began eating.

'Chicken,' answered the cook. And there was a strange glint in his eye as he turned and walked off.

'Chicken?' Zachæus muttered to himself as he scrutinised the food with his dim eyes. 'The hell it is, you liar! But meat it is, and there's sauce.'

And he ate the meat.

He finds found himself chewing at something he doesn't recognise. He can't bite through it, it's a bone with some kind of sinewy meat on it. When he's gnawed away one side of it he takes it out of his mouth and looks at it. Let that dog have the bone himself, he mutters, walking over to the door to examine it more closely. He turns it over, examines it from all angles. Suddenly he rushes back to his bunk and looks for the bottle containing his severed finger. The bottle is there, but the finger is gone.

Zachæus strides over to the bunkhouse. Deathly pale, his face twisted, he steps inside the doorway and in front of everybody he says:

'Hey, Polly! Isn't this my finger?'

He holds something up in the air.

The cook doesn't reply. Over at his table he begins to snigger.

Zachæus holds something else up in the air and says:

'And Polly, isn't this the nail that was on the finger? Don't I recognise it?'

By now all the diners at their tables had heard Zachæus' strange questions and were looking at him in amazement.

'What's the matter with you?' asks one.

'I found my finger, the severed finger in the food,' Zachæus explained. 'He's cooked it and served it to me with the food. Here's the nail too.'

From every table rose a great howl of laughter. Everyone began talking at once:

'Has he cooked your own finger and fed it you? Looks like you've had a bite out of it too. The whole of one side is gone.'

'My eyes aren't good,' answered Zachæus. 'I didn't know. It didn't occur to me . . .'

Then abruptly he falls silent, turns and goes out of the door again.

The foreman had to call for order in the dining-room. He got to his feet, turned to the cook and said:

'Did you cook that finger in with the other meat, Polly?'

'No,' answered Polly. 'God above, no. What kind of man do you take me for? I cooked it by itself, in a casserole all on its own . . .'

But the story of the stewed finger remained a source of amusement for the men the whole of that evening. People talked about it and laughed about it like madmen, it was the greatest triumph the cook had experienced in all his life. As for Zachæus, he was nowhere around.

He was out on the prairie. The stormy weather continued and there was no shelter to be had anywhere; but Zachæus kept on going, wandering further and further into the prairie. He had his wounded hand in a sling and was protecting it as best he could from the rain. The rest of him got soaked, from head to toe.

He walks on. Towards dusk he stops, looks at his watch by a flash of lightning, then turns and heads back the way he came. He walks through the wheat with slow, deliberate steps, as though he has carefully worked out his timing and his pacing. By eight he's back at the farm again.

It's pitch dark by now. He hears people in the dining-room eating their supper, and when he looks through the window he sees the cook, and it seems to him that the cook is in high spirits.

He walks away from the house and over to the stable and stands there sheltering and staring into the darkness. The grasshoppers are silent, everything is silent. But still the rain falls. Now and then, far off, a sulphur-coloured streak of lightning splits the sky and strikes down on the prairie.

At last he hears the men leave the supper table and head over towards the bunkhouse, cursing and running, to avoid getting wet. Zachæus waits patiently for another hour, then he heads off towards the kitchen.

A light is still on in there. He sees someone over by the stove and calmly walks in.

'Good evening,' he says.

The cook stares at him in astonishment. Finally he says:

'No more food today.'

Zachæus answers:

'That's fine. But give me a little bit of soap, Polly. I didn't manage to get my shirt clean the other day. I need to wash it again.'

'Not in my water,' says the cook.

'Oh yes. I've got it outside. On the corner.'

'I'm warning you not to.'

'Are you going to give me that soap?'

'I'll give you soap!' answers the cook. 'Now get out of here!

So Zachæus goes out.

He takes one of the water containers, carries it to the corner right by the kitchen window and begins making a fearsome splashing in the water. The cook hears and comes out to investigate.

Today he feels greater and more invincible than ever before, and he heads straight for Zachæus, sleeves rolled up, resolute and angry.

'What's going on here?' he asks.

Zachæus answers:

'Nothing. I'm washing my shirt.'

'In my water?'

'Of course.'

The cook comes closer, bends over the container to make sure it's his, and then feels in the water for the shirt.

Zachæus pulls the revolver out of the sling on his bad arm, aims it at the cook's ear and pulls the trigger.

The sound of a dull crack crosses the wet night.

5

Much later that night, when Zachæus came to the bunkhouse to take his rest, a couple of his workmates woke up. They asked what he was doing that had taken him such a long time.

Zachæus answered:

'Nothing. By the way, I shot Polly.'

His mates leaned up on their elbows to hear him better.

'You shot him?'

'Yes.'

'Well I'll be damned. Where did you hit him?'

'In the head. I shot him through the ear, upwards.'

'The hell you did. Where did you bury him?'

'West on the prairie. I put his newspaper between his hands.'

'Did you now?'

Then they lay down to sleep again.

A while later one of them asks:

'Did he die straight off?'

'Yes,' answered Zachæus, 'nearly straight off. The bullet went through his brain.'

'Yeah, that's the best shot,' the other says. 'If it goes through the brain, that's dead.'

After that it went quiet in the bunkhouse, and everyone slept.

The next day the foreman had to appoint a new cook. One of the old kitchen hands was given the job, so the murder worked out just fine for him.

Work went on through to the autumn, and nothing further was said about Polly. The poor bastard was dead and lay buried somewhere out in the wheatfields. That was that.

Come October the workers on Billybonny Farm headed into the nearest town to drink their farewells and go their separate ways. At such a time men were more friendly to each other than usual, and with warm hearts they embraced one another and treated everyone to drinks.

'Where are you going now, Zachæus?'

'I'm headed further west,' answers Zachæus. 'Wyoming maybe. Come the winter I'll go logging again.'

'See you there then! So long! See you, Zachæus. Have a good journey now!'

And in every direction men spread out over the great Yankee land. Zachæus heads for Wyoming.

Behind them lies the great prairie, an endless sea lit by the long, columnar rays of the October sun.

ON THE BANKS

For months on end we lay on the banks and fished for cod. Summer came, winter came and went and we lay always in the same place, in the middle of the ocean, on the border between two worlds, Europe and America. Four or five times that year we put in at Miquelon to sell our catch and load up with provisions; then we put out to sea again, lay to always at the same spot, fished cod—and then headed once again for Miquelon to unload. I never went ashore there; what was there to go ashore for? There were so few people in that tiny outpost, just a handful of fishermen and ships' chandlers.

Ours was a Russian ship named the *Congo*, a real Russian, an old barque with her gun ports still half-visible in her sides from her younger days. We were a crew of eight; two Dutchmen and a Frenchman, two Russians and I. The rest were blacks.

The *Congo* had four dories. In the mornings we rowed out in these dories and hauled in our lines, at three o'clock in summer, at dawn in winter. And in the evening we set them again, always at the same spot, seven or eight hundred fathoms west-south-west of the *Congo*.

Days came and days went—and we were always there. There was no variation in our existence; often we hardly knew Monday from Sunday. The only thing that distinguished us from the others fishing on the Newfoundland banks was the exceptional circumstance of our skipper having his wife on board with him. This wife of his was a young, extremely repulsive person with clusters of warts on both hands and a scrawny, scraggy little body. We used to see her almost every morning when we left the ship; she had just got up, was still sleepy and dressed any old how. Then it was nothing for her to steady herself with legs apart, lift up her skirts and ... well, I'd better not go into it. Yet even though she was so dirty and never said a word to us we were fond of her. Every one of us was fond of her, each in his own way, and not one of us would have been without her. That's just how fussy we'd become.

We weren't seamen, we were just fishermen. A seaman is always on course for somewhere, arrives somewhere and finally his journey comes to an end no matter how long it might take; but we just lay still, ever and always still, with all our anchors buried in the banks. It had been going on like this for so long that eventually we could hardly remember what dry land looked like. We changed so much. Perpetually being at rest made us strangely depressed, really very depressed; all we saw was sea and fog and we heard nothing above and below us but wind and weather. We cared about nothing and scarcely even bothered to think any more. Why should we think? Our endless intercourse with fish had turned us into fish ourselves, into strange, meaty sea-creatures that crept around on board a ship and spoke a private language of our own.

We didn't read either, read nothing. No letters could reach us out there at sea, and in addition the salty fog we breathed in daily and all our daily business with raw fish, the whole of this endless sojourn on the banks, had deprived us of any wish to read. We ate, worked and slept. The only one who hadn't completely abandoned his own head and who still tried in some way to 'keep up' was the Frenchman. Once a month he would take me to one side on deck and say in his serious voice:

'Do you suppose there's a war going on back home now?'

So indifferent had we become that we could hardly even be bothered to speak to one another. We knew only too well what the answers would be no matter what the question, and in addition to this we often had the greatest difficulty in understanding each other's language. Of what use was it that the official language on board was English? Both the Dutchmen and the Frenchman were too dull-witted and stubborn to learn it, and even the Russians, whenever they were trying to say something more than a few sentences long, always reverted in frustration to their own tongue and left the rest of us in the dark. All in all we were a helpless and isolated bunch of men.

And sometimes when we sat and hauled in the lines an emigrant ship would ghost by, a heavy, shadowy colossus which would suddenly appear from the fog then disappear into it again with a blast on its horn. There was something almost unpleasant about the sight of these great monsters which revealed themselves to us for a moment and then vanished. When it happened in the dark, with the ship's lights staring at us along the hull with round, glowing cow-eyes, we often cried out in fear and surprise; in calm weather we could feel the wafting of the wind from the massive ghost, and for a long time after our dory went on pitching in her wake.

Sometimes too when the visibility was fair van Tatzel, my partner on the dory, might catch sight of a sailing ship in the distance; but these never came so close that we could see anyone on board. We never saw anyone but our own: a cook, eight fishermen, an arthritic skipper and his wife.

Strange moods might sometimes arise as we sat and wrestled with the lines, hardly able to haul them in: to us it seemed as though our hooks were held fast in the grip of unseen hands far below which tried to overturn our dory. We cried out to one another, mad, our teeth chattering with fear; we forgot who we were and what we were doing, agitated and utterly confused by this struggle with invisible forces on the ocean floor which would not release their hold. When a fisherman suffered an attack of this special mood he was said on the banks to be 'singing for good weather', since the fog was thought to be responsible for the mood. And at times it might happen too, as we sat hauling, that strange and fantastical forms would nod to us from the fog, nod with great shaggy heads, floating and disembodied, and then disappear again. And soft, troll-like shapes drift about inside the white mass with long slow steps, big as mountains, floating with giant strides in whatever direction the wind blew them, rolling through the air on their feathery limbs and trailing vast threads behind them. On one occasion both van Tatzel and I saw something that made us stiff with fear. It was a dark evening and we were setting our lines when we saw a figure rocking up and down in the air. The whole of his head was aflame and he breathed like a storm. We both heard it. Shortly afterwards a steamer hurried by; we cried out when it gave a blast on the horn. Then it vanished . . .

But then late in the evening, after we had hauled in the lines and lay alongside the *Congo* with our dories fully laden, the good catch and our being done with the worst part of the job made us stupid and excitable in a different way. Often we would take a strange and unnatural pleasure in maltreating the fish. The two Russians in particular took a sickening pleasure in this. They took hold of the bigger fish by the head, stuck their fingers into the soft eyes and held them up like that, laughing lasciviously and looking at them. One day I saw one of the Russians biting a raw fish. He sank his teeth deep into it and held onto it for two minutes with his eyes tightly shut. These fat little fish bodies affected all of us. Opening up the smooth bellies excited us; we cut them open alive along the whole belly, were wilfully careless in gutting them with our hands and bloodied ourselves more than was necessary. The Frenchman never participated in these brutal sessions. But on the other hand he had an insane desire for the skipper's wife which he was quite unable to hide. He admitted it to all of us openly. 'I love her, God help me, how I love her!' he would say several times a day. One of the blacks, the one we called 'the doctor' because in his youth he'd studied a little medicine, was also passionately in love with her. I could have beaten him to death on the spot when he confided this to me, from jealousy. I wasn't a whit better myself.

As for her, she walked around skinny, slothful and filthy and noticed nothing. Didn't even glance at us. Once, when I had a little job to do aft, where she sat staring ahead of her on a canvas stool, I happened to trip on a stub of rope and almost fell. I was so startled that instead of just walking on I turned round and began staring at this stub of rope in a stupid, vacant way, and I must have looked ridiculous. But then why didn't she laugh? And why did she look at me the whole time and not laugh? She didn't react at all, showed absolutely nothing on her face. She's *roating* away! said van Tatzel in his broken English. My God she's just *roating* away!

And yet we wouldn't have been without her. Not for anything in the world . . .

Once the fish were cleaned and the lines set again we were done for the day and we lazed away an hour or two eating and smoking. Then we turned in for the night.

Now if we weren't too tired we might talk a little among ourselves and someone might even start telling yarns—everything in a crude and imperfect language, full of swearing and filthy language. The Frenchman had one about a man who 'couldn't look at a women without wanting her'. He told it several times, and always successfully. The Russians were crazy about it and laughed every time they heard it. The pleasure they took in the crude tale was as honest as a child's. It twisted their mouths and made them rock back and forth on their bunks in excitement. 'Yes—and then?' they asked the whole time, 'what happened next?' And yet they knew as well as the rest of us what happened next.

Van Tatzel, on the other hand, was nowhere near so successful when he told *his* particular story; we could seldom be bothered to listen to him. It was so difficult to understand him, he had so little English and what he did know was completely garbled. When he was trying to say something and suddenly got stuck he would look round at us all with his wrinkled face and not know how to get out of it. It was pathetic.

Van Tatzel was the older of the Dutchmen, an old pig of a man, somewhat deaf, but good-tempered and helpful. He always wore cotton-wool in his ears, summer and winter alike huge plugs of cotton-wool that were yellow with age and filth. He was an unusually big man whom the sea had turned into a child and he couldn't think past the tip of his own nose. Lying on his bunk smoking his strongest tobacco and spitting wherever he pleased he would always begin his tale like this:

'There was once upon a time an evening in Amsterdam', he says, 'an evening in Amsterdam. I'd just signed on and it was my last night ashore. I can't remember what o'clock it was, but it was certainly very late o'clock. After I left the beer-hall I was going to go aboard my ship so I rolled up my trousers first; I remember I made two rolls on each leg; but I was so drunk I fell down as I was doing this. So, I staggered on and had just turned down Leopold Street. Then I happened to . . . something happened to me. Because I wasn't too drunk to see her; she was right behind me, in the middle of the street—you don't have to believe me if you don't want to, but it was a woman.'

The old fool raises himself up in his bunk and looks at us. 'A real lady!' he says. And then he stops. His English won't take him any further, he's stranded.

'Did some woman really follow you through the streets of Amsterdam?' 'the doctor' asks teasingly from his bunk.

'Yes, a woman!' he says, delighted and laughing. It pleases him so much that he swears to it twice more, and we all laugh at him. He tries to carry on, stops again; it's just not possible for him to carry on. He strains with his old brain, struggles to find the words to tell us the thing; but not a word comes out. It's so important for him to communicate in particular this one point, and overwhelmed by the memory of this woman, driven to distraction by his inability to express himself he explodes suddenly in his own language and burbles out a great swarm of strange words that not one of us understands apart from his fellow-countryman, who lies snoring in the next bunk.

That was van Tatzel's story, the only one he knew, which always ended there. We had heard it so many times, beginning always in the same way with this evening in Amsterdam. It seemed a credible tale, and none of us doubted the truth of it . . .

So we lay a while and thought of this story, with the lamp swaying inside its brass rings, the sea roaring outside, the watch's wooden heels clacking as he passed on the deck above. Night fell . . .

But now and then I might wake up around midnight, half-suffocated by the fumes from all the breathing human meat that tossed in wild dreams around me and kicked off its blankets. The lamp shone down on the plump, grey-flannelled forms; the Russians with their wispy moustaches were like sleeping seals and their fat, naked feet like flippers. From every bunk came the sounds of sighing and murmured words; the blacks lay showing their white teeth, talking in their sleep, naming a name, puffing out their black cheeks. From the bunk where the younger of the two Dutchmen lay came the same name in a clucking of laughter, interrupted by snoring and brief whimpering noises. The skipper's wife. Everyone thought of her, passionate beasts that lay there and spoke of her even in sleep, each in his own language, sleepsnoring with eyes shut, murmuring lewd words, smiling, sticking out their tongues. Only van Tatzel slept quietly, deeply and quietly, like a dumb animal.

That same thick cabin air, the tobacco smoke, the smell of human sweat and of fish from the hold combined in a thick, narcotic fog that forced my eyes shut again the moment I opened them. And I fell asleep again, to a nightmare about an enormous flower that enfolded me and sucked me inside its wet leaves, choked me down, slowly, surely, hushed and silent. And the world around me vanished . . .

Then the watch came and roused us.

CHRISTMAS ON THE HILLSIDE

A lot of snow fell that Christmas. All that was visible of the little house on the hill were the roof and the two top timbers. It wasn't really much more than a shack, a smallholding with a cow, a sheep and a lamb. The family lived on their own there, in summer as in winter.

The man's name was Tor and his wife's Kirsti; they had five children whose names ranged from Timian to Kaldea. Kaldea was in service down in the village and Timian had struggled his way over to America. The three children still living at home were two boys and a girl, Rinaldus, Didrik and Tomelena. Everyone called Tomelena just Lena.

As was said earlier snow fell in great quantities that Christmas and old Tor had been shovelling away at it all day and was both tired and worn out, and once he'd read everything in the prayer book for Christmas Eve he lay down on his bed with his pipe in his mouth. His wife cooked and saw to the fire, moving about constantly in the room, always busy.

'Have the beasts been fed tonight?' asked Tor.

'Yes of course they have,' answered his wife.

Tor carried on smoking for a while and then said, smiling into his beard:

'Woman, what is that you're cooking and frying away at there the whole time? I can't fathom where you get it all from.'

'Oh I'm richer than you think,' answered Kirsti, laughing at his joke.

They took a dram with the evening meal, it was a family tradition, and it was Rinaldus's job to fill up the glasses. It was a solemn moment for him when he lifted up the carafe decorated with big painted roses in his little hands. All eyes were on him.

'Hold the rosebottle in the left hand when you're serving people older than yourself,' said his father. 'You're old enough now to learn the proper way to do things.'

So Rinaldus took the rosebottle in his left hand. He poured so carefully it was a pain to watch him, with his tongue sticking out and his head on one side.

The food was not everyday food. There were pancakes and syrup, and an egg for each of them. You could tell this was Christmas because they even had butter for the pancakes. Tor read aloud from Luther's grace.

But after the meal little Didrik got the day wrong and leaving the table he shook hands with his father and mother as thanks for his food. His father let him finish before saying anything; but when he was done Tor said:

'You shouldn't have thanked us for the food this evening, Didrik. It's not that there's anything wrong with it, only it's New Year's Eve when you're supposed to say thank you for the food.'

Didrik was so embarrassed that he cringed and almost cried when his brother and sister started laughing at him.

Tor stretched out once again on the bed with his pipe in his mouth and his wife did the washing-up.

'Some joke all that snow we got,' she said.

'And it isn't over yet,' answered Tor. 'There's a ring round the moon and the magpies are flying low above the ground.'

'Then I suppose it's out of the question us going to church tomorrow I should think?'

'No, God have mercy on you. You can't have read the almanac if you're talking about the weather tomorrow.'

'What are the omens then?'

'Not much better than a calf being born without legs. I don't even know if I dare tell you.'

'Oh no! Is it that bad?' exclaimed Kirsti.

'Bring me my glasses, Rinaldus,' Tor went on. 'Don't drop them on the floor.' And once again he studied the dangerous omens. 'You can see for yourself,' he said to his wife. 'It's like I said.'

'Jesus, God save us all then!' said Kirsti and put her hands together. 'So it means bad weather does it?'

'Oh it means bad weather all right! But that's nothing. If you really want to see an omen just look at this one here for 5 February. Nothing less than the Antichrist himself, with his two horns.'

'Jesus, God look after and keep us all! And with our Timian over in America too!'

After this it was quiet in the little room for a while. The wind began to blow outside and drift the snow. The children chattered to each other and amused themselves in a variety of ways; the cat wandered from one to the other, allowing itself to be stroked.

'I really really wonder what the king has to eat on Christmas Eve,' said Didrik at one point.

'Ha, I'll bet clumps of pure butter and sweetcake,' exclaimed little Lena, who was just eight years old and didn't know any better.

'Just imagine cake! And butter on it as well!' said Didrik. 'And I expect the king drinks up a whole rosebottle all by himself.'

But Rinaldus who was oldest and had read most in his encyclopedia hooted with laughter at this:

'Just *one* rosebottle? Ha, the king drinks at least twenty does the king.'

'Twenty?'

'At least twenty.'

'Don't be so daft, Rinaldus! He couldn't possibly drink more than two,' said his mother over by the cooking pit.

Now Tor joined in. 'What are you lot babbling on about?' he said. 'Do you suppose the king drinks ordinary plonk like we do? I'll tell you what the king drinks,' he said, 'the king drinks a drink that's called shampangan. Costs about five or six kroner just for one bottle, all according to what the price is in England. The king drinks it first thing in the morning and he drinks it last thing at night. Just shampangan and nothing else. And every time he empties a glass he chucks it against the wall and smashes it all to smithereens and then he says to the princess: Get rid of that! he says.'

'But in the name of God why does he smash all the glasses?' asks Kirsti.

'Ha, what a question! Do you think a man like that would put up with drinking out of the same glass day in and day out?'

Pause.

'When I think of all the things you know, Tor,' says his wife quietly. 'I just don't know where you get it all from.'

'Well, I have my off days too you know,' answers Tor. 'Still. But it wasn't so easy to get by the priest in my day as it is now. You had to know what you were talking about in those days.'

Then Tor got up, laid his pipe aside and asked where the powder was. He knew quite well where the powder was because he'd hidden it at the end of the bed himself last time he came back from the store. All the same he asked where it was and brought a hush to the room. Then he got it out and divided it into three equal portions and wrapped them in triangular pieces of paper. Then he put his cap on. The children swarmed around him and pleaded to be allowed to go with him, for they knew what was about to happen. Soon Kirsti was the only one left in the room.

Tor and the children waded across to the barn, where the powder was to be burnt. Snow whirled around them. Tor made the sign of the cross as he opened the barn door and crossed himself again once he was inside. It was pitch dark there, everything quite still, you could hear the cow chewing. Tor lit a torch and touched the flames to his three packets of powder, one for the cow, one for the sheep and one for the lamb. The children watched in silent wonder. No one spoke. Then Tor made the sign of the cross again and left. He called out to little Lena who had stayed behind to stroke the lamb that she better hurry up now. Then Tor and the children returned to the house.

'Quite some weather out there,' he said. 'Snow blowing all over the hill.'

He lay on the bed again until coffee was ready, while the children played with their little toys over on the table. Their voices got more and more excited and they laughed at the slightest thing. Tor spoke across the floor to his wife.

'I've been wondering what I should ... what a racket you kids are making, a man can't hear himself think ... I've been wondering where on earth I might try next for a bit of work,' he said.

His wife poured out the coffee.

'Something will turn up, with God's help,' she answered.

'Maybe I could get some threshing work down in the village.'

'Sure now, there'll be something . . . come and drink your coffee.'

When Tor had drunk his coffee he lit his pipe again. He drew his wife over to the door and whispered something to her, the children trying desperately to hear what it was. But when Lena poked her nosy little head practically in between the two of them she was ticked off at once and her brothers shouted in malicious glee:

'Serves you right!'

But little Lena was such a sweet and gentle child they didn't have the heart to keep it up, and straight afterwards Rinaldus gave her a big shiny button and his humble gift made her happy again.

Father went to the cupboard and took out a package. Wrapped up inside was something Timian had sent them from America, a fur stole lined with soft black leather and with tassels on it. Timian must have remembered how cold it was up on the hillside in the wintertime so he'd sent this home, which was the warmest type of scarf he'd ever come across. It probably set him back quite a bit too.

But who should have the stole? Tor and his wife had racked their brains over this question and the result was that they decided Rinaldus should have it. Rinaldus was the oldest, and anyway he already ran quite a few errands down to the village for them, so he needed something warm to have on.

'Rinaldus, come here!' said Tor. 'Here's a scarf from your brother Timian. It's a very special scarf, so you look after it so you've got something decent to wear round your neck when you go to confirmation. There, put it round your neck.'

There was a chorus of admiration and wonder. The soft stole was examined and touched for a full half-hour, and little Lena never tired of stroking it with her tiny blue hands. But she wasn't allowed to try it on, oh no she certainly wasn't allowed to try it on, she was much too little. What she did get was a candle, which she lit and then blew straight out again because she didn't want to waste it. Didrik was the only one who got nothing, but his father promised him that as soon as he found a little threshing work down in the village he would buy him a new bible story.

The snow continued to pile up against the window and sometimes snow even fell down through the chimney straight onto the fire pit. The hour was getting late, it was almost bedtime for the family from the hill; tomorrow would bring the same back-breaking labour of clearing snow again.

'Go on kids, up to the loft with you now,' said Tor. 'Don't forget your prayers and cross yourselves on the face and over the chest.'

And one after the other the children clambered up the ladder to the loft. Rinaldus was allowed to take the stole with him wrapped in paper, and Lena followed after carrying her candle . . .

At about midnight, when everyone was asleep, the mother down in the room heard someone moving about above her. She called out to ask if anybody was up. No answer, all was still again. A few moments later the sound of small feet across the boards, the most cautious footsteps you could imagine—it was little Lena sneaking over to try on the stole in the dark anyway and now she was scared stiff of being caught.

That beautiful stole! It was the softest thing ever seen in that little house on the hill, and Rinaldus wore it only twice to church and was very careful with it. All the same, with the coming of summer, the fur began to fall out of it, and there were maggots among the tassels.

LIFE IN A SMALL TOWN

If the rain isn't pouring down too heavily you can hear all week long, from dawn to dusk, the rhythmic beating of hammers on nails and bolts from the boat-builders' yards. This is the town's only communal sound. It can be heard everywhere, inside every house.

This is a small, placid place, an unruffled haven of conservatism, with its skippers, its liquor store and its church. The night-watchmen don't have a lot to do here. Brawling and disorderly conduct occur so infrequently as to surprise strangers, and if some deckhand or vagabond does take a drop too much one evening and starts singing or swearing in the street, it's as though the sheer quietness of the place itself deadens the sound. The watchmen pace the streets in easy silence and don't even turn their heads, because there's no need for it.

At night the town falls asleep. No one stays up late, no one parties. In the evening the two watchmen meet down by the mackerel market. This is their starting-point. They greet each other, walk a few paces together, have a little sit-down, a little smoke, then walk on for a few more yards—that's how they spend the night. They know everyone, and everyone knows them. If they encounter one of the townsmen making his way home a little later than usual they know at once whether he's coming from a christening or a bachelors' get-together. There's no fooling them. And if, as occasionally happens, a certain horse and wagon passes by in the still, dark night, with a woman in a hat on the front seat and a man on the seat behind her, they know what's going on there too. They put their heads together, whispering and nodding like two old biddies. They understand one another completely. On the stroke of six they go their separate ways and spread the news in every household where people are up—the midwife arrived two hours ago, and Skipper Gabrielsen's wife has had her baby.

The town also boasts two lame tailors, a beggar, the Salvation Army, a quay for steamers, a customs office and a savings bank. It's all there. In the middle of town is the Union, the town's Athenæum and club, where the town fathers congregate in the evening and read the daily newspapers. But reading is not indulged in to unnecessary excess here, and as well as textbooks and prayer books the bookshop also sells everything from combs to bars of chocolate. One man living here is said to have read *Peder Paars* from cover to cover in his youth; but it hasn't done him much good and he's ended up a bachelor and a layabout, as well as being a bit soft in the head. His name is Tønnes Olai. No one knows what Tønnes Olai lives off, but you never see him in the streets at mealtimes, so he must have some food in that old house he lives in winter and summer alike, alone and unnoticed. But mealtimes apart, he's always out in the streets. He's a small man with carroty red hair and beard, not much to look at, poor bugger, though in recent times he's begun to look a bit healthier, a bit more affluent. He's quiet and thoughtful in all his ways, in fact his head even droops slightly from being so well read and thoughtful. Since he knows everyone in town he feels obliged to greet them all, and most of them return his greeting, though the consul does so merely with a gesture of his index finger in the direction of his hat.

This man Tønnes Olai enjoys a certain renown locally. The ordinary fishermen and dock-labourers take a pride in knowing him and consider themselves his equal. They imagine that Tønnes Olai earns his living in some secret way that involves just the use of his head. He must be pretty smart, they reckon. No one has ever seen him do a day's work, and yet he manages to keep going, even seems to be prospering now and then. Must be because he uses his head.

But Tønnes Olai won't have any of it. What he *is* willing to admit is that he spends all his time out walking the streets, so he knows that town like the inside of his own pocket . . .

If you wake up one morning, don't hear the town's only communal sound coming from the boat-builders' yards, and it isn't raining, then you know the week is over and it must be Sunday. Then the townspeople put on their best clothes and go to church.

The path to the church is a sandy curve that climbs a hill. Countless footsteps have beaten that path, and the boot-heels of hefty skippers crushed its gravel to sand. The least puff of wind is enough to set it dancing, but Skipper Andersen's wife, who is rich, still wears the same long dresses she wore when young, and it's obvious how much sand she must waft up as she drags the train along behind her on the way to church. A lot of people curse her on account of this.

The young girls walk along wearing their bright clothes, and the married women something dark. And there's Jensen who works for Berg the merchant, and the chemist, and Olsen the customs man. And there's Rosen the photographer, who has only one leg and has never really found his niche in life. When the consul comes by he towers over them all. His hair is still dark, and though he has three grown children he never goes anywhere without a flower in his buttonhole.

The skippers walk along together in groups, both those who have just returned from a trip and those who have given up the sea for good. They're brown and gnarled and big and they walk like cart-horses pulling a heavy load. But their conversation is lively and their expressions carefree.

Afternoon comes.

One skipper persuades another to take a walk with him on the quay where the customs office is, and before long all of them have gathered here. Groups form, dissolve, re-form, people wander from one group to another and join in the chat. The talk is of mackerel, fresh mackerel, salted mackerel, pickled mackerel. A discussion on the subject of mackerel is reckoned to be successful if they can get it finished by six o'clock. Even if they don't manage to reach agreement they stop at six on the dot anyway. A steamer whistle out in the fjord is their signal, and from that moment onwards there's not a soul among them who can stand to hear the word mackerel even mentioned.

Rolling and heavy, the post-boat comes pumping into town.

And now everyone hurries down to the steamboat quay, for six o'clock is the great moment in the little town. People hop along on crutches and get wheeled along in wheelchairs to the quay when the post-boat comes to town. Four men stand ready to catch the hawser and tie her up. Half a dozen young ladies have got together to post a letter in her letter-box. A swarm of skippers' wives are waiting to see what sort of pedlar or travelling craftsman will turn up this time, and the Salvation Army are there too, in red, with their posters and a leaflet which is pressed into your hand. You read: 'Big prayer and Thanksgiving meeting at 7.30. Signed Cadet T. Olsen and Major A. S. Thorgersen. NB: Prepare to meet thy God!'

Then the bell rings for the first time on board, and shortly after that for the second time. A latecomer, a woman who doesn't want to miss the show, comes running along the quay holding her skirts in her hand. She's hot and she's out of breath.

Are you coming with us? the mate asks from the bow.

No, she pants.

It's just that she, like everyone else, wants to be there for the great moment. And thank God, she arrived just in time to see two crates of beer for the hotel get tossed ashore.

The bell rings for the third time, the gangway is lowered and the engine starts up.

And the mass of people ebbs away again, now that the great moment has passed, and it disperses back across the town, leaving behind only those interested in the contents of the mailbag, the young ladies expecting letters and the gentlemen awaiting their copies of the *Western News*. An hour passes, an hour full of hope and excitement and uncertainty, until finally everything has been handed out, and then these people too make their way home.

After supper the worthy town fathers stroll along to the Union to study the recently arrived newspapers.

That's how Sunday passes in the little town. Monday goes by in the same placid, peaceful manner, and that's the way things are for months on end.

But then came that dreadful year when the town was shaken to its foundations. It was a year from which, in a manner of speaking, only the church and one or two other institutions would emerge unscathed.

*　　*　　*

It all began in a perfectly simple and straightforward fashion. Rosen the photographer, the man with one leg who never found his niche in life, hanged himself. He moved from one place to another in the town but could never settle anywhere, because he was in debt to so many people. In the end he pawned all his equipment, just drank it all up. Then he hanged himself. But before he did this he'd had time to get engaged. His bride-to-be was a shopkeeper's daughter, so that made her one of the town ladies and she always wore a hat and carried a parasol, even though she was turned 30. It was also said that she'd helped her fiancé the photographer out of a tight spot on a couple of occasions, so now she didn't have much left to look after herself with. Other unmarried ladies of her own age said it was no better than she deserved—what did she think she was playing at?—and in the end they decided that it was precisely to avoid getting married that the poor photographer had hanged himself. He was a refined and intelligent man and no doubt realised how things would turn out.

But Rosen the photographer took Olsen the customs man down with him. Olsen didn't hang himself, of course, but he took a knock that finished him for life. That's what happens to ordinary people who try to live above their station. Olsen had been helping himself to the customs money, there were 300 kroner missing altogether. Well, quite a few people had suspected as much all along and knew it would end badly. Olsen the customs man was the type of person who just had to put on a cream-coloured suit and a straw hat as soon as spring came; and if there was one person in town who was compelled to carry a cane and have the point of a silk-handkerchief sticking out of the top of his breast pocket, well, that person would have to be Olsen. Didn't everyone know his mother, who was just a poor old widow-woman who lived over there and did washing and cleaning and helped out in the rich people's houses when it was Easter and Christmas? But Olsen declined to be any less refined than any other public servant, and he cultivated the society of such as Rosen the photographer and others like him who spent their money on bowls and beer and wore yellow shoes in the summer. Of course it ended badly, and Olsen lost his job at the customs.

The town bubbled with rumour and gossip, and Jensen who worked for Berg composed a little poem about these two events. Here the consul stepped in. Though Jensen didn't work for him but for Berg, the merchant, all the same he was said to have expressed his disapproval of Jensen's crude verses. He said in public that Rosen the photographer and Olsen the customs man were the only two people in town you could compare Jensen with, and if the consul said so then that was about all there was to it. The result was that Jensen's reputation was not after all enhanced by his verses; in fact, rather the opposite happened

And then there was this business about young Olava, the wife of Skipper Wollertsen, not being seen for a while. Of course, she was under no particular obligation to show herself in public; but surely a person had things to do in town at the bakers' and at the general store and friends to see and it wasn't necessary to break off all contact with the town. But Olava Wollertsen stayed indoors. What was she doing in there all the time?

She was a pretty young woman, married three years ago and with a husband at sea on one of the consul's ships who hadn't been home for two years. They had a child, and their little house with its roses in the windows was so clean and comfortable you would never imagine anything could go wrong in there. The young girl who helped out in the house couldn't see that Olava had got religion or joined the Salvation Army; and yet she kept herself shut away from people.

Several weeks passed. The weather was calm and the mackerel fishing good. But out at sea there were storms, and one morning two pilots came into the bay with a three-master they'd found in the night out beyond the lighthouse. She was drifting and her crew must have abandoned ship thinking that she didn't have long to go. What a big, handsome piece of salvage!

The three-master was a stunning sight as she came sliding into the bay. Young Else was out walking with a couple of friends and she was the first to see it.

'Look there!' she cried, pointing. She realised at once it was a stranger and not one of the town's own ships. 'They must have found it last night,' she continued. 'They'll get salvage on it!'

The friends had to admit she was right. Damn that Else, she was only young but already she knew so much.

'Let's go and tell the pilots' wives,' said Else. 'They'll get salvage money on it!'

And off they went.

Young Else was terribly proud of herself, almost thinking of herself as the one who had saved the ship. She strutted about in front of her friends and tried to think of more ways to surprise them.

She said:

'You know that Jensen who works for Berg? He's got a paint stain on his new trousers!'

Well, anyone could make fun of Jensen now that the consul had spoken out against him.

'No, he hasn't! Has he?'

'Didn't you know? Serves him right too, he's so stuck-up.'

'Ha ha—' they had a good laugh at that.

'And I don't suppose you know either that Olava Wollertsen is— like this.'

'Like what?'

'Like this!' And young Else stuck out her belly.

Her friends clapped their hands and said no, honest to God, surely that couldn't be true could it?

But young Else said she knew if was true for definite.

'Wollertsen's been away for two years, it's impossible.'

'Suit yourself whether you believe me or not. But just you remember what I'm telling you.'

The young girls couldn't quite work it out, but with the father being away for two years it couldn't very well be his child. And even though she wanted to astound them and know everything young Else couldn't explain it either.

From the pilots' houses the girls went directly down to the quay where the wreck was being tied up and having her lower decks pumped to keep her above water.

Then the consul went on board. The whole town was standing on the quayside watching him. A few idiots got in his way and he had to ask them politely to step aside.

He looked so distinguished with his dark hair and bright clothes and the flower in his buttonhole. He was carrying a large ledger under his arm and he went over the ship from top to bottom, making out his report and writing down everything he saw and noting the information the pilots gave him. A man from the crowd on the quayside was called up to carry the consul's ink-pot for him as he wandered about the ship writing things down . . .

That was such a strange year that nearly every month brought with it some new and notable event. The fire at the house of Eliassen the schoolteacher, for example, was a by no means commonplace occurrence. Here the good Eliassen really benefited from his own foresight, there was no denying that: just one year earlier he had insured his house, with contents and furniture and all his outhouses, for a very large sum of money, and now the whole lot had gone up in flames. Eliassen the schoolteacher was also treasurer of the Union and all the club's funds were lost in the fire. It seemed so unfair, some 200 kroner going up in smoke just like that. At the next general assembly it was moved that the treasurer be absolved of all responsibility for this money. At this Eliassen stood up and in a voice choking with emotion said he would rather see himself and his wife and children go naked than be absolved of so much as one øre. The Union had done him the great honour of electing him to this position of responsibility, and he knew where his duty lay.

Whereupon, in sheer enthusiasm, the members of the Union had a whipround and raised 200 kroner to buy new furniture for Eliassen the schoolteacher.

*   *   *

Autumn came, the weather turned cold, the nights dark. The two night-watchmen meet down by the mackerel market, they greet each other, have a little chat, then take a stroll along the street. It's night, and a dark one. The lamp over by the hotel shines with a feeble light. Then the one watchman grabs the other watchman by the arm and stops him. They both stand there looking.

They see a remarkable sight: Tønnes Olai walking along the street in his usual quiet manner and climbing the steps to the consul's offices. But this is the middle of the night! At the top he stops a moment and he lowers his head a bit, probably because all the thoughts in it are weighing it down. The two watchmen are on the point of stepping forward and posing a baffled question or two when they see the consul himself admitting Tønnes Olai. In all the 15 years they've been keeping watch in the town this is the most incredible thing they've ever seen. They just stayed where they were, rooted to the spot.

Tønnes Olai passed quietly through the door and remained silent as the consul turned the key. He was then conducted to the innermost room in the office. Here again the door was firmly closed behind them.

'It's hardly worth putting on a light,' said the consul. 'There's light enough coming from the hotel. But sit down. Sit down here.'

Tønnes Olai sat down respectfully on the edge of the seat.

'What I wanted to talk to you about,' said the consul, 'is this business about your knowing everything. You're all over the place at night. You've seen me a couple of times, several times at most. How many times have you seen me?'

'Seven times, Herr Consul,' answers Tønnes Olai.

'I haven't even been to her house seven times,' says the consul. 'A couple of times, I'll admit. A couple of short visits.'

Tønnes Olai answers:

'Seven times, Herr Consul. Sorry for mentioning it.'

The consul lights a cigar and of course does not offer one to the other.

'All right then, whatever,' he says and puffs out a cloud of smoke. 'But I hope we can be agreed upon what remains, my dear Jahnsen.'

The other doesn't fall for this and let himself feel flattered because the consul calls him my dear Jahnsen.

'Just Tønnes Olai, Herr Consul,' he answers.

The consul nods and blows out smoke.

'Right ... You told her that you've seen me leaving her house. That's number one. Number two, you told her that you expect the consul to look after you in this matter. How much do you want?'

With this he offers Tønnes Olai a cigar, which he declines. He urges it on him, but Tønnes declines.

'How much do I want?' he answers. 'It depends. I lead a simple life, don't require much. Herr Consul should bear that in mind.'

'The sum?'

'In regard to that I am entirely in the consul's hands.'

'Hm. Well I suppose, yes, you certainly are. I don't even need to come to any kind of agreement with you at all, Tønnes Olai. But I dislike being gossiped about and lied about and having people talk behind my back. I have a family. I want to shut you up, that is what I want. I am speaking frankly.'

Tønnes Olai says respectfully:

'Who will be the father, Herr Consul?'

The consul answers:

'The father? Surely she'll sort that out for herself?'

'It isn't easy for a lady on her own to sort out something like that,' says Tønnes Olai. 'Herr Consul ought to bear that in mind.'

'All right, what is it you're trying to say?'

Tønnes fiddles with his hat in his hand and thinks.

'Herr Consul could use me as the father,' says he. 'That is, if the lady herself would be satisfied with someone like me.'

The consul stares at him in the dark and immediately feels that this is a helpful suggestion.

'It is as I have always said, Jahnsen, you have an excellent head on your shoulders. I have often wished I had your head, Jahnsen.'

Still the other remains unaffected.

'In the daily run of things my name is not Jahnsen, Herr Consul. That involves an exaggeration. My given name is Tønnes Olai.'

'All right, all right, Tønnes Olai, as you like. But I have often wished I had your head. Your suggestion is valued. I mean, it is worth something, quite something, in purely financial terms. How much would you suggest yourself?'

Tønnes Olai thinks about this.

'A thousand kroner.'

The consul gasps.

'In God's name man, don't you realise I have a family? Be serious.'

'A thousand kroner, Herr Consul. Sorry for mentioning it.'

'Out of the question!' says the consul. He stands up, looks out of the window, thinking. Then he turns back to Tønnes Olai and decides the matter: 'Well then we can't do business. I'm sorry to have inconvenienced you so late at night. I shall get someone else.'

'In that case, what does the consul intend to do about me?' asks Tønnes Olai as he gets to his feet too.

'About you?' says the consul, suddenly quivering with anger. 'What am I going to do about you, you bastard? I'm going to have you arrested tomorrow. Get out.'

The consul opens the door and Tønnes Olai hurries out.

'Let me explain,' he says in a conciliatory tone, gesturing meekly with his hand. 'The consul couldn't do much better than use me.'

It strikes the consul that Tønnes Olai is right; but he is furious and says:

'I told you, I'll get someone else. Let that be the end of the matter.'

But it is so blindingly obvious that Tønnes Olai is right, and the moment he's out in the street the consul drags him back inside again and locks the door. They both return to the office.

'You said you had something to explain. Explain.'

'What are a thousand kroner to a wealthy man!' says Tønnes Olai.

'Well, I may not be a pauper—if it's any of your business. And I am not entirely without my share of worldly goods, a fact which I hope is generally recognised?'

'Oh goodness me, yes!'

'But a thousand kroner—no.'

'It might be arranged in a relatively painfree manner.'

'How? In small sums? Is that what you're trying to say?'

Tønnes Olai protests:

'In small sums—? Consul—! May the Lord strike me dead on the spot if I ...'

'Well that's what I took you to mean.'

'But it might be divided in two. Both of you. If Herr Consul can't manage it alone she might be able to help out. Share it, so to speak. She could afford it.'

The consul gets to his feet again.

'I want you out of here! Out, I said ... Have you, incidentally, discussed this with her?'

'I have mentioned it.'

The consul thinks about this and sits down again.

'It isn't because I can't,' he says. 'But it's one thing to be able and another to want to. It would be like giving away my own children's money . . . How much did she think she would contribute?'

'She didn't say. But she's a warm-hearted woman, in every way. Herr Consul ought to bear that in mind. I'm sure she won't be petty-minded.'

'Half!' says the consul firmly. 'D'you think I would quibble over that? She shall not be liable to pay more than one half!'

So they agreed on that.

'You can pick up the money tomorrow or thereabouts. When my cashier comes. I don't have the keys.'

The consul let Tønnes Olai out and then went back inside again, lit the lamp and sat smoking and brooding and working out his money . . .

The watchmen were still standing on the same spot. They had seen everything, Tønnes Olai being let in and being shown out again. But they had heard nothing and could make neither head nor tail of the whole business. So they decided to try to get hold of Tønnes Olai; but they slipped up there. Tønnes Olai had seen them and turned down the street just past the hotel, on the other side of the light, where no one could see him.

*   *   *

And again the watchmen meet in the evening and take it easy with a smoke and a chat and a stroll.

'I've gone back to flake,' says one.

'Me too,' replies the other and lights up.

'The price of that shag I was smoking just keeps going up and up.'

'You wouldn't even think of buying it, not the price it is now.'

'The price of every necessity of life just goes up. Pretty soon we won't even be able to afford to live here any more. Or am I wrong?'

'Or are you wrong? Listen, even if you were wrong you'd still be right anyway. When it comes to the necessities of life then all I can say is like the old proverb take care of the coppers and the notes will take care of themselves. My youngest daughter went to Confirmation this spring, but do you think we could afford a little frock for her? It's a serious business, getting confirmed; but she had to borrow a frock from her sister.'

'People envy us public servants. They say we've got job security. Now I'm asking you, Marcussen, what's the use of being public and being a servant when all the bare necessities of life are so expensive you can't even afford to live? The moment I get my wages they're gone again. The money might as well be invisible.'

'Well now let me tell you one thing, Thobiesen: if there's one person who knows that better than anyone else that person must be me. The money *is* invisible. It disappears while you're still looking at it in your hand. You can't afford to live.'

'It's not as if it was a bad year for mackerel this year. But everyone's complaining. I heard the bank's going to be doing a bit of foreclosing.'

'You don't say. Who?'

'I've heard several, Marcussen. Pretty soon the only one left standing is going to be the consul.'

'Yes the consul, he's well out of it. He's got his investments all over the place. If he gets in a bit of trouble here all he has to do is shoot in a bit of capital from over there. Then he's got his ships.'

The two watchmen drift along the street. Suddenly they hear a certain horse and wagon go by.

'She's out again then.'

They stop and watch the midwife driving by.

'Let's see where she's off to,' says Marcussen.

'I was about to say the same,' answers Thobiesen. 'Didn't she take a left past the hotel lamp? She must be going all the way out to Myren, she's off to Olava Wollertsen.'

'That bitch. That cow has behaved like an animal, her a married woman and all. What do you suppose Wollertsen is going to say?'

'Don't even mention it!'

'And she has the gall to summon the midwife!'

'I'm saying no more. And Wollertsen away from home these past two years . . .'

The midwife went to Olava Wollertsen's. By morning the whole town knew and now it couldn't be kept hidden any longer. And that sneaky Olava, how she had managed to keep her condition secret by staying out of people's way like that!

But the father—who was the father?

Well as for the father, Tønnes Olai made no secret of the fact that it was he who was the father—sorry for mentioning it. And there wasn't a soul in town who didn't puzzle over this for a very long time. No one could figure it out. If it had been a wild fling, if her heart had led her astray—because Olava was young and she was lovely—but *Tønnes Olai*? All you could say, it must just have been in a moment of pure lustful madness.

And Tønnes Olai admitted himself that he couldn't understand what she saw in him. But he defended her. Real ladies like her often behaved so strangely, he said. Now and then they could find themselves attracted to someone from well below their social class and station. That's what happened here. It makes you think.

But even after this Tønnes Olai continued to wander round the town as quietly and peaceably as before. And among his acquaintances the matter couldn't be said to have done his reputation any harm. That damn Tønnes Olai, they thought, he's a dark horse all right. You wouldn't put it past him to start up in business with a little shop and call himself Jahnsen. He's got the head for it, and he even looks like a little merchant already. Sort of an affluent look to him.

*   *   *

It was late winter when the whole thing finally blew up. Whatever else had happened paled in comparison with this catastrophe. The consul went bankrupt.

There was a meeting at the bank. Not for the first time, disquiet was expressed over some of the names the consul was using as guarantors for his loans. Finally, on the initiative of Berg the merchant, it was proposed that one application for the renewal of a loan be rejected. Berg proposed that one guarantor be replaced by another of higher standing. Such a suggestion was a gross insult to a man of the consul's status, for if *he* found the man worthy then the man was worthy. In short, Berg didn't get far with his proposal.

During this unpleasant little episode at the bank, however, the consul almost broke down. But he managed to control himself and preserved a calm exterior. He clung to a last hope, that a telegram would arrive from Skipper Wollertsen, currently sailing with a cargo of fruit, a telegram concerning a certain transaction involving a New York shipping firm.

'Herr Berg would like to see a better quality of guarantor,' said the consul. 'In my humble opinion the business of names is a pure formality. At the next meeting I shall have the honour of repaying the whole loan.'

There now. That's what you might call a dignified rebuke . . .

But the next meeting came round and the consul didn't pay back the loan. In fact, he stopped paying back any of his loans. The telegram from Wollersten hadn't brought him much joy—in fact it was almost incoherent: alarmed by the news contained in certain letters he had received Wollertsen had left his ship and was making his way home.

It left the consul with no choice . . .

He got up from his chair, flicked the dust from his lapels and had unfortunately an announcement to make to the honourable gentlemen of the board: heavy losses, bad luck with his ships, a depressed market, it all meant he could no longer maintain his position. His creditors had been informed. He resigned hereby from his position as honorary chairman . . .

The meeting broke up immediately.

The news spread through the town. It was as though a bomb had gone off in the little community and every home was rocked to its foundations. Women wept. The consul bankrupt—so who now was left standing on his own two feet? He was the wealthiest man in town, its bedrock. He had perhaps been autocratic and overambitious in his ways, with God alone able to stand up to him. And now God had stood up to him, and dealt him a crushing blow. Soon it became apparent that many, many others would be joining him in his fall.

It was ruin on a grand scale. Even the town's communal noise, the hammering from the boat-builders' yards, was silenced. Sure, Berg the merchant did manage to float one little company to build boats; but the hammers didn't dance as fast there, no it wasn't the same sound at all.

The whole town was crippled. It was the consul, with his house and his business, who had been the soul of the place, its pride and its ornament, and it was pitiful to see him now stop in the street, take out his bankrupt wallet and hand the shoemaker a 25 øre piece just like he always used to. There was black comedy in it, and there was self-mockery.

And when everybody else fell why shouldn't young Else fall with them? Should she have some special dispensation against falling? With the future so uncertain now she might as well say yes to Jensen who worked for Berg, even though she was much too good for him. It was painful to watch, the way her proud steps dragged as she walked up the aisle to the altar with him . . .

In short, the church was the only thing in town that escaped unscathed. And just as before Skipper Andersen's wife swept her way along the sandy path in that same old-fashioned long dress of hers, for she still had the health for it, and the money for it. Now the merchant Berg began his rise to prominence in the town. He took over as director of the bank and became mayor. But he never became a consul. He was from a humble background and had no sophistication. He was so bad it was an embarrassment to see and hear him when he spoke for the town in his official capacity. He called himself 'dorectoor' and he couldn't give a fluent and amusing speech not if his life depended on it. He practised and he slogged away at bowing and saying hello and how to express himself well, but no manner how hard he tried his manners and speech would never be the consul's manners and speech. What would the consul say when someone visited him? 'Pleasure to see you!' he would say, like the gentleman he was. And what would Berg say? He would bow like a horse and say something pretentious like: 'Good day, pleasure to make your acquaintanceship!' And when his wife was doing the washing he used to say that they were 'laundering' at home.

His wife didn't suit her new station either. She was forward all right, and even started getting letters addressed to 'Madame Berg'. Who was this Madame Berg? For quite a while the postmaster made out he didn't know who she was. But as time went by people got used to things. Berg the merchant was undeniably a wealthy man; with the years he grew wealthier still and acquired more and more businesses and in the end he did become a consul, and his wife beyond all dispute Madame Berg. And the next generation saw the town prosper once more under the auspices of the new dynasty.

As for the consul—the old consul—he started up an agency selling mackerel and life insurance policies; and this in the town where he had once been a prince! But God took mercy on him in his humiliation and his contrition and let his daughter Cordelia marry a rich man. And Cordelia was the apple of her husband's eye and his greatest support.

REIERSEN OF THE
SOUTHERN STAR

1

An old, tarred dried-fish sloop glides into the bay with a dinghy in tow. The sloop is the *Southern Star* and the skipper's name is Reiersen. Both sloop and skipper are familiar sights in the bay, they've been coming here for God knows how long, he dried fish in Salten, dried fish for the Spaniards, *bacalaos* they call it.

There was no one watching from any of the surrounding hillocks, only far away a few children playing at the edge of the bay by the boat-houses. It was different before, twenty years earlier, when the *Southern Star* anchored for the first time off the drying grounds. Then admiring women and children stood on every hillock while one fisherman after another rowed out to the *Southern Star* to greet it and hear the latest news.

There are four men on deck. Reiersen himself has taken the wheel, as he always does on important occasions. As he did in the old days he still steers his little fishing sloop with as much solemnity as if she were a great steamboat. His hair and beard are grey, but in former days hair and beard were black, that was twenty years ago, those first times he came to Salten, when he was a young man. His jacket is worn and patched, and Skipper Reiersen's reputation isn't what it was; but all during the approach he's the admiral of his ship and he roars out his orders like a lion.

'Cast anchor!'

And down goes the anchor.

The mighty rattling of the chain competes with the big man's voice. But times have changed. Postal steamers have started serving the trading place and folk no longer reckon much to honest old fishing sloops. When the children playing by the boat-houses heard the anchor drop they glanced briefly across the bay and then played on, just as if one had told the other that it was only Reiersen with his sloop.

With the day's work done, the sloop moored and the men gone to their bunks, the skipper sat on the deck and looked across the bay. It was a mild, light night and the sun gilded the water. He knew each skerry and had memories from them all, the happiest times of his youth had been spent here during the three summer months when he lay to and dried his catch. He was top man there, always did and always got what he wanted. On Sundays he went to church because that's where the people were, and on his way home afterwards he always had the company of the young girls. When the young fisher folk held their dances on summer nights Reiersen could be seen coming up the bay in his dinghy, standing upright in the stern, shoes polished and shiny, while the cook or some other member of the crew rowed him ashore. He danced like a lion and the cabin-smell of his fine blue clothes got the girls all excited. Oh yes, Reiersen had many talents, and he was everybody's friend. Whenever he came on the scene the local boys quietly gave up. He always beat them to the girls, but they never made a fuss about it, just hid themselves behind a wall and wept their tears.

Now Reiersen had a wife and five children up on Ofoten.

2

And the sea is calm as a mirror and night falls. But still Skipper Reiersen sits there thinking about the old days. What girls he'd had! Some of the best in the whole bay! The first year there was one in particular, scarcely past the age of confirmation, with dark hair and dark eyes. At any hour of the day or night you might see him in company with this sweet young thing, including times when most people thought maybe they both should have been on their own. And then as it was getting towards time for him to leave it was all over, Reiersen didn't dance with her any more, instead he kept the company of a great big fisher girl from further round the bay. She had big dimples and white teeth and her name was Ellen Helene.

Ah that Ellen Helene.

It lasted a year. It didn't usually last a year for Reiersen and that's why people said that *now* he'd been caught. Reiersen caught! Ha! They didn't know Reiersen. But he completely ruined Ellen Helene's engagement to the smith, and he got so far with her that he could call her his own sweet dear and not care who heard him.

The next year Reiersen came to the drying grounds he had a cabin full of store goods with him, flour and coffee, woollen scarves and linen, even rings for the fingers and expensive knitted mittens. He would never forget the sight of it all, it was as if there was a shop on board the *Southern Star*. Reiersen was even more of a great man after that. He paid both the hire of the drying grounds and the wages of the drying girls with these goods, and many's the neck scarf and shiny brooch with a stone encrusted he gave away to the girls. Ellen Helene didn't complain about it, it did no good to argue with Reiersen.

Yet not even Ellen Helene could avoid her fate, no matter how easygoing she was; she lost out to Jacobine, a frisky little thing who turned Reiersen's fish and was happy as could be in her work. Because why should it always and only be Ellen Helene for a man like Reiersen of the *Southern Star*? When the fish were to be packed that autumn Jacobine was alone in the fishroom and the skipper treated her to a drink and when she left the sloop he ordered two men to row her ashore. This about being in the fishroom, by the way, was almost the same as being in the cabin. Also, the people who lived thereabouts called it 'packing' fish and not 'loading' fish.

And with that the break with Ellen Helene was complete. Jens Olsen, her father, crossed with the great skipper over his fooling, he waved his fist at him and asked him a lot of rude questions. Reiersen was no one's pushover in those days, he waved his fist about too and said: 'If you my good Jens Olsen presume to insinuate yourself into the vicinity of my person then you will find out a little something or other you didn't know about Reiersen of the *Southern Star*.'

And yet not even Jacobine could capture Skipper Reiersen's fickle heart for any length of time. It was a night like this one, still and calm, he paces up and down the deck of his ship and hears the plashing of oars in the distance. A girl who had been out collecting eggs came rowing by.

'Boat ahoy!' shouted Reiersen.

She lifted her oars and listened.

'Heave to here, little one,' he said.

'It isn't your own sweet dear you're talking to,' came the reply from the boat.

'I know you,' said Reiersen. 'Have you got eggs in your boat?'

And the boat came closer.

'Yes well if it's eggs you want there's no reason why you can't have a couple,' said the girl.

And then after that Reiersen didn't say another word but swung down into his dinghy and from there over to the girl.

'It's me,' he said. 'Reiersen. You know me.'

He took the oars from her and rowed her over to the boat-houses. There was no one about and the night was warm and full of secrets.

'We might as well put the boat away now,' said Reiersen once they reached the shore.

And the girl answered:

'You're too kind I'm sure.'

But this about putting the boat away was said for a purpose and he had ideas of his own. Ha ha, you sly old Reiersen, you were thinking this and thinking that, and the girl was a real featherbrain and not a bit scared of the dark in the boat-house at night.

When they parted she only said:

'How are you going to get back on board again?'

'I'll swim,' answered Reiersen.

And he walked into the sea.

The girl's name was Pauline . . .

Ah but now all his girlfriends were gone, one dead, another in America, a third married. And all Reiersen had to show for it were memories. Pauline still lived on the bay, still single as before; but after she lost an eye a couple of years ago she experienced a religious awakening and now only the things of the spirit interested her. So ended all things in this world. As Reiersen had ended with a wife and five children in Ofoten . . .

One o'clock. In a while all the sea birds would wake. Reiersen yawned loudly and looked up. Well, best turn in now. Worn out and used out and too old for everything as he was. Tomorrow he would start cleaning his fish. That meant people on board, men and women in sea boots and oilskins, young girls among them with freckles and laughing faces, real children of Adam. Reiersen knew them.

And in the silence the greying family man stole a glance at his reflection in the compass glass before creeping down to his smelly hole of a cabin and turning in.

3

Boats come in the early morning, Reiersen paces up and down the deck, master in his own house, wearing his best clothes, with a fancy watch-chain made of hair dangling across his chest. Did he need cleaners? Yes, he needed cleaners all right. The price was discussed, certain conditions were set. The fishermen had developed the ill-mannered habit of haggling with a man like Reiersen, they demanded six skillings more than he offered. What sort of new-fangled invention was haggling? No, folk didn't think much of Reiersen of the *Southern Star* any more, times had changed, years had passed and his status had passed to the gold-buttoned chiefs from the postal steamers.

He gave the workers a dram of shop-bought whisky and a pastry. They thanked him and drank. He pinched the girls in the ribs, they pushed him off and laughed at him, they peered impudently down through the skylight and did just as they liked. What about it now, had he changed his mind, would he give them the extra six skillings?

The skipper is deeply offended and he deals with the matter summarily. He walks to the stern, and positions himself by the tiller, where his place is, where he is in command. Things will be done as they were in the old days, just as they were in the old days. 'Listen: you want cleaning work?' Surprised, the fishermen answer yes. 'Right!' said Reiersen. 'So and so much a dozen. Lay to. Start counting. Let's go!'

But it wasn't like in the old days. The fishermen dealt summarily with the matter too and climbed back down into their boats. And when they pushed themselves off and began to row homewards it was the skipper who had to give in and agree to their price:

'All right I'll give you the six skillings, who cares a damn anyway.'

The boats lay to again, the main holds on the *Southern Star* were opened and the fish, dripping with brine, thrown up. It took days, working round the clock, stopping only for food and sleep. The drying grounds were swarming with people, some cleaning, others carting the fish on wooden litters while still others spread the fish out over the rounded rocks to dry in the sun. As the hours passed the sloop emptied and began to ride higher in the water, until finally its whole belly was showing and only the keelson was underwater. The *Southern Star* was hosed down, she was empty.

These were idle days for Skipper Reiersen. He paid men to scrape and paint the sloop from top to bottom while he himself strolled about ashore, hands in pockets, mingling with the drying workers and joking with the girls. But he avoided Pauline, she was approaching 40 now and out of religious conviction said as little as possible; but when Reiersen's behaviour got too frivolous for her liking she gave him a silent admonition with her one good eye. Things went on like this for weeks and Reiersen didn't get anywhere with any of them, his age ruled him out and the boys from the bay had taken over from him. '*Yeugh!*' said the girls when he started acting up in front of them. And by that they meant—Don't bother!

But Reiersen had his plans. He didn't feel his age, and he knew quite well that he was still the same good old Skipper Reiersen he'd always been. He'd sailed the *Southern Star* from coast to coast and never holed her; he'd bought fish and dried fish; paid bills as long as a ship's rail and kept his log so well the devil himself couldn't understand it. Yet folk didn't pay him his due respect any more.

'Scrub down the cabin!' he said to the cook. Now he had his plan. Reiersen goes ashore and lets it be known among the drying workers that he needs two girls on board to do some mending for him, including repairing a few rips in the *Southern Star's* flag.

But none of the girls were willing to go on board. Reiersen's stranded again. He goes on about it for two days and doesn't get anywhere. Finally he hears a woman's voice saying:

'If I can be any help to you then I'll do what I can.'

It was Pauline who took pity on him.

Reiersen thought about it a moment, Pauline's eye is on him. What could he do with her? In the end he says yes thanks and Pauline gets in the boat with him. The girls left behind on shore stand sniggering.

To be truthful it had never been Reiersen's intention to stuff his cabin with the dull fear of God, he'd been looking for a day like the good old days of his prime, with laughing girls and drams and pastries. What was he to do now?

From closets and chests he digs out his frayed old clothes, brings the flag and Pauline settles down to work. She speaks hardly at all, Reiersen pours a drink for her and she drinks it, but she remains silent and busy.

'Hey Pauline,' he says, to please her, 'you're all right now you've found God.'

'You might say that,' she answered. 'It's about time you found Him too.'

Reiersen answers:

'It just might be that I'm not as far away from Him now as I once was.'

'Is that true?' she asks.

'I feel things are getting a little better lately, yes.'

'Thanks be to God for that,' she says.

But now her tongue was loose and the old maid went on talking about God. Reiersen regretted he'd raised the subject, it bored him and he soon ran out of good reasons why he was closer to God now than he had been before. It was just an impression he had, he said.

'Open your heart to it,' she beseeched him, 'open your heart to it.'

Reiersen poured another drink and offered more pastries.

'Those girls ashore were laughing,' he said, 'but now you can tell them how well looked after you were on Reiersen's boat.'

They both drank. But when he tried to nudge the conversation over in a more earthy direction she just sewed faster than ever and ignored him. He didn't dare remind her of the good days gone by twenty years ago, it was on the tip of his tongue but he didn't say it.

It got more and more boring, the hours passed and the flag was finished; but Reiersen had had no fun.

'That'll be enough for the time being,' he said when he could bear it no longer. He threw his old clothes back into the chests and closets and had Pauline taken ashore.

The day was ruined, his plan had foundered.

4

Another couple of weeks pass. It was getting on for autumn, the fish were dry and the day was approaching for them to be loaded on board again and packed. He chose a warm morning, the big rowboats were loaded to the gunwales with fish and men in their shirtsleeves rowed them out to the *Southern Star*.

It was an old custom that the packing of the fish be done by four girls. Who was going to pack this year? Everyone turned the job down. It was the responsibility of the workers' foreman, Endre Polden, and the skipper didn't get involved in it; but this latest example of disrespectful behaviour distressed him and he chewed his lip bitterly. Again Pauline took pity on him and said she would pack the fish if three others would join her. Reiersen turned on his heel and boarded the boat.

He went down below to his cabin, and all on his own he began to get stuck into a bottle. What else could he do under the circumstances? He'd just about had his day. Okay—then let this be the last year he sailed the *Southern Star* into this dump. There were other drying grounds in Salten. Him too old? We'd soon see about that. Cheers!

He drank. Drank his own health a number of times and bucked himself up. After half an hour he was in the sort of mood where he could have given a whipping to any gold-buttoned postboat functionary. He hears footsteps up on deck, swigs down another glass and climbs up from his cabin.

Were there packers down in the fishroom? He peers down, four girls there hard at work; Endre Polden had finally used his authority and forced them on board. Good! And now Skipper Reiersen decides to do something about it, watch closely now, he's up to something!

He hears how the laughter and chatter of the girls echoes through the empty ship and thinks: On you go and don't chicken out now. But Pauline wasn't chatting.

It was an established custom that on the day the fish were loaded on board Reiersen would treat the packers. Treat the packers? He'd made up his mind that treat the packers was exactly what he would not do this time. Now it was he who was in charge.

'Pauline!' he shouted. 'I'd like a word with you in my cabin.'

Pauline climbed up out of the fishroom and went with the skipper to his cabin.

'You were the only one who didn't refuse to go on board,' said the skipper. 'I'd like to treat you.'

'You shouldn't go to any trouble,' she answered.

But Reiersen wanted to go to any trouble. 'Cook—light the fire and make us some coffee!' And the skipper himself produced brandy and pastries. Pauline was like a guest at a feast.

'When you go back to the fishroom tell the girls that Skipper Reiersen didn't treat you too badly,' he said.

They drank and enjoyed themselves, Reiersen rubbed the old maid on the shoulder. She stood up and wanted to get back to her work.

'Sit,' he said, 'let's just sit here a while. This is the last time I'll be coming here to dry my fish.'

'You don't mean that?' she asked.

Reiersen nods:

'Last time.'

Something stirred in the old maid's heart, she lowered her eye and asked:

'What time are you sailing?'

'When the fish are all packed,' he answered. 'Tomorrow night, night after that.'

She sat down again.

'May God be with you!' she said to herself.

'Let's drink to that,' he answered. At all costs he wanted to avoid the conversation getting round to God again. He asked her straight out: 'Well Pauline, and when are you going to get married?'

She looked at him steadily and said:

'Are you making fun of me?'

'Making fun of you?' he retorted. 'Why's that?'

'Can I get married, me, with just one eye?' she asked.

Reiersen snorted:

'And why not? It's just a little disfigurement.'

In her heart she was grateful to him for these words and knew he was right. She had lost the one eye, but she was still just as good, she'd been unlucky, a child had poked her eye out with a knitting needle. So the years had passed and she'd had no one to help her but God. Occasionally she cried over the loss of that eye. But she was strong, and her health was good, that hadn't been taken from her yet.

Reiersen refills their glasses. He leans over her and won't hear no, that she can't drink any more. It was the last time he would be here in the bay, she was the only one who had stuck by him and he would remember her for that. Both were moved as he spoke. Reiersen took her hand and she sat there, firm and strong as a young horse. Suddenly he puts his arm around her neck and says:

'Remember that night in the boat-house? Twenty years ago?'

'Yes,' she replies throatily. She doesn't resist, he still has his arm around her neck. 'I think of you always may God forgive my sin,' she says.

Now just watch closely and we'll see who's clapped out or not.

'What are you doing?' she asks, astonished. 'Have you gone mad? A married man!' And when her rebukes don't help she gives him a crack on the head with her big fist that sends him tumbling into the yellow panelling. 'If I'd known that was on your mind I'd never have set foot in here,' she says angrily. 'Have you ever seen the like of it! A married man!'

She goes out of the door, up the ladder and climbs back down to her work in the fishroom. Her dream of Reiersen had been shattered and now she knew what type he was she would never think of him again and remember his jet-black hair when he was young. He respected neither himself nor God. In the boat-house twenty years ago! Yes, but wasn't it a completely different matter then, with neither of them married and not going against God?

But from that time onwards Reiersen was finished. Not even a 41-year-old one-eyed witch would have him, him, a man who once had every girl in the bay at his feet. Age had caught up with him, his account was closed.

And that was probably how he'd end up too, going in for a bit of seriousness and God-fearing in his old age; when all else failed he'd have that to turn to. After he sobered up he remembered his thoughts and he said to himself: day by day you're slowly becoming a better person, take just small steps and keep moving forwards; she may be right, Pauline, that it's about time.

When Endre Polden came on board that evening and reported that the loading and packing would be finished by tomorrow afternoon, the skipper replied gravely:

'Praise the Lord.'

Endre Polden looked at him uncomprehendingly. He asked:

'What time will you be sailing?'

And the skipper answered, again incomprehensibly:

'God willing, tomorrow night.'

And God willed it. Reiersen left as planned and sailed out of the bay. A thousand thoughts raced through his mind. He knew each tiny island, on this one here he'd had this adventure, on that one another, in his youth, in his prime. Ahgh, it was all over now . . .

Reiersen stands by the tiller, looking at his reflection in the compass glass. Suddenly he stands up straight like an admiral and he says to himself:

'Next year I'll try somewhere else. I'll be damned if I'm over the hill yet.'

ON BLUE MAN'S ISLAND

There are many populated islands out in the fishing grounds, among them a small one called Blue Man's Island, home to about 100 people. The island right next to it is much bigger, with 300 or 400 inhabitants, including the priest and the sheriff. It's called Church Island. In the days since my childhood it has also acquired a postal and telegraph system.

Wherever island dwellers were gathered it was always the thing to be from the big island. Church Islanders didn't even reckon much to folk from the mainland, though they had the whole of the country to be from. For miles around the people here are fishermen.

Blue Man's Island is so far out that the whole Atlantic washes its shores. It rises steeply and on three sides is impossible to climb. Only in the south, where it faces the sun at midday, have God and men made a negotiable track up the cliffs in the form of 200 carved steps. After every storm timber, planks and flotsam fetch up on the island and from these the boat-builders build their boats. They carry the wood up the 200 steps, build the boats next to their houses, then wait for winter to come, when the cliffs on the north side are blue and shiny with ice, and lower the boat on winches and pulleys down the glassy slope into the sea. As a child I saw for myself how this was done: two men stood at the top and paid out the ropes while another man sat in the boat and prevented it from getting caught up. It was a courageous, cautious process, conducted by a series of low cries of instruction and warning. And when it finally reached the water the one in the boat shouted up to his companions to steady up now, now we're down. This was all he said by way of announcing the great news that the launch was successful.

The man with the biggest house on Blue Man's Island was a trusting old boat-builder named Joachim. The Christmas dance was held in his front room every year, and there was easily space enough for four or six couples to dance at a time. There was fiddle music, and beside the fiddler sat a man who was just the man for the job by the name of Didrik, who lilted and hummed and beat time with his feet. The boys danced in their shirtsleeves.

Usually a young lad moved among the guests as a kind of host during the dance, he was the boat-builder's youngest son and himself a boat-builder. He was much respected on account of his craftsmanship and his intelligence, and Marcelius! thought one girl, and Marcelius! thought another, and his name was known even to the girls over on Church Island. As for Marcelius, he thought only of Fredrikke, the teacher's daughter, though she was so refined and well-spoken and beautiful that he would never be able to win her. The teacher's house was a big one too, and since he was not a mere fisherman but on the contrary a most important person he had curtains for his windows, and people would tap on his door with their fingers before going inside. But Marcelius's love was true and blind. He was at the teacher's house last year and there again this year, going to the kitchen door. 'Good evening,' he might say, 'can I talk with you for a little while, Fredrikke?'

'What do you want?' she says, though she knows well enough what he wants.

'Will you do that thing I asked you?'

'No,' says Fredrikke, 'I can't. And you're not to think about me any more, Marcelius, and not to keep hanging around me any more.'

'Sure, I know, the new teacher's after you,' answers Marcelius. 'I just wonder where all your refined ways are going to get you.'

And it was true, the new teacher was after Fredrikke. He was from Church Island and had been to the seminary. His father was only a fisherman like everyone else, but he was a rich and important one, and there were always cod and coalfish hanging up in his fish shed, and butter and ham and dried fish in his pantry. When his son came home from the seminary he was as elegant as the priest's son when he returned from his studies. He wore his sideburns long and had a handkerchief in his pocket and out of nothing more than a sense of his own importance he always had a loop of elastic hanging down from his hat. People had a laugh at him on account of that handkerchief, saying what a thrifty chap Simon Rust was now, look he'd even started saving the drips from his nose.

'He's just ordered a new boat from us,' says Marcelius, 'and I hope God gives him the joy of it too.'

'Why do you say that?' asks Fredrikke.

'Because I have to. He wants the gunwales painted green—okay, I'll paint them green. He wants a name on the boat too, but he'll have to paint that on himself.'

'He wants to give it a name?'

'It's a blasphemy, that's what it is. The boat doesn't even have a wheelhouse, it's just a plain four-oared rowing-boat ... So maybe you should reconsider if maybe you couldn't make yourself small enough to have me after all, Fredrikke?'

'No I can't, do you hear. Because he has my heart.'

'So he has your heart, does he?' says Marcelius, and he leaves.

Not long before Christmas Simon Rust arrived from Church Island to paint the name on his new boat. He stayed at the old teacher's house and every day Fredrikke wore her Sunday dress and a ribbon of watered silk around her neck. And once the name was in place there weren't many who could read the Latin inscription, but what it said was SUPERFIN. That was supposed to be the name of the boat. Not many people could understand such a fine word either.

And then it was the day before Christmas Eve, a deep and starry night. Marcelius went to the teacher's house and asked to have a word with Simon Rust.

'The name's dry now,' said Marcelius.

'Then we'll launch the boat tomorrow,' answered Simon Rust.

Marcelius went on:

'Is it true that you're engaged to Fredrikke?'

'That's hardly any of your business,' answered Simon the schoolteacher.

'Maybe so, but if you tell me the truth about being engaged to Fredrikke then you can have the boat for nothing.'

Simon Rust thought about this. He was careful with his money just the way his father always was. He called to Fredrikke, and asked her:

'Is it true that we're going to be engaged?'

And Fredrikke answered yes, because he had her heart.

And the night was so starry and Fredrikke's eyes seemed brimming over with joy when she said this.

On his way home Marcelius began regretting the waste of money in giving Simon a boat for nothing. But I'll be in the boat while it's being lowered and I'll make sure it's good and smashed up by the time he gets it.

He wandered on from house to house, didn't stop anywhere, just walked on and on beneath the northern lights and the stars. He walked right over to the north side of the island where his ropes and pulleys hung ready for the new boat to be lowered down into the deep. The Atlantic surged beneath him. He sat down.

Out at sea two small lights showed on a sailing ship. Further out another two lights from a steamer, heavy and black, making its way eastwards. He thought: maybe the best thing would be to join a ship like that and just sail away. Fredrikke was lost for ever, and it wouldn't be easy to carry on living there once she'd left Blue Man's Island. Oh God our father in heaven look after her and help her all her days! And as for wrecking Simon's boat he prayed for forgiveness for such a mean thought, and decided to do all he could to stop it bouncing on the rocks on its way down. That's the kind of man he wanted to be.

He got up and was about to head back home when he heard a soft cry, someone calling, he listened. He saw someone approach him.

'Fredrikke, is that you?' he said.

'Yes. I only want to make sure you don't do anything to harm yourself, Marcelius.'

'I'm just out walking,' answered Marcelius.

She took his arm and held it and went on:

'Because there's really no need to take it so badly. And anyway I haven't completely made up my mind yet.'

'Surely you have?'

'Oh what's going to happen?' she burst out. 'Just now he was absolutely horrible to me. I think you're a better person than Simon is. He tries to talk his way out of it. Just today he said: let's wait and see.'

Marcelius didn't answer her. They began walking. But in the middle of her unhappiness Fredrikke kept her head and she said suddenly:

'At least you mustn't give him the boat for nothing.'

'No, no,' answered Marcelius.

At the crossroads she gave him her hand and said:

'Now I better go home or he'll be cross with me. I think maybe he saw where I was going.'

Then they said goodnight to each other and went their separate ways.

The next day there was no wind and the sea was calm. Well before daybreak trusting old Joachim and his two sons had the new boat in position in the cradle on the north side of the island. Every able-bodied man had helped out so the fine new boat wouldn't get damaged while it was being transported. And now it hung there, trim and elegant in the cradle.

The old teacher had persuaded his brother-in-learning and colleague Simon Rust to postpone his return to Church Island until after the day's meal, and now it was time to leave. The atmosphere between the newly engaged couple didn't seem to have improved since yesterday, on the contrary they kept their distance from each other as they walked along the path, and she, who should have been so full of love, seemed instead to be filled with doubt. When they reached the pulley Joachim and his men were already gathered there. All bared their heads to the two schoolteachers and their party.

'Is everything ready?' asks Simon.

Joachim answers:

'Everything ready. Far as we can tell.'

Tormented by her doubt Fredrikke suddenly says loudly:

'You be careful, Marcelius. Can't someone else go in the boat for you today?'

Everyone is listening.

'Oh, he knows what he's doing,' says Joachim, the boy's father.

'What a sight that thing is with a name on it.'

'On the contrary it is an excellent name,' says her father tolerantly. 'This is something you don't understand, Fredrikke.'

Then Simon Rust says without any preamble:

'I'll go in the boat myself.'

Everybody tries to stop him, but Simon clambers up and sits down. For several minutes they plead with him. Simon answers, proud and eloquent:

'Fredrikke's mind must be put at rest.'

'Then at least rope yourself in,' says Joachim, and hands him a line.

Provoked, Simon cries, 'Lower away!'

The chocks are removed. The boat begins to descend. Simon takes the loop of elastic dangling from his hat and ties the end of it round a button.

Joachim shouts. Simon responds from further down the cliff, but neither one can seen the other. Simon is so sure of himself that his responses get shorter and shorter, because he really can't be bothered to make a fuss about such a simple business. In the end he falls completely silent. Marcelius has nothing to do and stands off to one side.

'He must be over halfway,' says Joachim. 'He's man enough for the job.'

Then there's a shout from far below, in a language no one understands. There's no 'avast a bit now' and 'now she's down', instead there's a 'Hey! Hey!' followed by forceful tugs on the signalling rope. Up on the clifftop they assume he wants them to hoist him up a bit and Joachim and his men haul on the ropes. Then a sharp, piercing scream rises up from below, there's the thud of the boat hitting the rock-face, it made a sound as though the whole island were coughing.

Everyone goes pale. At the same time the pulley ropes slackened. There is shouting, questions. Joachim says: 'Lower away!' And a few moments later: 'Haul up!' But everyone knows it's no good, the boat is empty, Simon has upended it and fallen into the sea.

And in the middle of all this the church bells sound out to ring in Christmas. What sort of Christmas was it going to be now?

But Fredrikke never lost her head, she grabbed hold of Marcelius and said: 'God forgive me, but I'm glad it wasn't you. What are you waiting for? Aren't you going to run over to the south side and get a boat out and see if you can find him?'

And when everyone realised she was right a great crowd of the men ran down across the island. Only Joachim, the trusting old boat-builder, stayed where he was.

2

I can't stand here holding onto the boat for ever, thought Joachim. Either I drag it up again, and I haven't the men for that, or I let it down into the sea. He thought good and hard about it, then he let go the line.

Curiously, the line paid out for less than half a minute before it went slack in his hands. The boat had reached the sea.

Joachim couldn't understand it. He hauled up again a fathom and paid out again. Again the boat reached the sea. Joachim was overcome by a great happiness and looked round for someone to tell the news to. If the boat was no more than a couple of fathoms above the surface of the sea then Simon Rust could not have been crushed by it. The question now was, had he drowned?

'Hurry lads!' Joachim shouted over to the south side. 'He might be all right!'

And still holding the slack rope he felt a tug on it, as though someone had taken control of the boat down below. It's probably just the undertow making the boat pitch, thought Joachim. He shouted down:

'Are you all right?'

But there was just the heavy soughing of the Atlantic, and he got no answer.

He held onto the line the whole time. He could have made it fast and waited at his ease; but Joachim thought this was not the time to be saving his strength. Here before his very eyes a man of great learning and deep insights might have been lost to them. Just so does the value of life overrule every consideration of common sense.

A long quarter of an hour went by. With the wind in the right direction Joachim could hear the chiming of the bells over on Church Island, heightening the mystery and the seriousness of the occasion for him. Then he heard far below him the voices of the rescuers. His own boys were rowing the boat so he knew they would soon be on the scene. Joachim held his breath and listened.

'There he is!' says Marcelius.

'Is he there?' the father asks from the clifftop.

Shortly afterwards he feels his line being untied from the boat, he leans over the abyss and shouts:

'Is he alive?'

'Yes he is!' answered Marcelius. 'You can haul up your line.'

'Thank God for that!' muttered Joachim. He hauled the line up, put a plug of tobacco into his mouth and made his way down to the landing place on the south side to meet the others. On the way the mostly trusting old boat-builder entertained a few thoughts of his own on the subject of Simon Rust and his narrow escape. That Simon was a clever man and a deep-thinking trickster: maybe he turned the boat over himself and jumped into the sea when he had no more than a couple of fathoms to go. Shame on his trickery! thought Joachim.

He met the teacher and his daughter at the landing place and said:

'He's been rescued.'

'Rescued?' cried Fredrikke. 'Are you joking?'

'He's been rescued.'

The old teacher too said 'Thank God for that' and was very happy. But Fredrikke was quiet and pensive . . .

When the boats reached the landing place Simon Rust was sitting at the oars and rowing with all his might; he was soaking wet from head to foot and freezing cold.

'Did you hurt yourself?' asked Fredrikke. 'Where's your hat?'

'We didn't find it,' said Marcelius.

'Then you might let him borrow yours for the time being,' said Fredrikke with a show of concern for Simon.

'He wouldn't have it,' answered Marcelius.

'No, you'll have to forgive me but I wouldn't take it,' said Simon too and was very proud of himself, though he was shivering with cold.

The old teacher asked his colleague and brother-in-learning all about the accident, and Simon told him; it seemed to Joachim that when these two had the stage to themselves the language they spoke was a rare and profound thing: Simon Rust explained that he had learnt to swim at the seminary, and it was thanks to this that he was saved. Yet he had known something of the torments of Tantalus in the moments before the rescue boat hove into sight. He wanted to tell the whole story just exactly as it had actually happened, so that later there would be no rival version of events.

'There's just one thing I'd like to know,' he said, addressing Fredrikke. 'How did you, Fredrikke, react when the boat turned over?'

'React?' said Fredrikke.

'What was the first thing you said?'

Fredrikke quickly regained her composure.

'I was the one who told people to hurry down and rescue you.'

'That's good then,' said Simon.

Marcelius was silent. He understood that now Simon Rust had all her heart again.

'Let us go home at once and get you a dry suit of clothes to put on,' said the old teacher. 'It is in truth a divine miracle that you have survived such a catastrophe.'

Everyone helped to drag the boats ashore and Marcelius treated them both alike, putting chocks under Simon's boat as well as his own so that the wind wouldn't turn them. He let the others go on ahead and set off unhappily for home.

In the evening Fredrikke paid a visit to the house next door, but she didn't call in to see Marcelius. He stood on the doorstep to watch out for her, and when she came by he said:

'Good evening. I see you're out walking in the northern lights?'

'I have an errand,' she answered. 'What do you think of that miracle today?'

Marcelius answered:

'I'll tell you just what I think: that business today wasn't any kind of miracle at all.'

'Really. But if you'd been thrown out of the boat, would you have been able to save yourself?'

'He wasn't thrown out the boat. He just jumped out a couple of fathoms above the sea. My father says.'

'So he jumped out did he? Really. You would have been even less likely to do that.'

Marcelius was silent.

'Because you can't swim,' continued Fredrikke. 'And you don't have the learning he has. And you can't play the organ.'

'So I suppose then that you two are going to have each other,' said Marcelius.

'I don't know what will happen,' she answered. 'But that's almost the way it seems.'

Marcelius said bitterly:

'I don't care, you and him you can have the boat for nothing, like I already said.'

Fredrikke thought about this, then answered:

'Yes all right, if we do get engaged then we can have the boat for nothing, as you say. But if he decides to break up then you and me will probably end up together and in that case we'll make him pay for the boat.'

Marcelius showed no surprise at her decision. He asked:

'When will I know?'

Fredrikke answered:

'He's going home tomorrow, so he's bound to say something then. But of course I can't ask him, you know.'

But Marcelius had to wait several months before he knew for certain.

Simon Rust went home for Christmas and he didn't come to any agreement with Fredrikke before he left. Later he went courting several places on Church Island and always got a yes on account of his father's wealth. But Simon didn't commit himself anywhere and kept himself a free man through it all. Finally he even tried the governess at the rectory, but she was a lady and much too good for him, so Simon Rust got a no there.

Fredrikke heard all about this and it bothered her more than she cared to admit.

On Twelfth Night there was to be a dance as in previous years at Joachim the boat-builder's house, and as usual Marcelius played the host. The fiddle player was booked and Didrik who was just the man for lilting and humming was also booked in good time before. The boys had already invited the girls and Fredrikke had promised Marcelius she would come.

Then one day a four-oared boat came to the island and old Rust the fisherman had sent it with a message that Fredrikke was to come over to a dance on Church Island that evening. Fredrikke got ready at once and put on her very finest clothes for the party.

Marcelius came to the house and said to her:

'Well well, I suppose now you'll be making up your mind?'

'Yes, now I'll be able to make up my mind,' answered Fredrikke.

She sat in the boat all the way over and looked as though she knew exactly what she was going to do.

Rust the great fisherman came to meet her and in the evening when the dancing began she was a favourite with all the Church Island boys. As for Simon, the son of the house, he fooled around as usual with this one and that one and wanted to keep Fredrikke guessing as before.

At intervals throughout the evening coffee and drinks were served to the guests and old Rust was a generous host; he spent the time sitting in comfort in an alcove with several other old fishermen. Simon Rust took a glass or two so as not to seem superior, but with him being a schoolteacher and all it wasn't really proper for him actually to dance with the fishermen's daughters.

Late on everyone went home and Fredrikke was left alone with Simon because she was going to spend the night there. But even now Simon wasn't any more affectionate towards her than before and she would have to be stupid if she took the little digs he was giving her in the side for undying love.

'I'm just standing here to cool down,' said Fredrikke.

'You shouldn't do that,' answered Simon, 'it could easily have unfortunate consequences for your health.'

'God knows why that barn door is open,' said Fredrikke and pointed.

Simon didn't know why either.

'Let's close it,' she said.

Fredrikke looked inside the barn and said:

'Let me see how much feed you've got.'

Both of them went inside.

'We've got hay on this floor here and we've got hay on that floor there,' said Simon.

'Where?'

Simon climbed down into the hay and showed her.

Fredrikke climbed down after him.

3

Still Fredrikke kept up Marcelius's hopes with a sort of half-promise that she might yet be his, and so he went on patiently waiting. But by Shrovetide in March Fredrikke knew what she wanted and she said to Marcelius that no, there was nothing else for it, Simon was the one who would have her.

'Yes, yes,' said Marcelius.

And he didn't mention the boat again. She might as well have the boat for nothing now, he didn't care a damn. He had had good time to prepare himself for such a fate, and for the rest of the spring Marcelius could be seen carrying on at his work as before. But in his mind his mood was much changed and he spent a lot of time on his own.

And the days grew long, the sun and fair weather melted the snow and soon there was no more launching of boats down the glacier on the northern side. For a couple of weeks the boat-builders were idle; but once the spring storms were over and the Atlantic calm again the boat-builders began fishing in the home waters round the island. On one such trip Marcelius and his brother earned a lot of money from the salvage of a schooner that had lost her mast and was drifting abandoned at sea.

There was no doubt about it, Marcelius's reputation on the island was much enhanced after this, and since he went daily to tend the wreck where it lay moored off the landing place he became almost like the captain of the abandoned ship. He was contacted by the Danish ship-owners and the salvage they paid him was a lot of money by the standards of Blue Man's Island. It caused a sensation, and people said that Marcelius the boat-builder was going to set himself up in business on the island and call himself Joachimson.

One day he visited Fredrikke and said:

'So you really are going to have Simon?'

'Yes,' she said, 'I am.'

She walked back over to his house with him, knitting as they walked. She said:

'If this had been in the old days I would have asked you to row over to Simon and fetch him here for me. But you're such a big man now, Marcelius.'

Marcelius answered:

'I'll show you I'm no bigger now than I was before.'

And he rowed over to fetch Simon.

After Simon had been and gone Marcelius again went to Fredrikke and asked, in his blindness:

'So you're both still absolutely certain?'

She answered:

'Yes. And now there's a special reason to get it arranged as soon as possible.'

'Then there's no point in asking any more.'

'You know how a heart is,' said Fredrikke. 'I've never loved anyone as much as I love him.'

Marcelius didn't respond to this, it was all just fancy book-talk. He invited her in for coffee, but she said no thanks, he wasn't to put himself out. As she was about to leave she remembered the boat.

'You don't expect any money for that boat now do you?' she said. 'Now that you're rich? Simon told me to ask.'

'No I don't care about the boat,' he answered. 'I've got enough, thank God, of money and importance. When are you going to publish the banns?'

'In two weeks.'

'Have you thought of going out for the island sheep this year?' he asked.

She answered:

'Let's wait a couple of weeks for that too. It's still too early, the snow hasn't gone yet.'

'I was only asking,' he said.

The island sheep were Icelandic sheep, with thick rough coats.

They were turned out onto an island where they lived the whole year round and foraged for themselves. Once a year, in the spring when the weather was mild, they were rounded up for shearing.

Two weeks later the banns were read for Fredrikke and Simon Rust in the church on Church Island. People had waited a long time for it, and at last these two had become a couple. That same evening Fredrikke paid a visit to Joachim the boat-builder's house and she was in a joking and light-hearted mood.

'Good luck and God bless!' said the boat-builder's wife. 'I heard your name from the pulpit today.'

'Are you sure you heard right?' said Fredrikke for a joke.

'Good luck and God bless!' said Marcelius too. 'Have you thought any more about the island sheep?'

Fredrikke laughed and answered:

'You're in such a hurry to get the island sheep done this year. What's the matter with you? You were talking about it as early as May.'

'I felt it was something I had ask to you,' he answered.

'As a matter of fact the reason I came here today is to tell you that you can have someone to go with you to the island sheep tomorrow,' said Fredrikke.

He asked quickly:

'Someone to go with me? Then I suppose you can't be bothered yourself this year?'

She had half a mind to give it a miss this spring; but Marcelius's crafty question made her flush slightly and she answered:

'Can't be bothered? And would you mind telling me why I can't be bothered?'

No, Fredrikke wasn't the kind of girl to take to her bed every time she had a little morning sickness. This year just like every other year she would help round up the sheep.

As soon as he heard this Marcelius went outside and wouldn't come back in again until she was gone.

Marcelius climbed down the couple of steps to the rocks where the boat-building yard stood. There was a long hollow fitted out as a slipway with stocks for all kinds of boats from ketches to the biggest rowing boats. Here he tidied up and swept the floor. It was the end of May, there was daylight until after eleven at night. He strolled on down to the landing place. His four-oar lay there resting on its chocks as though it was looking at him. It was midnight before he returned home.

He did not take off his clothes but remained sitting at the side of the bed. His elder brother was already sleeping. Marcelius went to the window and looked out for a long time. 'Well well well well well,' he murmured. 'Oh Jesus, Jesus.' Then he went back to the bed. He lay down fully clothed, curled up, and didn't sleep all night. As soon as he heard his mother starting the fire downstairs he got up, woke his brother and went down. It was only four o'clock.

'You're up early,' said his mother.

'I'm thinking about those island sheep,' he answered. 'If we want to get them all sheared today we need an early start.'

They got ready all three of them, the brothers and the mother, and then walked over to the teacher's house and waited outside for Fredrikke. Fredrikke had just the maid with her. That made five of them in the boat.

The brothers rowed strongly and steadily and the women talked together. The sun rose and the sheep-island floated still and heavy on the sea. From a long way off the sheep had seen the boat coming, they stood as though amazed and stared, and they stopped chewing. So as not to alarm the timid creatures they made as little noise as possible in the boat.

But the sheep had forgotten the visit of a similar boat the year before, they had never in their lives seen such a sight. They let the boat approach and in their wondrous silliness did nothing about it; only once the boat landed did a large, shaggy wether begin to tremble. It glanced quickly at its fellow-sheep, then at the boat again. Suddenly—when the five people stood still a moment on the beach and the boat was hauled up—it seemed to the wether that this exceeded any danger it had ever come across before, it whirled round and ran wildly for the interior of the island. All the other sheep followed after.

'Those sheep won't be any easier to catch this year,' said the women to each other.

The whole group moved up the island. The first thing was to get hold of a lamb, that way the mother would be easier to catch. They worked until well into the morning before they managed to catch a full-grown animal. A flock was driven down towards the boat, in their mortal terror they ran straight into the sea and Marcelius waded out and caught them one after the other.

'Now you've got wet,' said Fredrikke.

While all three women sat and sheared the brothers stood by with three more sheep which they had collared. Marcelius was standing near Fredrikke. The spring sun shone warm and bright on them all.

'That was my second,' said Fredrikke as she stuffed the wool into a sack and stood up.

'Let's see if we two can catch a sheep on our own,' said Marcelius with a strange tremor in his voice.

Fredrikke went with him and they walked out of earshot of the others.

'I think they must be in another place,' said Fredrikke.

Marcelius answered:

'Let's just look here first.'

They came to the northern side, which was in shade; but they saw no sheep there.

'They must be right out on the point,' said Marcelius, and he hurried off. But Fredrikke wasn't as light of foot as she used to be and she couldn't keep up. Marcelius took her by the hand and helped her along, at the same time speaking in an unnaturally loud voice and saying:

'Now you'll see, now you'll see!'

'Don't shout so loudly you'll scare the sheep,' said Fredrikke, who was thinking about the work.

But he kept dragging her along and talking in a loud, wild voice:

'Now you'll see! And I'll teach you how to play the organ.'

'What's the matter with you?' she asked and tried to read his face.

And his face was unrecognisable.

Then she tried to resist and make herself heavy, slipping down the cliff in her shoes as Marcelius dragged her along. She realised that she was about to be killed and her courage faded away. Without a word or a scream she was dragged to the point and thrown over the edge. So stiff with fear was she that she hadn't even grabbed hold of Marcelius's clothes, so he remained standing where he was on the point, even though his intention had been to go over the edge with her.

He looked round cautiously to see if the others had followed, but there was no sign of anyone. He peered over the point. Down below the sea sighed heavily. It had already swallowed Fredrikke. Marcelius straightened his waistcoat and made ready to jump. Then he abandoned that idea and began looking for a way down. While descending he sought carefully with his feet for toe-holds, so that he wouldn't slip. Halfway down it occurred to him that it would scarcely matter if he fell and hurt himself. Yet he continued to look for footholds with great care.

The sea came right up to the cliff-face, and when he was no more than two fathoms above it Marcelius stopped. He took off his jacket and waistcoat and left them on the rocks so that someone else would be able to use them. Then he put his hands together and asked God to have mercy on his soul for the sake of the Lord Jesus Christ. Then he jumped.

CHRISTMAS PARTY

A sleigh approaches at speed with its bells jingling. Frost, snow and stars.

A young couple aboard the sleigh. They don't converse; she doesn't answer a word he says. At the bridge where the wind is fiercest he asks if she is cold. She answers curtly that she is cold. Passing the great fields he says:

'Well, almost there now.'

They were almost there, the lights from the yard were already in sight. The hired hand, the labourer stood in the farmyard.

'Good evening, Brede,' say the strangers.

'Good evening,' replies the labourer and takes the reins.

The young wife steps down from the sledge, pulls off her mitten and offers her hand to the labourer. They knew each other. Her hand was cold, his was warm.

They don't converse, he says merely:

'It's Martha.'

She goes straight into the house with her husband and Brede leads the horses to the stable.

A few minutes later Brede goes into the kitchen and sits down on the long bench. He's a strong man, young, tall, well built. Noise and laughter from the living rooms penetrates to the kitchen; evidently there is a party going on. The maids are busy with the food.

The door opens and Martha comes in.

She greets all the servants and pats the dog, then she turns to Brede and asks him to look for her mitten which she must have dropped out by the sledge. As she speaks the light from the lamp falls on her face, she is buxom, young, blonde. Brede looks at her for a moment then goes out in silence.

Shortly afterwards Martha goes out too. She meets Brede by the sleigh.

'Have you found the mitten?' she asks.

'No,' he answers.

They both search for a while. She says:

'You haven't changed much this past year.'

'Oh yes,' he answers, 'this has been a long year.'

'Yes,' she says too, 'this has been a long year. Not once have you been over our way.'

They don't find the mitten. They stand at the foot of the steps. He says:

'You're cold, Martha, you have so little on.'

'I don't care,' she answers softly.

Her husband comes out. His face is lively, amused, he's had several good drinks. Martha glances at him quickly then goes in.

'Come and have a drink, Brede,' says her husband cheerfully.

They both go into the kitchen and a bottle is brought. By the third glass Brede is unwilling to continue, but the husband presses him. He drinks a fourth glass, gets to his feet and leaves the kitchen.

He makes his way to the servants' quarters. Two of the other workers are sitting there playing cards by candlelight. It is almost eight o'clock.

Brede sits on his own. Presently he hears footsteps in the hall.

It's the boy with the food, he thinks. Martha appears.

'Aren't you playing cards?' she asks Brede.

'No,' he answers.

'Then will you help me with something out here?' she continues.

Brede follows her out.

'What is it?' he asks.

She doesn't answer. It's dark in the hall. She has taken hold of his hand and he can hear her heart beating.

'It's strange to see you again,' she says.

Brede doesn't respond. She asks:

'Perhaps you don't care for me any more?'

'No,' he answers. 'Go in now, Martha.'

A minute passes. Suddenly she lets go of his hand, shoves it away from her and in anger says:

'Well, get out of the way, let me pass.'

He stood aside, confused and surprised. He looked out into the yard, she had already disappeared.

The food came, Brede went into the kitchen and sat down with the other servants at the long table. In the middle of the meal Martha's husband enters again with the bottle. His face is even redder, more animated. He treats everyone, but above all Brede. Martha comes in too. She laughs loudly and walks with her husband.

'Give Brede a drink,' she says.

Her husband fills Brede's glass. Brede drinks every time; then suddenly he says.

'Why do you want me to drink so much?'

'Drink,' answers the husband.

Brede gets up angrily from the table, grabs his hat and leaves.

'After him!' shouts Martha.

All laugh. Martha runs out after him, her husband follows with the bottle, laughing and cheering. More and more people leave the house to watch, among them Martha's father, owner of the farm, who holds his belly and shakes with laughter. Brede sets off running towards the barn, sees he's being followed and begins resolutely to climb up the tall barn-ladder. Higher and higher he climbs, all the way to the top, and then onto the barn roof. He sits down in the snow. The moon has risen, the evening is clear and bright.

'Be careful, it's dangerous up there,' shouts Martha.

Brede doesn't answer.

'It's dangerous up there, isn't it?' she cries again. Her face is anxious.

Brede doesn't answer. The moon lights up his big body and casts a shadow across the roof.

'After him, Paul!' says Martha angrily, slowly.

Her husband begins to climb up the ladder. He laughs and speaks to those below, climbs on, reaches the topmost rung, sticks his head up over the edge of the roof and nods to Brede.

'Brede,' he says.

'What do you want?' answers Brede. 'I'll chuck you down on top of her.'

Paul climbs up onto the roof.

'Yes chuck me down on top of her, you're the very man who could do that,' he says. He speaks to Brede in a friendly, agreeable way, slaps him on the shoulder. He offers him a swig from the bottle. Brede accepts to please him.

They remain sitting up there. The guests at the party go back in again to their food. Brede drinks and drinks from the bottle. Paul embraces him. They drink to their friendship.

'You knew Martha before me,' says Paul, blinking, laughing. 'The two of you almost grew up together.'

Brede asks suspiciously:

'What do you want me to tell you? Ask her yourself.'

'Give Brede another drink,' Martha shouts up.

'Do you want to get me wrecked, is that it?' Brede asks back.

The bottle is empty. Brede sits swaying on the roof. Down below Martha stands and sees everything.

'Christmas comes but once a year,' Paul says with a simple expression on his face. He begins to climb slowly down the ladder.

'Wait!' Brede shouts to him. 'Is there any left in that bottle?' He waves his arms and looks down stiff-eyed into the yard. He scoops snow from the roof and showers it over Paul, laughing and cheering at the top of his voice.

When Paul reached the bottom his wife said:

'Take the ladder away.'

Brede hears her up on the roof and answers:

'Yes take the ladder away. I'll jump down.'

He stands up and prepares to leap, slips, falls backwards onto the roof. Dull and drunken he lies there and sees the ladder being lifted away.

All is quiet on the farm. He looks down, sees no one and assumes he is alone. The ladder is lifted up again and put back where it was but he doesn't notice, his eyes are closed.

'Bring the ladder back,' he says to himself. The cold affects him, he falls asleep and wakes up with a start. 'Come back with the ladder and I'll give you something,' he says into the air. 'I've got something for you.' Confused and hopelessly drunk he braces his hands against the roof and lets himself slide down into the yard.

Someone screams, men's voices join in, he is surrounded.

'But the ladder was there,' says Martha in horror. 'I put it back, there it is.'

Brede rolls round a couple of times in the snow then gets to his feet. He has bloodied his forehead, but the fall clears his head and he begins to laugh in surprise, wiping the blood off with a comical expression. Unable to stand still he staggers about until one of the other workers grabs his arm to steady him. His jacket comes undone and a mitten falls out.

Martha's eyes open wide and her face lights up in ecstasy. She approaches, picks up the mitten and puts it in her pocket. 'He had my mitten,' she says quietly. 'He had it all the time.'

She goes in with Brede and bandages him. Gradually his drunkenness abates and his strong head reasserts itself. But he still has outbursts of raving, and when his legs are examined it emerges that one of them is broken. Martha kneels in front of him and quickly loosens his shoelaces . . .

Two years later Martha was widowed. The year after that the stiff-legged Brede became her husband.

A REAL RASCAL

I met him in a cemetery. I did nothing to encourage him, but he latched onto me at once. I simply sat down on a bench on which he was already sitting and said:

'Am I disturbing you?'

That's how it began.

'Not at all,' he replied, and made room for me. 'I was just sitting here contemplating the kingdom of the dead.' He gestured with his hand over the graves.

This was in Christ's Cemetery.

As the morning progressed it had grown more and more lively up there. One by one the bricklayers and workers arrived, and the old watchman was already sitting in his little shed reading newspapers. Here and there women in black busied themselves planting or watering flowers or trimming long grass. And high in the chestnut trees the birds sang.

He was a complete stranger to me. A young man, big and broad-shouldered, unshaven, his clothes rather worn and shabby. The furrows in his brow, the authority in his voice, his way of blinking thoughtfully after he said something, all of this gave him an aura of being older than his years.

'You're a stranger here?'

'I've been away from home for the past nine years,' he replied.

He leaned back, stretched his legs and looked out across the cemetery. German and French newspapers stuck out of his pockets. 'A cemetery like this is such a sad place,' he said. 'So much death in one place. So much energy expended and so little achieved.'

'What makes you say that?'

'This is a military cemetery.'

Aha—pacifism again! I thought.

He continued:

'But the most disgraceful thing of all is the celebration of the dead, these rituals of grieving.'

A pious futility . . .

He gestured rapidly and sat up straight.

'Do you realise there's a fortune in granite here? And then these expensive bouquets of flowers just thrown on the dirty ground. We buy comfortable benches to sit and weep on, conjure images of holy heathendom from the quarries up on Grefsen Hill—this cemetery is a petrified treasure trove. It's one of the least rundown areas in town . . . It makes you think, doesn't it,' he continued. 'Once it's put here this wealth stays here, it's untouchable, because it's dead. All it requires thereafter is management, that's to say, proper looking after—the tears, the flowers withering and dead on the sandheaps, the wreaths that cost up to 50 kroner each.'

A socialist! I thought. A travelling tradesman who's been abroad and learned to raise his voice against capital—capital!

'Are you a stranger in town as well?' he asked.

'Yes.'

Again he leaned back on the bench, blinked and thought, blinked and thought.

Two figures pass by, old, both with sticks, backs bowed, reverent, talking to each other in whispers—parents, perhaps, on their way to a grave. A puff of wind lifts the dust and the powdered remains of flowers into the air and rustles through the dried leaves along the footpaths.

'Look!' he cried suddenly, without changing position, indicating the direction with his eyes. 'See the lady coming towards us? Watch her when she passes us.'

Nothing simpler. She almost touched us with her black dress and her veil brushed against our hats. She was followed by a little girl carrying some flowers and a woman with a rake and watering-can. All three disappeared around the corner leading to the lower part of the cemetery.

'Well?' he said.

'Well?'

'You didn't notice anything?'

'Nothing unusual. She looked at us.'

'Begging your pardon, she looked at me. You smile, you want to reassure me that there won't be any argument between us on that score. The fact is, she passed by here a few days ago. I was sitting here talking to the gravedigger, trying to sow a little seed of doubt in his mind about his highly respectable job . . .'

'Why did you do that?'

'Because he disturbs the lie of the earth to no good purpose and creates untold difficulties for the forms of life that have to live on it.'

A poor, confused freethinker! Where in the Bible does it say that the dead shall not be buried in the earth? Now you're beginning to bore me. All this I said to myself.

'I sat here talking to the gravedigger. "It's a sin," I said. The lady was just passing. She heard me and looked at me, because I was talking about sin in a holy place. Apropos: did you notice the old woman carrying a rake and a watering-can in her worn-out old hands? And her back, how bent it was? That creature has literally worn herself out digging up the earth, ruining it, the source of life. And did you see, just three paces behind that lady on her way to grieve at a grave—but that's not what I meant: did you see what the little girl was carrying?'

'Flowers.'

'Camellias. Roses. Did you notice? Flowers that cost a kroner each. Lovely flowers, that live preposterously sensitive lives. A little bit too much sunshine and they're dead. In four days' time they'll be tossed over the fence into the garden there, and be replaced by new ones.'

At this point I gave the freethinker my answer:

'At least they don't cost as much as the pyramids!'

It didn't have the effect I had expected. He seemed to have heard the argument before.

'In those days they didn't need it,' he said. 'And Egypt was the granary for the whole Roman Empire, the world wasn't so small then as it is now—and I know a little bit about how small it is now—or rather, not me personally, but someone I know. Anyway, the pyramid in the desert is one thing, a well-maintained modern grave is another. Look around you! Hundreds of graves, expensive monuments and monuments that were just granite borders on the ground, from Grefsen Hill at 3 kroner 60 the ell, with turfs from Ekeberg costing 2 kroner 50 per square cord. Not to mention the inscriptions and the fancy carving on the stones themselves, polished or unpolished, carved or hewn, red, white, green; and just think of all that turf! I was talking to the gravedigger about it, the demand's just too great, you can hardly get it now. And I ask you to remember the importance of turf on this earth: turf is life itself.'

I objected then that life itself could not and should not be stripped of all idealism. There was after all an ethical aspect to our practice of reserving a certain amount of turfs for our dead. And as a matter of fact I still believe that today.

'Look here,' said the man heatedly, 'whole families could live on what's wasted daily up here, children cared for, the destitute provided for. I know for a fact that that young woman down there is planting camellias that cost the same as two dresses from the market—for a little child. When grief can afford that kind of indulgence it becomes gluttony.'

I was convinced that he was a socialist, possibly even an anarchist who enjoyed turning serious matters upside down. I listened to him with less and less interest.

He went on:

'Then you've got the watchman sitting up there. Do you know what his job is, apart from spelling his way through the newspapers? It's to guard the graves. Law and order even for the dead. I told him when I came here earlier today that if I happened to see some child up here stealing flowers in order to pay for her schoolbooks, some frightened, skinny little girl nicking a camellia for her food then I wouldn't tell on her, I'd help her. ''That would be what I would call a sin,'' said the old watchman. ''A sin,'' he said. A starving man stops you in the street one day and asks you what time it is. You take your watch out—now look at his eyes! Like lightning he grabs the watch from you and off he runs. You've got two options. You can report the incident and in a couple of days' time you'll have your watch back after it turns up in some pawnbrokers. And within twenty-four hours you'll probably have your thief as well. Or you

can say nothing. That's your other option. Say nothing . . . Actually
I'm rather tired, I've been up all night.'

'Have you now? Well, time's getting on, I'd better be getting off
to work.'

I stood up to go.

He pointed down in the direction of the sea and the docks.

'I've been down there among the shop doorways and back alleys
trying to find out how the hungry and the needy sleep at night. But
listen—the world is full of so many strange things:

One day nine years ago I was sitting here—in fact I believe it
was the exact same bench—and something happened to me that I've
never been able to forget. It was late on in the day, most people had
gone home. A stone-carver who'd been lying flat on a marble stone
over there carving some inscription had finally given up for the day,
put on his jacket, stuffed his tools into his pockets and left. A wind
got up, it was already billowing in the chestnut trees and a tall iron
cross that was hereabouts—it's gone now—was swaying slightly. I
buttoned up my jacket too and was about to go when the gravedigger
came hurrying round that corner over there, no coat on, no hat, and
asked if a little girl in a yellow dress carrying a satchel had gone
by.

I couldn't recall having seen her. What was the problem?

"She's stolen some flowers," said the gravedigger. He hurried
off.

I sat here until presently he came back again.

"Did you find her?"

"No. But I've closed the gate."

A proper search was about to be made, the little girl was bound
to be still inside the cemetery and now he would track her down.
This was the third incident of pilfering that day. Schoolchildren,
bright young girls who understood quite well that it was wrong.
What do they do with them? They sell them. Make bouquets out of
them and sell them—nice kids, eh?

I went along with the gravedigger and helped for a while in his
search for the child. But she'd hidden herself well. We had the
watchman with us, and the three of us searched everywhere without
finding her. As dusk fell we abandoned our search.

"Which grave was robbed?"

"That one there. A child's grave. Can you imagine?"

I walked over. Now as it happened I knew that grave. I knew the dead little girl too, in fact we had buried her earlier that day. The flowers were gone, even my own, I couldn't see them anywhere.

"We've got to keep on looking," I said to the others. "This is an outrage."

It really wasn't the gravedigger's responsibility, but he took part anyway as a matter of principle, and all three of us resumed the search. Suddenly, down where the path turns, I caught sight of a little person, a child, sitting hunched up on the ground, just behind Dr With's large, polished stone. She was staring at me. Her little neck was right down between her shoulder-blades.

But I knew her: it was the dead girl's sister.

"Little friend, what are you doing here so late?"

She didn't answer and she didn't move. I helped her up, picked up her satchel, and said I would take her home with me. "Little Hanna wouldn't like it if she knew you were sitting here this long for her sake."

So she came with me. I spoke to her:

"Did you know that some naughty little girl has stolen the flowers from Hanna's grave? A little girl in a yellow dress, have you seen her? Never mind, we'll catch her later."

And she walked along beside me, still without answering.

"Ah, you've got her!" I heard the gravedigger shout. "You've caught the thief!"

"What?"

"What? You're holding her hand."

I had to smile.

"No you're wrong there, this isn't the thief. This is the little sister of the girl who was buried today. Her name's Elina, I know her."

But the gravedigger was convinced he was right. The watchman recognised her too, she had that red scar on one side of her chin. She'd stolen flowers from her sister's grave and the little wretch couldn't even bring herself to say she was sorry.

Now I ask you to note this particularly: I had known these two sisters for a long time. We lived in the same decrepit building and I had often seen them playing under my window. Now and then they might argue furiously and hit each other; but they were good children both of them, and they always sided with each other against outsiders. This was hardly something they could have learned at home, since their mother was more or less a slut who was never there, and they had never known their father—as a matter of fact I think they each had their own father. These two children lived in a tiny cubicle not much bigger than that stone over there, and as my room was right opposite theirs I could see into it when I stood at my window. Hanna was the leader, she was a couple of years older and very mature in many of her ways. She was always the one who took out the tin box when they were going to have a slice of bread, and in summer when it got so hot in the yard it was Hanna who had the idea of fixing a sheet of newspaper over the window to keep out the worst of the heat. And quite often I heard her going through her little sister's homework with her before they left for school. Hanna was old before her time, and her life was a short one.

"Let's look in her satchel," said the gravedigger.

And sure enough, there in her satchel were the flowers. I even recognised my own two or three among them.

What could I say? She stood there, the little sinner, an unapologetic look on her face. I gave her a shaking and asked her for an explanation; she said nothing. Then the gravedigger said something about the police and went off with her.

Up by the gate she seemed finally to realise what was happening:

"Hey, where are you taking me?" she burst out.

The gravedigger replied:

"To the police-station."

"I didn't steal them," she said.

Hadn't she stolen them? But she had them in her satchel, we'd seen them—But she repeated feverishly that she had not stolen them.

At the gate the sleeve of little Elina's frock got hooked up and almost torn off, you could see the white of her skinny little arm inside it.

And so it was off to the police-station, and I went along. A few statements were taken, but no further action was taken against Elina, as far as I know. As for me, I didn't see her again after that, because I travelled away and didn't come back for nine years.

But now I've found out more about the matter. We were completely wrong to treat her as we did. Of course she hadn't stolen the flowers; but what if she had? What I'm saying is this: why not? Have you ever heard of anything worse than the way we treated her? Yet no judge would have found against us, we merely apprehended her and brought her to justice. I've seen her since then. I could even take you to her.'

Here he paused.

'If you'll listen carefully to what I'm going to tell you then you might understand. "Listen," the dying child had said. "When I die there will probably be flowers for me, maybe quite a lot; because Teacher will probably send one, and that nice fru Bendiche will maybe send a whole wreath."

But that sick child knows as much as any adult. She's grown too fast to live and her illness has made her even sharper. When she speaks, the other one falls silent, her little sister, struggling to understand what's being said to her. They live alone and their mother is never home. But now and then fru Bendiche sends them a bite to eat, so they don't starve to death. The sisters never fall out now, it's a long time now since they last argued and their occasional spats in the playground are quite forgotten.

"Flowers are nice enough, but they wither too," says the dying girl. And what's the point of having withered flowers on your grave? The dead can't see them, and they won't keep you warm either. But could Elina remember the shoes they saw that time at the market? "Now they would keep you warm."

Elina remembered the shoes. And to show her sister how clever she was she described the shoes exactly for her.

It wasn't long now till winter. And there was such a draught coming through the floor over by the window, and the washing cloth froze on its peg on the wall.

Elina could have a pair of shoes like that.

The two sisters look at each other. Elina isn't stupid enough to believe this.

Yes, because she could take her flowers and sell them. Yes she could. There were always people out walking the streets on a Sunday who wanted to buy flowers. They were always driving out into the country with flowers in their buttonholes, and you were always seeing gentlemen driving along in hansom cabs with flowers in their buttonholes.

Elina asked if she could buy a little hat.

Yes, if there was any money left over. But first she was to buy the shoes.

So it was agreed. It had nothing to do with anyone else, it was an agreement between the two children. But Elina had to be sure and take the flowers that same day, before they began to fade.

How old was she, the sick child? About 12 or 13, I should think. It isn't always the age that matters. I had a sister who learnt Greek when she was *this* big.

All the same, Elina came off badly from the whole business. She wasn't punished, the police just gave her a bit of a scare and in that respect she got off lightly. Then the teacher began looking after her. Looking after a child means singling that child out, testing it, always watching it out of the corner of your eye. Elina has to stay behind at break time: "Little Elina, please just stay behind a moment or two, I'd like a word with you." Then she's rebuked in a firm, gentle fashion. Day in and day out reminded of this business, told to pray to God for forgiveness.

And something snaps inside her.

Elina becomes sloppy. She turns up with her face unwashed, she forgets to bring her books to school. An object of suspicion, followed always by these doubting eyes, she develops the habit of avoiding the teacher's gaze, of not looking anyone in the eye. Instead she steals quick, secretive looks at people that give her an air of flirtatiousness. And on the day of her Confirmation the priest gives her a booklet on the subject of one sin in particular, and the whole street has its ideas on the sort of future awaiting her. Then she leaves that block, moves out of that little room. The sun shines over the town, people wander the streets with flowers in their buttonholes; and she takes a drive out into the country in one of these hansom cabs . . .

I met her again last night. She lives down there, she stood in a doorway and whispered to me. She had no choice but to recognise me, I had heard her voice and seen the red scar. But my God, how fat she had become!

"Over here, it's me," she said.

"Yes it's me," I said. "How big you are now, Elina."

Big? What sort of thing was that to say? She didn't have time to stand about chatting, if I wouldn't go in with her then I had no right to hang around there scaring other folk off.

I reminded her of my name, of the yard we once lived in, talked about little Hanna, all I could recall. "Let's go inside and really talk together!" I said.

Once we were inside she asked:

"Have you got a little something for a drink?"

That's what she was like.

"Just think if Hanna could have been here now, we could have sat around the three of us and chatted away about all sorts of things."

Elina hooted with laughter.

"What are you babbling on about? Are you a child?"

"Don't you think of Hanna any more now?" I asked.

She spat in annoyance.

Hanna! Hanna! Did I imagine she was still a child? All this Hanna stuff happened long ago. What sort of nonsense was all this? Should she fetch us something to drink?

"Please do!"

She gets up and leaves the room.

I heard voices from the neighbouring rooms, the popping of corks, music, little squeals. Doors opened and banged shut. Now and then a voice out in the corridor shouted out an order to a serving maid.

Elina returned. She wanted to sit with me, sit in my lap. She lit a cigarette.

"Why can't I sit in your lap?" she asked.

"Because that's not what I want," I answered.

"Right then, you can just pay for the wine and go."

I said:

"Sit down quietly now and let's talk. Naturally I'll recompense you for your time." And I gave her some money, I didn't count exactly how much but it was a fair amount.

At once she calmed down and took a seat. But there was no

question of our having a conversation. If I asked her about something she invariably began by singing a snatch of song, or lighting another cigarette. She did not want to hear anything at all about the old days. That dirty old yard, was that anything to remember? Could she take a glass of wine out to the servant in the corridor?

"Of course."

"I'll tell you something, it's actually my mother. I got the job for her. She does well out of it."

She took the wine out to the corridor and returned.

"*Skål*, old pal!" she said.

And we drank the wine.

Again she said she wanted to sit in my lap.

"Doesn't it get boring here after a while?" I asked.

"Boring? No. Why won't you let me sit in your lap?"

"How long have you been here?"

"I can't remember exactly. What's the difference? *Skål*."

We drank. Again she sang a snatch of song, out of tune, some nonsense from a new show.

"Where did you hear that song?"

"At the Tivoli."

"Do you go there often?"

"Yes when I can afford it. But now I can't any more. The landlady's after me for money today. She takes such a big cut, she takes so much before there's any left over for us. You couldn't spare a bit more cash could you?"

I had, thank goodness, enough to let her have some more.

She took it without a thank-you, without any kind of response at all. But perhaps she felt a little bit happy inside. She asked me to order another bottle of wine. Obviously she felt I had to be taken for all I was worth.

The wine arrived.

But now she wanted to show me off. She wanted to call in a couple of the other girls and let them have a drink of the wine. The girls came. They wore short, starched skirts that rustled whenever they moved. Their arms were bare and their hair cut short.

Elina introduced me and remembered easily what my name was. In an affected manner she told them I had given her a lot of money, that I was a dear old friend and that all she had to do was ask and I would give her as much as she wanted. That's the way things had always been. That's how rich I was.

The girls drank and grew merry too, they competed with one another in making suggestive remarks and howling snatches of song. Elina got jealous when I addressed a remark to one of the others, she turned awkward and unpleasant. But I did it on purpose, to get Elina to be more forthcoming and give me some kind of insight into her state of mind. My ploy hadn't the desired effect, however. She tossed her head and said she had an appointment. Finally she grabbed her coat and got ready to leave.

"Are you going out?" I asked.

She didn't answer, just hummed, with a superior expression on her face, and put on her hat. Suddenly she opened the door into the corridor and called out:

"Gina!"

That was her mother.

She came shuffling along in her slippers, knocked, came in and stood waiting by the door.

"I told you I want that chest of drawers dusting every day!" said Elina haughtily. "Look at this filth! That sort of cleaning won't do for me I'll have you understand. And these photographs here should be wiped down every day too."

Her mother said "Yes!" and was about to leave again. Her face was a mass of wrinkles and her cheeks hollow. She listened obediently to her daughter, intently, so as to miss nothing.

"Now just you make sure you don't forget!" said Elina.

Her mother answered "No, I promise!" and then she left. She closed the door quietly behind her so as not to make any noise. But apart from that she looked like a pretty rough sort of character.

Elina stood there dressed and ready to go out. She turned to me and said:

"Well, I think it's best if you pay for the wine now and leave."

"Thanks," said the girls, and drained their glasses.

I was somewhat taken aback.

"The wine?" I said. "Hey wait a minute. The money I gave you was for the wine. Maybe I've got a little more.'' I searched my pockets again.

The girls began to laugh.

"So that's how rich he is! All that money you got off him, Elina, and now he can't pay for the wine! Ha ha ha!"

Elina was furious on my behalf.

"Get out!" she screamed. "I don't want you in here any more. Money? He's got money coming out of his ears. Look here at what he gave me!" And with a triumphant gesture she threw notes and coins down on the table. "He's paid for the wine and for me, see? You two have never seen so much money all at once, have you? I could pay the landlady for two months with that. What I said was just to tease him a bit, I was just mucking him about. Now get out of here!"

And the girls had to leave. Elina began laughing, a nervous, rasping laugh, as she locked the door after them.

"I don't really like them coming round," she said apologetically. "They're just a couple of tarts, boring, not really my friends. Didn't you find them boring too?"

"No I didn't," I replied, to make her even more ashamed of herself. "They answered whenever I asked them a question, told me whatever I wanted to know about them. They were decent girls."

"Then you can leave as well!" shouted Elina. "Go on, go after them if that's what you want. I'm not stopping you." And just to be on the safe side she scooped up the money lying on the table and put it away.

"There's something I'd really like to ask you about," I said, "if you would be kind enough just to sit down quietly and listen to me."

"Something to ask me about!" she answered witheringly. "I've got no business with you. I suppose it's about Hanna again? All this crap about Hanna makes me want to puke. I can't live off it."

"But don't you wish you could break away from this life?" I asked.

She pretended she hadn't heard me, again began fussing about the room, tidying away things, whistling to keep up her spirits.

"Away from this life?" she said suddenly, stationing herself directly in front of me. "Why? Where would I go? Who do you suppose would marry me? Who would have someone like me? And I refuse to work as a maid."

"You could try leaving the country and make a fresh start."

"Rubbish! Nonsense! Stop it! What are you, a missionary? Why leave the country? I'm doing okay, I'm managing all right. Listen, let's have some more wine? Just us two? Not those others . . . Gina!" she shouted through the door.

She demanded more wine, drank, grew less and less accusatory. I couldn't get any sense out of her, she just sat there humming snatches of the latest songs and thinking to herself. She drank more, and her laughter became repellent. She kept asking if she could sit on my knee, waggled the tip of her tongue at me and said "Look!" Finally she asked me straight:

"Are you staying the night?"

"No," I answered.

"Well then I'm going out," she said . . .'

The narrator fell silent.

'Well?' I asked.

'What would you have done, faced with a choice like that? Would you have stayed or left? See, that's the question. Do you want to know what I did?'

He looked at me.

'I stayed,' he said.

'You *stayed*?' I gasped, my mouth agape. 'The night? With the girl?'

'I am a disgrace,' he said.

'But for heaven's sake, what were you thinking of? Were you drunk?'

'That too, in the end. But of one thing I'm sure, I'm no more disgusting and repulsive than other people. This was a woman whose background I knew, and it was a touching and a disturbing story, and besides I felt the strangest urge to be utterly shameless. Do you understand? So I did. I was. And oh what a sea of shamelessness we did wallow in!'

This unprincipled cynic shook his head in recalling his own conduct.

'But now I'm going down to see her again,' he continued. 'Surely it's still not too late. I suppose you'll say I don't have the right? But maybe I'm not as disgraceful as you think. Last night, for example: remember, if it hadn't been me it would have been another, and a swap like that would almost certainly not have worked to her advantage. If she were able to choose her company I think she would have felt herself quite safe with me. I'm considerate, understanding, and I never forget for one moment to offer resistance. The strange thing is that it was precisely this aspect of my character which excited her most. She told me herself. "It's lovely the way you try to resist," she said. What is one to do when faced with such a woman? And remember too that the spoiling of her heart was a direct result of that business with the flowers. That's where it all started. If one were allowed to take flowers from a grave she would be today an honest woman. But see, we chased her, and caught her. And I helped! I helped!'

Again he shook his head in abject despair.

Presently he awoke as though from a trance.

'But I've kept you. And now I'm tired myself. Do you happen to have the time on you?'

I reached for my watch. It wasn't there, I had left it at home.

'Well thanks anyway, it doesn't really matter,' he said as he stood up, stretched his legs and pulled down the knees of his trousers. 'Look, here comes that lady again, the grieving is over, the little girl isn't carrying the flowers any more. They're down there, the roses, camellias. In four days' time they'll have withered. So if some little girl wants to take them to pay for a pair of shoes then I don't regard that as stealing . . .'

The man looked straight at me for a full minute. Then he took a step closer to me and began laughing, silently, his mouth wide open.

'See, that's the kind of story to tell 'em,' he said. 'There's a market for stuff like that. Thank you for your attention, dear listener!'

He doffed his hat, bowed, and walked off.

*   *   *

I remained where I was in a state of utter bewilderment. He had confused me completely, made my head spin. That bastard had spent the night with the girl. *Girl?* A pack of lies. He'd made a fool of me, his heartbreaking little tale was a fiction from beginning to end. Then who was he, the scoundrel? If I ever come across him again I'll tell him what I think of him. Probably he read it somewhere and learnt it off by heart. Wasn't too bad. Man had talent. Ha ha ha, well I'll be damned, he really had me going there!

I went home, still confused. I remembered to look for my watch. It wasn't on the table. Suddenly I slapped my forehead: the watch had been stolen! Of course! He'd stolen my watch while he was sitting there beside me! Ha! damn you! Damn you, you rascal you!

I had two choices. I could either report the theft and get my watch back a day or two later from some pawnbroker. Not long afterwards no doubt the thief would be collared. Or I could say nothing. That was my second choice.

I said nothing.